Don Lazaro slowly stood and began to unbutton his black shirt, his movements purposeful but not hurried. He pulled off the shirt and let it drop to the floor. His chest and arms were well muscled. The olive skin over his belly rippled beneath the coat of sleek black hair.

Lucina lay back on the couch, resting her head upon a pillow covered in antique Persian silk. She moved over a little to make room for the master to sit beside her.

"You are as lovely as a flower, my dear girl," don Lazaro said, brushing the hair back from her forehead.

Lucina turned her head to one side as he gathered her into his arms, making it easier for the *vampiro* to slide his gleaming white teeth into the soft skin of her neck. . . .

By Michael Romkey
Published by Fawcett Books:

I, VAMPIRE
THE VAMPIRE PAPERS
THE VAMPIRE PRINCESS
THE VAMPIRE VIRUS

THE VAMPIRE VIRUS

Michael Romkey

FAWCETT GOLD MEDAL • NEW YORK

A Fawcett Gold Medal Book
Published by Ballantine Books
Copyright © 1997 by Michael Romkey
Excerpt from *The Vampire Hunter* by Michael Romkey copyright © 1997 by Michael Romkey

All rights reserved under International and Pan-American Copyright Conventions. Published in the United States by Ballantine Books, a division of Random House, Inc., New York, and simultaneously in Canada by Random House of Canada Limited, Toronto.

Grateful acknowledgment is made to Harcourt Brace & Company and Faber and Faber Ltd. for permission to reprint an excerpt from "The Waste Land" from COLLECTED POEMS 1909–1962 by T. S. Eliot. Copyright © 1936 by Harcourt Brace & Company, copyright © 1964, 1963 by T. S. Eliot. Reprinted by permission of the publishers, Harcourt Brace & Company and Faber and Faber Ltd.

http://www.randomhouse.com

Library of Congress Catalog Card Number: 97-90278

ISBN 0-449-00261-6

Manufactured in the United States of America

First Edition: January 1998

10   9   8   7   6   5   4   3   2   1

For Carol, Ryan, Matt, and Drew, with love

I wept not, so to stone within I grew.
　　　—Dante

PART I

✧

Zonatitucan

Uno

DR. JANIS LEVY stood with her head thrown back, stunned to silence at the sight of the limestone pyramid rising abruptly from the rain forest's crouched shadows.

She tugged against the snap clasps on her forest-green day pack, rummaging inside for the canvas-bound field notebook, impatient because it was buried beneath the blouse she'd worn over her T-shirt until the day became too hot.

April 21, Zonatitucan. Here at last! The city is magnificent!

The full moon had cleared the sawtooth mountains on the horizon, its color bloody red from microscopic particles of volcanic dust suspended in the upper atmosphere. The lunar face seemed to be balanced atop the 150-foot-tall temple, a halo of light crowning the altar where warrior-priests once ripped living hearts from the captives they sacrificed to the gods of war and nature.

It's good luck that I've arrived on the night of vernal equinox. The central temple and plaza are aligned with the stars along north-south axis. The moon appears to sit upon the biggest pyramid's altar—a sight that has not lost its power to inspire awe despite the centuries that have passed since its construction. This huge structure (I estimate the height at 150 feet) is most likely a Pyramid of the Moon, similar to the one at Teotihuacán. But if so, where is the corresponding Pyramid of the Sun? Strange variation. The Maya worshiped the sun, the giver of life, not the moon.

Astronomy, religion, and architecture had been inextricably linked for the Maya. At Chichén Itzá, the builders of the Pyramid of Kukulcan had been sophisticated enough to design the structure so that the sun's shadows drew the outline of the serpent god descending from the summit along the north staircase balustrade, connecting with the effigy of the creature's snarling head at the temple's base. (The same phenomenon could be observed by moonlight at three in the morning; Janis had published a paper on the subject in *The American Journal of Archaeology*.) Kukulcan appeared twice yearly, at the spring and autumnal equinox, the beginning and end of the agricultural cycle, the seasons of life and death in the old religions.

Unable to read hieroglyphics at present. Strange dialect, probably due to separation from sister cultures. The glyphs representing the city's warrior-priest-kings incorporate the stylized image of a bat. The bat must have been the ruling dynasty's totem.

She paused to study a statue of a jaguar devouring a human heart. A typical motif, though this was the first winged cat the archaeologist had ever seen. Janis noted that the flat, scalloped wings had no feathers. The wings of a bat.

Using the mechanical pencil to point, Janis counted the terraces to the step pyramid's summit. Nine was the usual number, the ritual number that symbolized the nine levels in Mayan hell. She counted again, confirming she'd been right the first time: there were *ten* levels to this pyramid. Perhaps the unprecedented tenth terrace represented transcendence over death. If so, it would be ironic, she thought. Zonatitucan's builders had proven to be no more immortal than the other Mesoamericans the Spanish had crushed in their fever to loot the New World's treasure.

Architecture and hieroglyphics exhibit High Aztec influence, unusual this far south. Of course, the city itself shouldn't be here.

The sound of pencil scratching against paper was the only thing disturbing the hush that had fallen over the ancient city, the animals in the rain forest cautious in the stranger's presence.

Extreme isolation from trade routes and nearest pre-Columbian cities in Honduras. A ring of 14,000-foot mountains surrounds the valley, several volcanically active. Zonatitucan is accessible through a single pass and therefore easily defended. Yet I see no sign the conquistadors were ever here, and there is no mention of the city in the literature. My guess is the Spanish somehow missed this Zonatitucan entirely. . . .

The rain forest had been unusually kind to the city. Instead of the overgrown ruins Janis had expected, the central plaza and its buildings were amazingly intact. It was as if it had been five years, not centuries, since the Maya had melted away into the jungle. No wonder the Indians in Paradisio believed the place was haunted.

The dense rain forest surrounding the city teems with life—parrots, gargantuan ferns, rhododendrons the size of houses, tapirs, monkeys, jaguars. (Haven't seen any of the big cats yet, but I know they're there.) An exotic, primordial place, with great natural beauty . . .

Janis counted twelve significant intact structures in the moonlight, satellites orbiting the central Pyramid of the Moon, plus numerous smaller constructions— subtemples, government and ecclesiastic offices, warehouses for grain and trade, apartment dwellings, a game court enclosed in long stone walls where the Indians had played a ritualized version of lacrosse, sometimes using a human head instead of a ball, the losing team's members forfeiting their lives. The rain forest pressed in on all sides, the stone temples bone-white in the soft lunar glow.

The city is a true mystery. What is it doing here, so far south, in such an inaccessible place? How did it, alone, escape Spanish conquest? Where did its people go?

There would be a book in this, of course, Janis thought.

A book and so much more.

Zonatitucan was the greatest archaeological find since Howard Carter unearthed Tutankhamen's tomb in Egypt's Valley of the Kings in 1922. Excavations would yield a collection of golden idols, skull masks inlaid with turquoise mosaics, jade statues, ritual knives, jewelry, and weapons. And if the rulers' tombs were undisturbed—the ever-expanding field of possibilities made Janis giddy with excitement.

The archaeologist's face would appear on the cover of *Time*, *Newsweek*, *Science*, and *National Geographic*.

Janis shrugged off the fantasy, and yet she knew it all was true. The entire world would applaud the amazing discovery Dr. Janis Levy had made deep in the remote rain forests of Costa Rica.

What solemn pageants took place in this sacred plaza? Who were the city's rulers? What battles did they fight, what city-states did they conquer?

Her neat script became slanted and hurried.

I can almost hear the slow beating of war drums as the prisoners are led into the plaza and made to kneel before the Pyramid of the Moon. Above me, the vanquished warrior is held down on the high altar. He screams as his chest is cut open, but the terrible cry is cut short when his beating heart is plucked out to honor the gods of the rain forest. The head is cut off his corpse, a trophy for the temple's skull rack. His

*headless body cartwheels down the stone staircase to
land in front of the other prisoners, who tremble as
they wait for their turn to be led up the steep terraces
to cross over into the underworld.*

Janis studied the semispherical shapes of hundreds,
perhaps thousands of skulls stacked one on top of another
behind the altar. A bat flew across the moon, fluttering
almost drunkenly.

"It is a disturbing place to visit for the first time at
night."

The voice startled Janis.

"I didn't hear you, don Lazaro." She put her hand over
her pounding heart.

Don Lazaro Ruiz Cortinez had a way of coming up
quickly and quietly, so that he sometimes seemed to
materialize beside her. Don Lazaro was a direct descendant of the Spanish aristocrat sent to Costa Rica in 1511
to found its first city, Cartago, and govern what was then
a Spanish colony. He appeared to be about the same age
as the archaeologist—thirty-five. He had handsome, even
noble features, olive-colored skin, dark eyes, and long,
thick, black hair he wore combed straight back.

"I beg your forgiveness, Dr. Levy," don Lazaro said,
his sonorous Spanish accent cultured and sensual. "Do
you find the city interesting?"

"To put it mildly," Janis answered, putting her hand on
Lazaro's arm. "It's been a long time since anything like
this has been discovered."

"Discovered? Oh, I see what you mean. For me, Dr.
Levy, Zonatitucan is something that has always been
here, like the mountains, the moon, the rain forest. I sup-

pose I should be embarrassed to have missed the ruins' significance. I should have listened to my protégé. Roberto has been telling me the same thing for years."

"Roberto?"

"You have not met him. He is away at school in the United States. Tell me again about the pictures, Dr. Levy. Photographs of the earth taken from outer space."

"They're NASA weather-satellite photographs, thermal images showing vegetation patterns. I was looking at them for a paper on climate and pre-Columbian culture. The funny part is that I'd specifically asked for images of only Mexico, Guatemala, and Belize, but they were careless and mixed in shots of Costa Rica."

"*Fantástico*. But how is it the other scientists did not see the city in the photographs?"

"The meteorologists who ordered the series had no interest in curious rectangles in the middle of the rain forest. They only paid attention to what they wanted to see."

"Ah," don Lazaro said, the word a spoken sigh. "I confess that it makes me a little sad to think that noisy tourists soon will be scrambling up the temple stairs. It seems almost disrespectful, like stepping on a grave."

"The first priority must be to ensure that the site is protected, don Lazaro. It's a minor miracle looters haven't already found the city. I can have a grant within days to pay for guards here twenty-four hours a day to keep out trespassers."

Including unauthorized archaeologists, Janis added to herself.

"The second step will be preservation. Extensive structural surveys need to be made so that we can immediately stabilize any buildings that are in jeopardy. I'm sure you agree that we must do everything within our power to keep a city of such enormous archaeological and historical value from crumbling away into the rain forest. The stone looks solid enough to the casual eye, but limestone can be deceptively fragile, especially in this climate."

Lazaro looked down at her, following her words without any hint of agreement or disagreement.

"Tourists are the last people granted access to an important archaeological site. Everything must be secure and stable before a site is opened to the public. It could be decades before Zonatitucan is ready for visitors."

"But the others will come sooner."

"I'd like to have security people within the week. Once word gets out, Zonatitucan will become a magnet to thieves and artifact pirates—at least it will until they learn the site is protected. I'd expect to return with a staff of conservators within a month to begin a general survey."

Lazaro stared down at her, saying nothing. His mouth had become a tightly drawn line. The inner conflict was obvious enough to Janis. She realized he was thinking about refusing to give her permission to study the site.

"It is impossible for me to emphasize enough how important this discovery is, don Lazaro," Janis said, her voice beginning to quaver. "There is no way to put a value on what there is to learn in this city. Since Zonatitucan is on your estate, it belongs to you, in the legal sense. But the knowledge locked up in this site belongs to the entire world. It would be a tragedy if the world wasn't allowed to share in this with you, don Lazaro."

"How could I refuse so eloquent a plea?" he said after a painfully long pause.

"Thank you," Janis said. "From the bottom of my heart, thank you."

"There is no need to thank me," don Lazaro said, looking away.

"I'll be spending a lot of time here from now on. I hope I won't wear out my welcome at La Esmerelda."

"My hacienda will always be open to you," Lazaro said.

Their eyes met again. Janis felt something melt inside. An invisible key was turning, unlocking urges she had trained herself to control so that they wouldn't interfere with her career. Lazaro's eyes glittered in the moonlight, a mesmerizing set of matching black pearls, the yearning in them too powerful to resist. His desire was becoming her desire.

"Would you think any less of me if I asked you to kiss me?" she asked.

"I never refuse a lady's request," Lazaro said softly.

Janis closed her eyes as his mouth joined hers. She did not have to worry about them being interrupted. The Indians who worked for Lazaro—proud, almost fierce, unsmiling men—seemed preternaturally sensitive to their employer's wishes. They would be sure to stop a discreet distance away and remain hidden in the rain forest, silently holding their packs and guns, waiting for their master's silent signal to advance.

"I only wish the others didn't have to come," Lazaro whispered. "I wish we could keep the secrets of this place to ourselves."

"I know, Lazaro. But it wouldn't be fair. I know you understand."

"I understand perfectly," Lazaro said.

His hand tilted her face up to his again. Her moist lips softly parted as his mouth came closer, brushing past her lips, her cheek, a trail of burning kisses moving down the soft, tanned skin of her throat to the delicate hollow between her neck and shoulder.

"Lazaro!"

Janis gasped at the quick, sharp stab of Lazaro's teeth penetrating her neck, cannulating her jugular vein to release the torrent of blood coursing there. The spike of terror and confusion rising in her almost immediately subsided beneath the overpowering tide of ecstasy that washed through her and over her, carrying her away on a sea of purest bliss.

Janis's dilating eyes fixed on the Pyramid of the Moon as she sank backward into the vampire's arms, surrendering to the onrushing darkness, dragged down into the vortex of secrets that captured everyone who came to Zonatitucan.

Dos

LISA LEANED ACROSS the blanket and kissed Roberto, surprising him for once.

This was not going quite as he'd planned. He detested America, where everything—even relations between a man and woman—was rushed compared to the pace of life at La Esmerelda in the mountainous Costa Rican rain forest.

The dying day had faded to an arc of iridescent purple low on the western horizon by the time they finished making love. Roberto lay looking up at the sky, feeling her eyes on him, studying him, thinking about him. She would speak soon.

"What are you hiding behind so much silence?" Lisa asked, a minute later. "Is it just machismo, or do you have a secret?"

Roberto pushed up on one arm, the ponytail from his thick, jet-black hair falling over one shoulder.

"I have many secrets. We all do."

"Such as the fact that you've discovered a way to decipher Zona hieroglyphics."

"That is one secret," Roberto agreed.

"Dr. Blanco will be insanely jealous. He's been trying to figure out how to read the Fieldman tablets for years."

"The writing is a distinctly northern dialect. The Fieldman tablets are artifacts from a northern Zona trading and diplomatic outpost. The culture was centered far from where the tablets were recovered."

"How far south?"

"Costa Rica."

Lisa sat up on the blanket. "That's impossible."

Roberto shook his head.

"There is no record of advanced pre-Columbian society that far south."

"There is now."

"Wait until Blanco hears that!"

"My translations indicate Zona culture was in flower before the rise of even the Toltecs. The Zona Feathered Serpent and Jaguar Prince glyphs are similar to what you see in much older Toltec writing. That means—"

"That the Toltecs, Aztecs, and Incas descended from the Zona," Lisa blurted, cutting him off. "You realize that we're talking about a wholesale rewriting of history. Blanco's new three-volume chronicle on the Aztecs is out-of-date before the ink dries on the pages. He'll want to kill you when he finds out."

Lisa laughed happily. She didn't like their autocratic department chairman. Nobody at Harvard did.

"I want to thoroughly investigate the implications before anybody else hears about this."

"That's a damned smart strategy, Roberto. Blanco wouldn't wait a heartbeat before trying to steal an undergraduate's breakthrough."

Roberto's chin jerked up, and his eyes narrowed on something distant in the darkness.

"What is it?" Lisa said, casting a nervous glance at the trees as she reached for her clothes.

"The frogs."

She heard them now, the bright trilling song from the creek down the hill that bisected the park.

"Chuwen is speaking to me."

"I can't imagine what Chuwen would have to say to you, Roberto," Lisa said, pulling the T-shirt on over her head.

Chuwen, the Mayan frog deity, was the god of corruption and decay.

Roberto reached for the second bottle of wine. "Archaeology has fascinated me since I was five years old. That is when I first visited Zonatitucan, the extensive complex of Zona ruins that sits in a remote valley on my patron's estate."

Lisa stared at Roberto. "Who else knows about this?"

"Only my patron and the people who work for him, none of whom ever leave the province. My patron never receives visitors. He is an exceptionally private man."

"Like you."

"No," Roberto said, frowning in the gathering darkness. "I am not at all like him."

"How have you managed to keep quiet about this?"

"Zonatitucan is sacred to the Zona," Roberto said, drawing the cork from the wine bottle. "I am a Zona. The blood of the people who carved the so-called Fieldman tablets runs through my veins."

"But a discovery of this magnitude can't be kept secret."

"Of course not." He filled her glass. "But the situation must be carefully managed. I will not allow Zonatitucan to be desecrated by Dr. Blanco and other ham-fisted bone shovelers hunting for gold artifacts and scraps of information to shore up their petty theories."

Roberto raised his glass. "To Zonatitucan."

"To Zonatitucan." Lisa touched her glass to his.

"The Spanish stole my people's culture. Soon they will be forced to make amends."

"It's a lot to make amends for," Lisa said, wrinkling her brow as she took another sip of wine.

"The twenty-year k'atun period is coming to a close. The planetary conjunctions indicate tremendous upheaval. The Zona will rise up in the rain forest and overthrow their oppressor."

"I'm surprised you can think about politics at a time like this. You're sitting on top of discoveries that will let you write your own ticket at Harvard, Oxford, or any top university you care to choose."

"I have no interest in politics," Roberto said. "It is the knowledge contained within the temples in Zonatitucan—and the power that knowledge will unleash—that I want to possess. My ancestors learned to defeat Death. They were immortal beings, a race of demigods."

"Only in their myths," Lisa said. She took another swallow, as if the wine would loosen her thickening tongue.

"The Zona ruled the rain forest for a millennium. Their civilization rivaled anything found in ancient Egypt, Rome, or Greece. Then came the Spanish, destroying everything in their path. The conquistadors robbed the Zona of their immortality."

"A myth," Lisa said, her voice deeply slurred.

"Power sits patiently in the rain forest, biding its time, awaiting the warriors' return. My patron is just an ignorant Spaniard. He will never understand."

"You're not making sense," Lisa said, speaking with her eyes closed, the words running together so that they sounded like one word with many garbled syllables.

Roberto took the glass of drugged wine from Lisa's hand before she dropped it.

"Do you believe in vampires?"

She stopped swaying from side to side long enough to look at Roberto.

"I thought not. I myself detest the term. People have such ridiculous misperceptions today about the *vampiro*."

Lisa closed her eyes and collapsed backward onto the blanket.

"You may think that I'm mad, but I assure you I am the sanest person you will ever know. It is only my relentless sanity that has made it possible for me to perceive the truth as it really is. You and the others are too narrow-minded to know what I know, to see what I see. You have been programmed to disbelieve. It will be your undoing."

Roberto retrieved the paring knife from the picnic basket. He'd sharpened it that morning. The handle was slightly sticky with dried fruit juice from the apple Lisa had peeled earlier. How intently he'd watched her hold the ripe red fruit in her hand, working carefully at it with the blade, juice running over her fingers, making them wet, until she licked them clean. Perhaps there was a dim spark of prescience in the stupid American woman's soul.

Roberto sat cross-legged beside the unconscious woman, his eyes fixed on the starry sky beyond the trees. There was nothing left to do but wait for moonrise, as specified in the Zona guardian ritual he'd learned from the Fieldman tablets. He'd need a guardian's assistance to get the upper hand with his nemesis, the *vampiro*. Harvesting Lisa Scanlon's heart as an offering to the *luna* wouldn't give the young sorcerer enough power to summon a guardian, but it was a start.

Roberto had prepared himself. He knew he could do anything, if he put his mind to it. But he wasn't apprehensive. Just the opposite. Roberto was, in his own quiet way, excited about the work he would do in eight more minutes when the full moon came up over the horizon.

Tres

BAILEY SQUEEZED HER Honda between a BMW and a Mercedes and ran into Peabody's, a dollar bill, quarter, dime, and nickel clutched in her right hand. There was a line at the counter, but Cindy had her coffee waiting at the register, a perk Bailey was afforded for being a regular customer.

A grande-sized coffee at Peabody's cost $1.40. That was a lot for a cup of coffee, but cappuccino was her one extravagance. She could have been making mortgage payments on a quarter-million-dollar house in an upscale Atlanta suburb for what it cost her every month to pay back the money she'd borrowed to attend medical school and postdoctoral epidemiology studies at Johns Hopkins University.

As soon as she arrived at her office, Bailey threw her briefcase and sunglasses onto a desk piled high with journals, files, and printouts and took her coffee straight to the conference room, a single folder tucked under one arm. She was the last person into the room. Gerald shot her a look, but Bailey ignored him. She wasn't a morning person, but she made up for it in other ways. Besides, scheduling Monday-morning staff meetings at seven made little sense. Gerald was the only person who ever looked fully conscious when the sessions started.

The pecking order in the division determined where people sat around the big conference table. Senior staff members were at the far end of the table, grouped around Dr. Gerald Terry. The less senior people occupied the chairs closer to the door. Bailey, the new kid on the block, sat with the exit immediately behind her, at the opposite end of the table from Gerald.

The boss was a bantam of a man in his middle fifties who boxed to keep in shape and had been known to whip bigger, younger men. His steel-gray hair was cut short, the way he'd worn it when he was a colonel in the army.

At Gerald's immediate right was Scott Russo, the division's comptroller and Gerald's chief foil. Gerald and Scott were the odd couple in the Centers for Disease Control's Tropical Disease Research Center. Scott was about thirty pounds overweight, and when he laughed at Gerald's jokes, his eyes disappeared into his cheeks and his face turned purple. Scott had a daughter starting college at Brown. Bailey hoped Scott had a good life insurance policy.

"What do you have for us today, Ron?" Gerald asked in his Texan drawl, looking to his left.

Bailey's coffee had cooled off enough to drink. She popped off the plastic top and took a sip as Ron Peterson began to talk about chimpanzees in the Ivory Coast mysteriously getting the Ebola virus every other autumn. The coffee was Guatemalan. Peabody's rotated a dozen different blends, featuring one coffee daily.

Ruth Heymann made a presentation on the World Health Organization's plan to create a "SWAT team" of

United Nations doctors with special passports that would allow them to go anywhere at the drop of a hat to study emerging diseases. The bureaucrats had allocated $1.5 million for the program. It would take ten times that amount to get the project off the ground, Bailey was about to say, but Ellen Bush beat her to it. You had to be quick to make points at the staff meetings, Bailey thought, consoling herself with a sip of coffee.

Hank Bettleman had a new strain of plague in India. Hank always had something interesting to tell them. He was lucky to be responsible for India, where puzzling new diseases seemed to crop up every few weeks.

The rest of the meeting was routine stuff. An outbreak of salmonella in three western states had been linked to contaminated ice cream. There was another long discussion about antibiotic-resistant tuberculosis, followed by more hand-wringing about the safety of the blood supply. They'd talked about the last two topics so much in the past few months that Bailey found it almost impossible to follow the discussion.

"Do you have anything for us today, Dr. Harrison?"

Bailey blinked and sat up straight. Gerald was smirking at her, his eyes glittering. He was either mocking her or treating her like one of the boys. It was impossible to know which.

"As a matter of fact, I do, Dr. Terry," Bailey said, meeting his cold gray eyes. "Two weeks ago the body of an archaeologist was brought back from Costa Rica—"

"Dr. Janis Levy."

How the hell did Gerald know that?

"I read about her in the newspaper, Bailey," Gerald said, guessing her thoughts. "I don't *really* know everything."

Several people laughed quietly.

"The autopsy was performed in Miami," Bailey said. "The cause of death was undetermined. There was no indication of gross injury or disease. Decomposition was extremely advanced after several weeks in the rain forest."

Bailey opened the file folder on the table in front of her and glanced at it, mainly for theatrical value; she had already committed the details to memory.

"The subject had had a complete physical, including a stress test, before the trip and was, by all measures, completely healthy and in excellent physical condition."

"Cut to the chase," Gerald said.

"The tissue samples contain evidence of significant but unidentified viral activity. Numerous fragments of an unclassified retrovirus were present. The retrovirus contained a potent DNA load. Even viewed in fractured segments, it looked more like human DNA than anything else, which is certainly unusual and perhaps significant. There were peculiar anomalies with nuclei of the reconstituted red blood cells."

Gerald glanced significantly down at his watch.

"The pathologist and an employee at the funeral home where the remains were taken developed flu-like symptoms. The mortician was briefly hospitalized. The tests on them both came back negative. Nevertheless, it looks like whatever killed Dr. Levy infected the pathologist in Miami and the mortician in New Jersey. I think the virus, whatever it is, could turn out to be something ugly."

"You *think*, Dr. Harrison?"

Bailey glanced down at her empty cup. "There wasn't

enough test material to be certain," she said. "I only had a few desiccated genetic fragments to work with."

"So you think you should maybe go to Costa Rica, take some blood samples, nose around some, and see what there is to see."

"Yes, I think it's certainly worth checking out."

"You might discover a dangerous strain of influenza or an exotic new disease and name it after yourself."

Bailey ignored the laughter, more interested in the fact that Gerald wasn't looking at Scott Russo. That was the tip-off. If Gerald was going to refuse her permission to go, Scott would be the one who would speak up and say that the budget wouldn't allow it, that the cost/benefit ratio didn't merit the expenditure. It was shrewd of Gerald to use Scott to insulate himself from unpopular decisions.

"How's your Spanish?" Gerald asked.

"Muy bien, gracias."

"Have you booked your reservations?"

Bailey shook her head.

"What are you waiting for?" Gerald demanded.

"It's next on my list," Bailey said, grinning back at her boss.

The chance to do fieldwork was what being a bug hunter was all about, her reward for having spent a year looking through a microscope in a windowless lab, waiting for her chance. It would be her first trip away from the Centers for Disease Control's Atlanta headquarters, her maiden excursion into the bush to seek exotic and dangerous new diseases and look for ways to unlock their secrets and render them harmless.

Dr. Gerald Terry stood up, signaling the meeting's

end. Suddenly everybody was on their feet, gathering up their papers and chatting. Bailey stood up with her folder and her empty coffee cup.

"Happy bug hunting, Bailey."

"Thanks, Dana."

"Just don't drink the water," Ruth Heymann said, patting her on the shoulder as she squeezed past.

"Dr. Harrison?"

Bailey looked across the room at Scott Russo.

"Fly coach."

Cuatro

✧

BAILEY CLOSED THE *New England Journal of Medicine* as the jet began its descent and looked out the window. At first, water was all she could see. Land, when it appeared, was a ribbon of sugary sand dividing the sapphire-blue Caribbean from the jungle.

The ringing tropical light started to hurt her eyes. She reached into her breast pocket for a pair of wire-rimmed sunglasses.

The flight was coming in from the east, over the lowlands north of Limón, above mosquito- and alligator-infested swamps best suited for banana plantations and penal colonies. The plane seemed to continue its descent, but it was an illusion: the ground was rising to the airliner as the malarial flatlands gave way to heavily forested mountains.

The jet dropped suddenly. The bald man sitting in front of Bailey gasped as San José appeared in her window, a city of one million sprawled across a deep basin in the Sierra de Tilaran central highland.

San José looked like a cross between Miami and a Mexican border town, a haphazard combination of modern, 1950s, and colonial architecture. Bailey expected more of a skyline, but frequent earthquakes apparently kept builders from putting up tall buildings in a city where more than half of Costa Rica's population lived.

Bailey got her equipment through customs without trouble, barely getting to use her Spanish. She bought a postcard and stamp in the gift shop, jotted a note to her mother on the back, and put it in a mailbox. The man at the car rental agency helped load the gear into the Toyota Land Cruiser. Bailey politely refused his offer to find her a driver. She knew how to read a map.

Bailey inched through San José's gridlocked traffic, looking at the people on the streets. Hispanics, blacks, tall European-looking blondes, Indians scarcely five feet tall with wide noses and coal-colored hair. The people appeared healthy and well-nourished, without the goiters and distended bellies common in Third World countries. Costa Rica was a paradise compared to Guatemala or Nicaragua.

Outside San José, the expressway narrowed to the two-lane Pan-American Highway. Traffic thinned out to a light but steady stream of Jeeps, sedans, and trucks overloaded with cargo. Bailey drove for ten miles behind a bus with a crated pig lashed to its back bumper. The road snaked up and down the mountains, her speed averaging no more than fifty miles an hour. The rain forest pressed in on either side of the highway—trees a hundred feet tall, rubber plants with leaves as broad as canoe paddles, prehistoric ferns that could have easily concealed a lurking velociraptor.

Between Volcán and Palmar Sur, Bailey turned the Toyota off the highway onto the dirt road that would take her deep into the rugged Cordillera Talamanca.

The Land Cruiser bounced along the rutted track, the space between rancheros getting farther and farther apart until at last there was nothing left but the narrow road, the mountains, the forest, and the four-wheel-drive vehicle, lumbering along like a tireless beast of burden. There seemed to be no people in this remote part of the country— no ranchers, no loggers, no Indians. There weren't even any other travelers on the lonely road. The rain forest seemed to be completely uninhabited, a primeval world where the only tenuous evidence of civilization was a narrow strip of man-made road pushed this way and that across the landscape by the more powerful forces of nature.

Bailey stopped at an overlook to stretch her legs. Off the side of the road, at the bottom of a thousand-foot cliff, a river meandered through a leafy gorge toward a thundering waterfall. The river rushed over the precipice and plunged two hundred feet into the heart-shaped lake at the foot of the cataract, filling the air with a spray of rainbow mist that sparkled in the afternoon sunlight.

Bailey climbed back into the Land Cruiser and checked the map. There were another fifty miles to go, with nothing between her and the town at the end of the road but two more hours of driving. A butterfly the size of a bird was floating across the road as Bailey looked up. Watching the creature rise into the sky on iridescent wings, she noticed the wisps of clouds forming high above the mountains.

She tossed the map onto the passenger seat and put the Land Cruiser into gear.

The days began and ended in the rain forest with cloudbursts. The road would turn to gumbo when it was wet. She wanted to be in Paradisio by the time the deluge let loose.

Bailey drove more quickly than before, rattling the gear packed behind her as much as she dared. The clouds knit themselves together and began to come down out of the sky, hiding the peaks, filling in the empty spaces between the ridges with steaming billows of white and gray.

The road angled steeply into a valley. Bailey's ears popped as the elevation changed. The green canopy closed in over the four-wheel-drive truck, hiding the angry sky. Bailey fiddled with the truck's controls until she found the switch that turned on the headlights.

The road curved around a colossal tree covered with vines that had grown from the top down. The vines' roots had sucked all the nutrients from the ground, leaving the tree a dead shell of itself, a skeleton whose only continued purpose was to prop up the vegetation that had killed it.

A roar of thunder split the air. The storm hit before Bailey could get the windows up; the rain spattering her bare arms was surprisingly cold.

The Land Cruiser crawled along the slippery clay track, Bailey gritting her teeth every time the tires began to spin. There was an electric winch on the truck's front bumper. If worse came to worst, she could pull the cable out, hook it around a tree, and pull the truck free from the mire.

She drove on until she got to a place where water was running across the road. The forest stream was probably only a few inches deep most of the time. Judging from the angle of the road, she guessed the fast-moving water was now about a foot deep. However, the water was coming up as she watched, the stream swelling fast with mountain runoff.

It was now or never.

She jammed the accelerator to the floor. When the truck hit the stream, water exploded into the air, making it impossible to see a thing. Bailey took her foot off the gas a moment later and slammed on the brake, trees looming in front of her, dark, dripping, vertical shapes that seemed to race toward the truck in the rain.

Bailey sat there a minute, listening to the windshield wipers slap back and forth.

She'd made it.

Bailey had to back up a few feet to get the truck back on the road. She drove up a small rise and around a small curve and saw the few flickering lights that were Paradisio.

A flash of lightning lit up the sky, revealing Paradisio to be scarcely more than a village, a dozen buildings and maybe a hundred shacks huddled between the two mountain ridges and climbing the steep slopes on either side.

The Indians stood in doorways, watching the stranger drive along the muddy street, splashing slowly through the deep puddles of water. In the lightning flashes Bailey saw their expressionless faces. Only their eyes moved as they followed the Land Cruiser's progress through town.

The only electric lights were at the Hotel Paradisio, single bare lightbulbs flickering in front of the hotel and adjoining cantina.

Bailey parked in front of the hotel. When she turned off the engine, she could hear the hotel's gas generator somewhere out back, sputtering along in the rain. She grabbed her backpack and opened the door and jumped out, instantly drenched.

"Buenas noches, señorita."

The clerk behind the plywood reception desk was a smiling black man wearing a Day-Glo orange Bob Marley T-shirt and shoulder-length dreadlocks. The displaced Rastafarian spun the hotel register around for her, introducing himself as Vincent.

"Every morning and every night the rains come," he said. "It's hard to believe, but we mostly dry out during the day. The earth here is like a sponge."

"I like a good storm," she said, signing the register. "It makes it easy to sleep."

"What brings you to our village ... Dr. Harrison?" Vincent asked, turning the register back toward him, reading her name.

"Research."

"Sounds interesting, Doctor."

"I'll tell you all about it sometime, Vincent, but right now I'd really like to get into some dry clothes."

"We'll put you in room thirteen. It is not much, but it's the best we have to offer."

"I'm sure it will be fine."

Vincent handed her the key but did not move. The Hotel Paradisio was apparently the kind of hotel where the guests were expected to help themselves.

Bailey went back outside for her suitcase, not hurrying now, already wet to the bone. She'd have to bring in the heavy equipment cases, too, not wanting to risk having them stolen from the truck. If anything happened to the gear, replacements would have to be flown in from the States.

Vincent sighed heavily when Bailey lugged in the suitcase, water streaming down her face.

"Why don't you let me give you a hand with your things, Doctor."

"I can get it."

"No, Doctor, I insist," Vincent said unhappily.

He ferried the gear, which was packed in sturdy flight cases, into the lobby, then he and Bailey carted it upstairs.

"You can get something to eat in the cantina next door," Vincent said, breathless and soaked, after he'd transferred the last case into Bailey's room.

"Maybe I will later." She peeled off some money for Vincent, anxious to get out of the sodden clothing.

Vincent had been right about the room: it wasn't much. There were two windows looking out over the street in front, where Bailey's Toyota was the only vehicle in sight. The floor and walls were bare white-washed wood. There was a bed in the corner with mosquito netting draped over it. Underneath the bed was a chamber pot. There was a single straight-backed wooden chair at a small, rough writing desk, a kerosene lantern, and a dresser with a basin and water jug. A single naked lightbulb hung from the ceiling at the end of a length of gummy-looking black wire.

Bailey pulled the tattered blinds and stripped out of her wet clothes, draping them over the chair. A hot shower would have been wonderful, but she didn't hold out any hope for that. Bailey washed up in the basin instead, using the single washcloth and homemade soap, then pulled on some underwear and a T-shirt, lifted the mosquito netting, and got into the bed. The bedclothes smelled of mildew, which was no surprise, the way it rained in Paradisio. Bailey stretched out on top of the covers, intending to rest a few minutes, then dress and go to the cantina for supper. She was asleep almost before she closed her eyes.

Bailey didn't remember where she was when she woke up a few hours later in the darkness. She put out her hand, felt the mosquito netting, and everything fell into place again.

She pushed the button that illuminated her runner's watch. It was only nine. It was so quiet that it seemed much later. Even the generator was silent, either broken, out of fuel, or shut down for the night.

Bailey sat up in the darkness. It was starting to rain again, she thought, but then she realized it was only the wind in the trees, blowing the moisture from the leaves. Insects were beginning to sing, a pleasant, high-pitched chirring, night music in the rain forest.

Cinco

✧

FATHER XAVIER SAT at his desk, listening to the rain as he finished his correspondence.

It rained every morning in Paradisio, and every evening, too. The twin deluges were bookends that bracketed daily life in the village. The clouds boiled up from the fecund, humid earth, building towering thunderheads that drew together around the mountain peaks, shouldering out the sun, the sky descending until the clouds dragged their ragged bellies across the treetops.

And then, with a crack of thunder, the explosion of rain.

There was nothing gradual about rain in Paradisio. It started full bore, as if God Himself had thrown open the celestial faucets, cutting sheets that stung the skin like needles and pounded noisily on the village's corrugated metal roofs.

And then, as abruptly as it had started, the rain would stop.

The clouds would blow away, leaving the weather cool, clear, the humidity washed from the air until an hour or so before the next rain, when it would become sticky and close again, the cycle preparing to repeat itself. Rain-sun-rain-stars—the pattern recurred without variation in Paradisio. It was all well and good for the trees and the cowboy loggers who worked for don Lazaro, but unimaginably tedious for a cosmopolitan man who had lived all his life in Mexico City.

Father Xavier looked up, startled by the silence.

It had stopped raining.

The priest finished the second letter, sealed it in an envelope, and added a stamp. It was almost eight o'clock. In Mexico City, he'd be drinking a cup of café au lait and picking apart a croissant. After a look at the daily papers, he'd head off to the hospital to visit ailing parishioners. There were no croissants in Paradisio. His newspapers arrived infrequently, three or four of them at a time, always at least a week out-of-date. There was no hospital to visit in Paradisio. The Indians didn't seem to get sick. There was only poor old don Merino, a Mexican expatriate like Father Xavier, dying in his house up on the mountain.

The priest hoisted the canvas backpack onto the desk and looked inside to reassure himself the housekeeper had stocked it with the fruit he would eat for lunch and two one-liter bottles of mineral water. Living in the rain forest had turned Xavier into a methodical man; there were no neighborhood bodegas to stop into for a cool drink when you got thirsty.

Father Xavier unlocked the middle desk drawer where he kept the Browning 9mm semiautomatic. He checked the clip and racked the stainless-steel slide. After making sure the safety was on, he put the weapon into the backpack, along with the letters he planned to mail and a Bible.

Paradisio's residents were not religious. The local Indians belonged to the secretive Zona clan and were only nominally Christian. The only reason Father Xavier ever saw any of them in church was that the local *caudillo*, don Lazaro Ruiz Cortinez, made it known that he wished them to attend.

Don Lazaro was Costa Rica's largest landowner, the direct descendant of a conquistador to whom the Spanish crown had granted most of the province. The *caudillo* owned the rain forest surrounding Paradisio and most of the town itself, including the Hotel Paradisio and its cantina. Although to Father Xavier's knowledge don Lazaro had never set foot in the church, his donations kept it open.

Grabbing a straw hat, the priest stepped outside, where the entire world appeared to be green, wet, and dripping. He adjusted the angle at which the hat sat on his head, came down the steps, and began to pick his way up the muddy street that led through the middle of Paradisio.

Overhead, a few patches of blue struggled to break through the dense gray mass.

The Hotel Paradisio lobby was deserted.

Father Xavier slapped the bell on the reception desk with the palm of his hand and waited. There was no sign of Vincent. The door to the hotel manager's tiny office was open. Xavier looked in at the clutter of empty whiskey and beer bottles, tools, a wad of filthy towels—a real rat's nest.

The smell of burnt rope hung heavily in the air. Marijuana, the Rastafarian sacrament. The Jamaican read the Bible daily. He liked to discuss Scripture with Father Xavier, though the priest hadn't been able to convince

Vincent that the Bible didn't instruct him to stay perpetu-
ally stoned on ganja.

Xavier rang the bell again. Still nothing.

A thief could walk in, pluck any of the keys from the
hooks on the wall behind the reception desk, and help
himself to the guests' personal belongings.

Xavier swung the backpack around to the reception
desk and got out his letters, depositing them in the card-
board box that served as the village's drop for outgoing
mail. The hotel registry was open on the desk, the edge of
its leather binding spiderwebbed with mildew. Father
Xavier noted the new entry, reading it upside down. *Dr.
Bailey Harrison, M.D.* was inscribed in black ink in neat,
feminine handwriting on the green-ruled paper. And then
after the name, in Vincent's scrawl, *Room 13*.

Bailey Harrison—the name sounded American. The
priest smiled to himself. Doctors, not hotel keepers, were
the ones whose penmanship was supposed to be illegible.
The expensive Toyota truck parked in front of the hotel
must belong to the lady doctor.

Father Xavier rang the bell a third time, still without
result. He picked up his backpack and turned to go.

"Good morning, Father Xavier."

The priest tipped his hat to the woman coming into the
hotel.

"Good morning, señorita."

Yanira Rojas lived in the Hotel Paradisio. She was one
of the prostitutes Vincent had imported to entertain the
cowboys who drank in the cantina. Aside from Vincent,
the prostitutes were the only people in Paradisio with
whom Father Xavier had any real rapport. They were all
in exile, something they had in common. Yanira and her

fallen sisters never missed Mass. Whores, in Father Xavier's experience, tended to be religious.

Just past the modest church with its red-tiled roof, he left the rutted road and headed up the path, stopping long enough to get the pistol out of the backpack. The forest was filled with snakes and jaguars. He'd once encountered an eight-foot bushmaster on the trail to don Merino's house, though fortunately the snake had hurried back into the forest at the first sign of him, as afraid of the man as the man was of the serpent.

Father Xavier checked the pistol's safety again, then stuck the gun into his pants under his belt buckle. He wasn't taking any chances, especially not since Father Juan, his predecessor in the parish, had disappeared into the rain forest without a trace.

The priest was careful to stay in the middle of the trail. The vegetation was still dripping, and unless he was careful, he'd look as if he'd showered with his clothes on.

Don Merino lived on a ridge halfway up the mountainside. He had come to Paradisio to avoid certain legal complications, settling there because the people didn't care where you'd come from or what you'd done. Don Merino had admitted his crimes to Father Xavier in a general way. The specifics would come in time. Don Merino was dying; he wouldn't go to his grave without making a full confession.

Who could know? Today might be the day.

Father Xavier hiked for an hour, stopping to drink some water at the spot where the trail split in two. He'd always taken the left trail to don Merino's, but the one on the right had seen the most traffic recently, the path beaten down from heavy use. Maybe it would be faster. If he could trim an hour from the trip, he'd get home before the evening rain came. It seemed worth the gamble.

Father Xavier's thoughts turned to his parish's benefactor as he headed up the new trail. Perhaps he should gas up the Jeep and drive out to La Esmerelda to pay don Lazaro a visit, since the rich man almost never left his estate to come into town. It was possible don Lazaro required only a little friendly encouragement to get him into church. Souls were like plants: they had to be cultivated before they could flower.

It was evident to Father Xavier that don Lazaro was a good man.

In addition to funding the parish, don Lazaro's money ran a school in town that provided a rigorous, almost Jesuitical education to the local children. The teachers were all Indians, local tribe members don Lazaro had sent away to college in the United States. There were ten-year-olds in Paradisio who spoke better Latin than Father Xavier—something that only added to the air of unreality that pervaded the strange little town.

The priest had met don Lazaro only once, bumping into him in the street one night outside the cantina. Xavier replayed the meeting in his mind, as he had done many times. Don Lazaro had been dressed entirely in black, from his shirt to his knee-high riding boots. The *caudillo* was blessed with a striking appearance. Don Lazaro had a movie actor's good looks. Yet it was his eyes that Father Xavier remembered best: so dark, so fierce. They'd only spoken briefly, exchanging banal pleasantries, yet Father Xavier had come away with the distinct impression that don Lazaro didn't like him. Or was it priests in general that the rich man didn't like?

Father Xavier stopped on the trail to adjust the backpack and mop the sweat from his face and neck. The trail had become steep. Walking was like climbing stairs.

The path widened into a small clearing, the canopy of trees overhead draping it in deep gloom. At the far end was a broad stand of trees, their concave trunks grown together into a single living altar, a vaulting pillar that jutted up from the rain-forest floor to support the verdant roof high above. Vines interlaced themselves among the six-hundred-year-old trees, binding them together, giving their association a peculiarly sexual appearance, as if Xavier had happened upon trees while they were tangled in a passionate embrace, vines binding, bulging, twisting, caressing, emerging from one cavity to disappear into the fold of another.

A rectangular, mossy rock in the center of the clearing stood about as high as the priest's waist. The ground cover around it was trampled down, as if a crowd of people had come up the trail and walked in circles around the rock again and again.

Father Xavier moved closer and saw that the rock had designs carved in its surface, the images heavily disguised beneath a covering of moss and mottled lichen. It appeared to be Aztec-style writing. Getting down on one knee, his hand on the stone for balance, he could make out dim outlines of the distinctive, highly stylized hieroglyphics: warriors and jungle creatures carved without perspective in the familiar two-dimensional, side-on fashion. The central figure was a king or god, a knife in one hand and a serpent in the other. A jaguar skin was knotted around the figure's waist, his head covered with plumes and crowned with the image of a bat.

There weren't supposed to be pre-Columbian ruins in Costa Rica. In fact, if Father Xavier remembered what he'd learned in college correctly, there weren't any ruins south of Honduras, at least not until you got all the way to Peru and the remains of the Incan culture.

The artifact was an unusual discovery. No wonder so many people had come all the way from the village to have a look. It hurt Father Xavier's feelings that nobody had shared the exciting news with him.

Father Xavier got back on his feet, rubbing his thumb and fingers together, feeling the sticky wetness. He glanced down at his hand as he was about to rub it dry against his khaki pants.

His hand was wet with blood.

Father Xavier stood perfectly still, not even breathing, immobilized by a disconnection between his eyes and mind.

The priest knelt down and quickly, almost frantically, rubbed his hand through the leaves and stems matted close to the ground.

A branch snapped in the rain forest.

Father Xavier jerked the pistol from his belt as he scrambled to his feet. He turned in a quick circle, holding the gun in front of him in both hands as he carefully searched the dense vegetation, forgetting the safety was still on. He caught a glimpse of something that could have been a jaguar watching him, but it was gone before he could be sure.

The priest made the sign of the cross with his left hand, his eyes sweeping the impenetrable snarl of foliage. He held the gun held in front of him, not realizing how useless it would be if he pulled the trigger.

Somewhere in the rain forest, a howler monkey shrieked.

Seis

LUCINA SAT ALONE in the kitchen, playing a game of dominoes with herself. The clock above the sink said eleven. She hid a yawn behind her small hand. One more hour and she could go to bed. Alvaro had said goodnight to Lucina at ten, after turning down the master's bed and laying out his black silk pajamas. Lucina was probably the last servant awake at La Esmerelda. She knew she was the last one on duty.

Lucina's responsibilities at La Esmerelda included sitting up in the kitchen until midnight in case the master wanted something to eat or drink. In the two years she had worked in the hacienda as the cook's assistant, Lucina had never known the master to request anything of her. He always retired to the library after his evening meal with a cup of coffee and whatever book he happened to be reading at supper. The master was considerate of his servants. Whenever he wanted a glass of port or cognac or one of the Cuban cigars he kept in a special humidor, he got them for himself.

Lucina looked up at the bell that would ring if the master wished to summon her. She had heard it ring only once, when Obdulia was teaching her her responsibilities. Lucina wished it would ring now and save her from her boredom. The bell, however, remained stubbornly silent.

Lucina pushed aside the dominoes, wishing Maria Therese still lived in the hacienda. Her friend used to sit up late with her, playing dominoes and gossiping.

"Poor Maria Therese," Lucina said to herself, shaking her head.

Maria Therese claimed to enjoy her life as Anonimo's wife, but she couldn't possibly mean it. Anonimo was old enough to be Maria Therese's father. Maria Therese had succeeded in making her favorite suitor, Carlomango Cordoba, crazy with jealousy, but to what end? Marrying Anonimo had only meant that the foolish girl would be kept apart from Carlo forever.

Perhaps Lucina could catch Carlo's eyes. A delicious idea, Lucina thought, though a bad one. It would hurt Maria Therese very much to see her and Carlo together. Lucina could never do that to her friend.

Lucina began to stack the dominoes neatly away in their wooden box.

If she did not marry Carlomango Cordoba, then who? Roberto?

Lucina frowned with her eyes. A Zona, she had been taught it was rude to display emotion through facial expressions.

Though Lucina had had a terrific crush on Roberto when she first came to La Esmerelda, he no longer seemed like a suitable boy. Being away in the United States had changed him. He had become even more serious and brooding than his patron. Roberto and the master had had a furious argument about the dead *gringa*. Roberto had quit school after that. He refused to come back to the hacienda. Instead, Lucina had heard, he was living alone in a miserable shack on the mountain above Paradisio, studying sorcery.

Roberto had better hope the master never gets wind of *that*! Lucina thought.

The chair legs scraped dully against the tile as she pushed herself away from the table. It was early, but she would collect the coffee cup and saucer and any other glasses the master had used in the library. It would give her something to do for a few minutes.

Lucina walked down the long corridor toward the door at the end of the wing where the library was situated, listening to the sound of a classical guitar coming from the master's inner sanctum. She paused outside the door, tapping lightly on the varnished mahogany. The knock was more courtesy than a request for admission. The master was often too preoccupied to notice the interruption.

Lucina stood there a minute, listening to the wonderful music coming from behind the door. The song was beautiful and exotic—a sad melody built around a progression of minor-chord arpeggios.

Lucina quietly opened the door and slipped inside.

The master held a guitar in his arms as if it were his lover.

The master did *everything* well. He was the best horseman in the province and the best shot. He wrote exquisite poetry, which he sometimes recited to himself in a quiet voice as he strolled in the gardens at night, not realizing Lucina was listening, she thought. He was also an excellent artist. The master had given Lucina a water-color painting of a butterfly three months earlier as a sixteenth-birthday present. She treasured the picture, hanging it on the wall opposite her bed so that it would be the first thing she saw when she awoke in the morning.

Don Lazaro stopped playing and looked up at the girl.

Lucina thought he was angry with her for interrupting his concentration, but the light in his eyes was soft. He had always treated her more as a guest than a servant. Such a kind man, she thought. It was indeed a blessing to have gotten a position in the master's household.

"Do you like the music?"

Don Lazaro's words seemed to awaken Lucina from a dream.

"*Sí*, don Lazaro. It is very beautiful."

"It is a gypsy love song from southern Spain. The music is supposed to convey the pain a young woman feels longing for a lover."

Lucina hardly knew how to respond to that, but her reply became unnecessary when don Lazaro's fingers began to move again over the strings. The guitar came to life in his hands, a magical living creature with a voice of its own pouring feeling straight into Lucina's heart. The girl moved to the couch and sat down, responding to some subtle invitation from the master, her entire being focused on the symphony unleashed by don Lazaro's long fingers.

He leaned forward over the guitar, eyes closed,

seemingly as bewitched as his guest by the music's alchemy. The gypsy song built toward a climax of fiery scales starting low in the guitar's register and burning with impossible speed up the fret board, ending with a staccato burst of harmonics that resonated in the air for nearly a minute after the piece had ended.

Don Lazaro continued to lean forward over the guitar, barely breathing, drained. At last he set the guitar gently on the floor, leaning its neck against the arm of the chair, careful that the instrument was balanced and would not fall. The instrument was once again an inanimate object of wood strung with nylon strings, the magic leaving it when the master put it aside.

Don Lazaro slowly stood and began to unbutton his black shirt, his movements purposeful but not hurried. He pulled off the shirt and let it drop to the floor. His chest and arms were well muscled. The olive skin over his belly rippled beneath the coat of sleek black hair.

It was only then that Lucina realized she had been summoned to the room by the magical sounds the master had coaxed from the guitar. She lay back on the couch, resting her head upon a pillow covered in antique Persian silk. She moved over a little to make room for the master to sit beside her.

"You are as lovely as a flower, my dear girl," don Lazaro said, brushing the hair back from her forehead.

Lucina smiled, the trembling stopping as her body became perfectly relaxed, perfectly ready for the master. She had hardly dared to dream this would happen, that she would become one of the chosen. Lucina turned her head to one side as he gathered her into his arms, making it easier for the *vampiro* to slide his gleaming white teeth into the soft skin of her neck.

Siete

✧

VINCENT LEANED BACKWARD, balancing on the hind legs of the bar stool, smoking a spliff as he coolly surveyed the room on the opposite side of the bar. The unreliable generator was broken again. The single hurricane lamp at the end of the bar served mainly to pull the shadows out of the corners, draping them languidly around the dimly lit room.

It was a dead night in the cantina. They were all dead, except Saturdays. Saturday was payday for the timber and mining crews that worked La Esmerelda. The cowboys would take their weekly baths, dress up in their best chinos, western shirts, and "town" boots, and pack the cantina, staying until Vincent threw them out—don Lazaro's rule—in time to sober up for church.

They weren't real cowboys, of course. That's just what everybody called them. And not the Spanish word *gaucho*, but *cowboy*.

Vincent exhaled a blue cloud of ganja smoke and squinted through it. The only customer in the cantina was a middle-aged ranch hand drinking quietly at a table with one of the girls. The cowboy had a hand up Yanira's skirt

48

under the table. She looked back at him with a vaguely bored expression.

Father Xavier came into the bar, going toward his usual spot in the corner. The priest didn't look at Yanira. He and the prostitutes had an arrangement: they ignored one another when the girls were working. Vincent thought it a little strange that the whores liked Father Xavier so much, but then the priest was probably the only man in town who wasn't screwing them.

Father Xavier turned away from Vincent long enough to transfer something from his belt to the side pocket of his jacket before he sat down. Why was the priest carrying his gun in Paradisio? There was rarely trouble, even with drunken cowboys. Don Lazaro didn't allow it.

"How you doing tonight, Father Xavier?" Vincent called across the room.

The priest looked up, a startled expression in his eyes. He nodded.

"Your usual?"

"Mescal, *si me hace el favor*."

Vincent poured two fingers of mescal instead of the priest's usual beer.

"Everything okay up at don Merino's place? How's that crazy old *bandido* getting along?"

"Don Merino is dying."

"Sure he is, but how's he doing? He ready for another case of rum?"

"I don't know," Father Xavier answered, his mind elsewhere.

Vincent laughed when the priest gasped at the harsh, raw taste. "That one's on the house. You want a beer chaser?"

Father Xavier shook his head and motioned for Vincent to pour him another.

"Strong medicine. Something wrong?"

The priest shook his head, his eyes on the table.

Liar, Vincent said to himself.

Vincent poured the priest another drink and went back behind the bar, lighting a cigarette, leaning backward on the stool to contemplate the situation. Father Xavier must have seen something funny. There were things that went on in the rain forest that were best ignored. Live and let live was Vincent's motto. The smart thing to do was look the other way, pretend the witchery wasn't there.

Dr. Harrison came into the cantina through the door connecting it with the hotel. She hesitated in the doorway, smiling at Vincent, the bead curtain swinging back and forth behind her.

Too bad she liked to dress like a man—khaki shirt and shorts, hiking boots, heavy red-striped gray socks folded over the top. She'd have looked a lot better in a blouse that left her stomach naked, like the one Yanira wore. Dr. Harrison had a nice face and a tight body. Her blond hair made her look exotic, like an angel descended from heaven to save them from boredom. You didn't see many blondes in the rain forest, Vincent thought.

Dr. Harrison crinkled up her nose at the lingering smell of marijuana hanging in the air, her eyes settling again on Vincent, with his magnificent dreadlocks and T-shirt decorated with the Jamaican flag. Vincent gave her his biggest smile. If he wanted to smoke ganja, he'd bloody well smoke ganja.

Father Xavier lurched up out of his chair as if jolted by a cattle prod.

"Hello," he called out. "You must be Dr. Harrison."

"Please call me Bailey," she said, going over to shake his hand.

The generator sputtered unexpectedly back to life, filling the cantina with light that brightened and dimmed several times before settling into a steady glow. Scratchy mariachi music poured forth from the ancient radio behind the bar, strings and trumpets and a man singing the painfully overwrought lyrics of a love song. Vincent greatly preferred reggae, but this was the only music the cowboys would tolerate.

" 'Let there be light,' " Father Xavier said, making a poor joke.

Dr. Harrison laughed politely, pretending not to notice that the priest was a little bit drunk.

"By any chance, did either of you meet Dr. Janis Levy when she came through here?"

"She spent a night here," Vincent said. "That's all I know about her, except that she's dead. She wasn't very friendly."

"I met her once," Father Xavier said, his forehead becoming lined with worry wrinkles. "It was here, as a matter of fact, in the cantina."

Vincent squinted through the dissipating blue haze at Dr. Harrison. He hadn't noticed it before, but now he saw it, experiencing one of the insights ganja sometimes brought him. Dr. Bailey Harrison was going to be trouble. Big trouble.

"Was she a friend of yours?" Father Xavier asked.

"I never met her."

The priest seemed to be completely confused. "Are

you an archaeologist, like Dr. Levy? I thought you were a medical doctor."

"I am. I'm an epidemiologist, to be more specific. I research outbreaks of disease that could lead to epidemics, if left unchecked. I work at the Centers for Disease Control in the United States."

"I've read stories about smallpox and other diseases science is eradicating," Father Xavier said, swirling the glass of mescal. "It hadn't occurred to me that new ones come along to take their place."

"It happens all the time. AIDS. Or Ebola. Diseases pop up seemingly out of nowhere. Usually, it's in the tropics—often in rain forests."

"Jah protect us," Vincent muttered.

"God and the CDC," Dr. Harrison said.

Father Xavier crossed himself.

"Which brings me back to Dr. Levy," she said.

The cowboy and Yanira got up and started for the hotel. Vincent followed them into the hotel to collect the money before they went upstairs. Money up front was Vincent's first principle of business. When he returned to the cantina, Dr. Harrison was telling the priest about some new virus found in Janis Levy's body, or what was left of it after the *policía* found it in the rain forest.

Vincent sat down again and lit another cigarette, letting the conversation swirl past him while meditating on how nervous he'd been when the *policía* were in Paradisio searching for the missing archaeologist. There were warrants for Vincent's arrest in both Jamaica and the United States. He'd sit in prison a long, long time if the law ever got its hands on him.

"How long have you been in Paradisio, Father Xavier?"

"About six months."

"Have you seen any signs of unexplained illness?"

"None at all."

"What about your predecessor? Did he ever mention strange fevers?"

"I never met the man," Father Xavier said after throwing the rest of the mescal down his throat. "He disappeared somewhere out in the rain forest. Nobody knows what happened to him, but I doubt very much he's still alive."

"You realize what that could mean."

"What?" Father Xavier asked Dr. Harrison, stupid from the mescal.

"He might have contracted the same virus that killed Dr. Levy."

Dr. Harrison seemed to almost relish the possibility, Vincent thought.

"I think it's more likely that something much more ordinary happened to poor Father Juan," the priest said, his head seeming a little loose on his shoulders. "He probably had a heart attack or fell and hurt himself. Or perhaps he had a disagreement with some of the local Indians and came to a bad end."

The priest glanced at Vincent, meeting his eyes for only a brief, nervous moment.

"Wouldn't there be other sick people in Paradisio from this virus, Dr. Harrison?" Vincent asked.

"Not necessarily. The Indians may have an acquired immunity. The virus could be deadly only to outsiders."

"How is that possible?"

"The reverse has already happened, Vincent. Measles didn't exist in the New World before the Spanish arrived. What was a relatively mild disease to Europeans wiped out tens of thousands of Native Americans."

"And this time it's the other way around," Vincent said, crossing his arms in front of himself and pointing in opposite directions. "The Indians are immune, but we're not."

"It's one possibility. You're not from here, are you, Vincent?"

"He's Jamaican."

"That's right, mon. Born and bred in Kingston town."

"How long have you been in Paradisio?"

"Too damn long," Vincent answered.

"Have you ever been ill?"

Vincent slapped his chest. "I'm healthy as a horse."

"Good," Dr. Harrison said with a laugh. "However, I have no doubt the virus is here. I've seen fragmentary evidence in the tissue samples taken from Dr. Levy. I'll find it. It's only a matter of time."

"You go looking for trouble, ma'am, trouble come looking for you."

"It's my job to find this particular trouble, Vincent," she replied.

"But how?" the priest asked.

"I'd intended to start by taking blood samples here in Paradisio to build a database. I tried to get some of the Indians to let me draw their blood. They were a little hostile to the idea, to say the least. For a while I thought they were going to be taking blood samples from *me*. I ended up setting some mosquito traps around town, so the day wasn't a complete waste. That could turn up something.

Mosquitoes are a fairly active disease vector, collecting pathogens from the blood of a variety of birds and mammals. But what I really need is some blood samples from the people who live here. Any idea how I can convince the Indians to cooperate?"

"The Zona Indians are as stubborn a people as any you will ever meet," Father Xavier said. "If they don't like needles, you've got your work cut out for you."

"What about you, Vincent? Any ideas?"

"You can't force the Indians to do anything they don't want to do. They'd as soon die first."

"Maybe there's a doctor or nurse-practitioner in the area I can get to help. These people don't know me, they don't trust me, and it seems pretty clear they aren't going to cooperate."

"There's nobody like that around Paradisio."

"What do these people do when they get sick, Father Xavier?"

"They don't get sick."

"Great," she said, when Vincent knew what she really wanted to do was swear. "I suppose it doesn't ultimately matter. I'll find the real answers in the rain forest."

"You're going into the forest?" Father Xavier said, almost gasping with disbelief. There was no doubt about it, Vincent thought. The priest had seen something he wasn't meant to see.

"Of course I am, Father. I need to visit the places Dr. Levy visited, collecting specimens and seeing what I can scare up. It's the best chance I have of finding the key to what killed her. I need to see where her body was recovered."

"Won't it be dangerous?" the priest asked.

"I know the risks and how to minimize them. Dr. Levy was an archaeologist. She must have been looking for some kind of ruins near here. Do you know where they are?"

Father Xavier's face went white. "No," he said. "I have no idea whatsoever."

"What about you, Vincent?"

Vincent made the elaborate ritual of lighting a cigarette to give himself time to think. She was a persistent woman. She'd find out regardless of what he told her. Nevertheless, he decided, she wasn't going to find it out from him. He didn't want her blood on his hands.

"She didn't tell me a thing except that she didn't like the Hotel Paradisio."

"Then I'll find the ruins on my own," Dr. Harrison said, staring straight at Vincent, letting him know she didn't think he was telling her the truth. "I need to hire a guide. Can you recommend someone reliable, Father?"

"I don't know any guides," Father Xavier said.

"We don't get tourists in Paradisio, Dr. Harrison," Vincent said. "There are no guides here."

"Then what about you taking me? I'm willing to pay enough to make it worth your while to be away from the hotel for a few days."

"I'd like to help, Dr. Harrison, but there isn't enough money in the world to get me into that rain forest."

"You're afraid of the rain forest?" Her tone was lightly mocking, as if she thought she could shame him into helping her.

"You're damned right. There are snakes and jaguars and spiders and scorpions and who knows what waiting in that forest, waiting to kill you dead. The forest's got these little green bugs you can hardly see that will bite you and make you so sick you'll wish you were dead. Damned right I'm afraid of the rain forest."

"Come on, Vincent. Name your price."

"Listen, Dr. Harrison. That other woman went into the rain forest alive and came out of it dead. You want to go messing around out there, you find somebody else to do it with you."

"What about you, Father?"

"I wouldn't be any use to you," the priest sputtered. "I barely know my way around the village. I will ask around for you, but I wouldn't hold out much hope. The people here are not known for being cooperative."

Dr. Harrison got up from the table and came across the room to lean on the bar. "I'll give you one thousand dollars in American money for a week of your time," she said in a low, bargaining voice.

Vincent swung his dreadlocks.

"Fifteen hundred."

"Don't think I'm not tempted, but sorry, Doctor, no."

"Two grand."

"The Indians say the rain forest is haunted," Vincent whispered, "especially where the *policía* found what little bit of Dr. Levy there was left to scrape up out of the dirt."

"You don't believe in demons, do you, Vincent?"

"What I don't believe, Dr. Harrison, is that I can spend your money after it gets my ass killed."

"Twenty-five hundred dollars. That's my best offer to take me into the rain forest to find the place Janis Levy died. I'll pay you cash."

There was a movement in the doorway where Roberto

Goya de Montezuma seemed to materialize, his back framed by the darkness in the open door.

"Sorry," Vincent said, looking past her at Roberto, "but I can't help you."

Dr. Harrison turned toward Roberto and spoke in Spanish. "Excuse me, *señor*. My name is Dr. Bailey Harrison. I'm looking for someone to serve as a guide on a research trip into the rain forest to where some ruins are apparently located. I will pay very well, if you or anyone you know can help me."

Roberto's face was expressionless, but Vincent could see the cold hatred in his eyes. Vincent was not afraid of Roberto, merely wary. Roberto had the eyes of a man who would cut your throat as you slept without thinking a thing about it.

"I'm a physician," Dr. Harrison explained, trying to convince Roberto to help her. "My work is extremely important. Lives depend on it."

Roberto stood toe-to-toe with Dr. Harrison, looking down into her hopeful face. For a moment Vincent was afraid Roberto was actually going to accept her invitation, but he turned without a word and went back out the door.

"Doesn't he understand Spanish?"

"Roberto understands *everything*," Vincent said.

Dr. Harrison raised her hands, then dropped them, slapping them against her hips.

"Then I'll go alone, if I have to."

"No, please don't say that," Father Xavier pleaded.

"It's more dangerous than you understand," Vincent said. "You shouldn't even consider going into the rain forest alone."

"I am not going back to Atlanta empty-handed just because I couldn't make it the last few miles after traveling all the way to Costa Rica." She crossed her arms and raised her chin. "If no one will help me, I'll find the ruins myself."

Dr. Harrison was flat-out determined to get herself killed, Vincent decided. He made it a habit to never involve himself in other people's problems, but the pretty American had no idea what she was dealing with. If Vincent didn't help her, she was as good as dead. The problem was that she was as good as dead even with his help.

"I will take you to Zonatitucan."

The silhouette of a tall, lean man stood in the doorway where Roberto had been a few minutes earlier.

Vincent felt himself sink into the stool, gravity seeming to increase as the ganja high grabbed him by the back of his neck, pulling his brain down into his spine. What strange luck that the boss and Roberto would turn up in Paradisio on the same night—and stranger still that they hadn't run into each other in the tiny town. There was bad blood between the two of them now, ever since Roberto had come back from the United States.

"Good evening, don Lazaro," Vincent said.

From somewhere out in the night came the sound of a child singing—the high, clear, unaccompanied voice of an Indian child sweetly singing the lyrics to Mozart's opera *The Magic Flute*.

"I will take you to the ruins," don Lazaro said, stepping into the cantina, his black riding boots clicking on the plank floor in counterpoint to the aria.

Dr. Harrison's eyes did not leave his as she came toward him to gratefully accept his outstretched hand and his kindly offer of help.

PART II

La Esmerelda

Ocho

THE SERVANT CARRIED her suitcase with little apparent effort, though she could hardly lift it. The Indian was no taller than Bailey, but he was much stronger. It was impossible to tell his age from the unlined nut-brown face. About forty, she guessed, but he might as easily have been seventy.

An antique four-poster bed sat at an angle in one corner with two nightstands, a dresser, and a mirror made from matching mahogany grouped around it. The leather couch looked comfortable. It sat in front of a fireplace faced with colorful mosaic tile fitted together to form an Aztec winged serpent.

"You can leave that on the floor by the bed, please," Bailey told the man in Spanish.

The M. C. Escher engraving hanging over the fireplace was one she had seen before. The interlocking series of alligators emerged out of a drawing in the artist's sketch pad, crawled over a book, and merged back into the drawing. The engraving was an original, numbered and signed.

The books on the coffee table were about art and architecture—expensive, oversize volumes meant to be leafed through while passing an idle hour. At a right angle to the couch and fireplace were an overstuffed chair and ottoman, a pole lamp behind the chair and a small table beside it to hold a cup of coffee. The claw-foot writing desk was inset with a wine-colored leather writing surface and stood under the window that looked out on the gardens.

Bailey put the backpack on the floor beside the desk, leaned across the desk, and switched on the green-shaded banker's lamp. An onyx tray held a selection of pens, markers, and a dozen No. 2 pencils, each sharpened to a perfect point.

The Indian bowed slightly without speaking or smiling or meeting her eyes when she thanked him. He turned on a switch by the door as he went out, closing the door behind him. Overhead, in the center of the high-ceilinged room, fan blades began to slowly turn.

Through a half-open doorway was her bathroom, retrofitted into what must have once been a dressing room. A small watercolor painting of a wildflower hung on the wall above the light switch. Bailey leaned forward to read the signature on the miniature: *Lazaro*.

Bailey turned the gleaming brass faucet, and hot water poured into the marble basin. It was strange, even a little disappointing, to have traveled so far into the wilderness only to find such refined amenities. Bailey began to wash her face with perfumed French beauty soap.

Dr. Janis Levy had also been don Lazaro's guest. She slept in the bed where Bailey would sleep and had probably stood at the same sink and washed her face with French beauty soap upon arriving at La Esmerelda.

Bailey's hands found the towel while her eyes were

still closed. She patted her face dry, staring at herself in the mirror.

She was not going to end up like Janis Levy.

They paused by a shallow pond along the path that led to the stables.

A floating blanket of lotus blossoms reached a third of the way to the center of the pool, followed by a stretch of water so placid that it might have been glass. At the opposite side was a tall stand of saw grass. The rangy brown stems were topped with billowing crowns that floated above the water, reflected in it like clouds in the azure sky.

"I have everything I need here—my music, my books, my art."

"Your home is very beautiful, don Lazaro. But do you ever feel as if you're missing something, living so far from the madding crowd?"

"As I said, Dr. Harrison, I have everything I need."

"What about the things you don't need?"

Bailey noticed the slight tightening of the muscles around don Lazaro's eyes.

"Such as what? The noise? The congestion?"

"I think I would miss them after a while. As much as most people fantasize about running away to a desert island, there's something to be said for being caught up in the thick of things, even though it is hectic and some-times unpleasant."

"I suppose I occasionally regret being so far removed from the pulse of the world," don Lazaro said. "I suppose it is only natural. Nevertheless, the quiet pleasures of life here are not to be underappreciated. After you have spent some time at La Esmerelda, you will come to understand. You may discover yourself wishing you, too, could remain here forever."

The air in the stable was a mix of straw, manure, and horse that was earthy rather than rank. There were two long opposing rows of stalls. A brass plate on each gate named the animal that looked out at the two visitors with curious or frightened eyes and a flurry of bumps, paws, and equine sound.

"They are magnificent animals. Proud and strong, some with an instinct so keen that you would swear they could read your mind."

Lazaro scratched a horse's nose. The animal turned its head to one side as if it were flirting with him, nuzzling his hand. He glanced backward at her and grinned, giving Bailey the peculiar sensation that he was reading *her* mind.

"Yet the horse is a fragile creature. You have to care for them as if they were children. My trainer sleeps with them, watching over them through the night. God forbid that a jaguar should get into the stable during the night."

"Is that why you have armed men wandering the grounds, trying to look inconspicuous with machine guns slung over their shoulders? Are they guarding your horses from jaguars?"

"The big cats are too intelligent to come around the hacienda during the daylight. Only the bravest chance it after dark. Still, it does happen, from time to time."

"I dislike guns."

"You must not forget where you are, Dr. Harrison. That is the best advice I can give you. The rain forest has great natural beauty, but it can become a place of death more easily than you can imagine."

"A gun wouldn't have helped Dr. Levy."

"Poor woman. I did what I could to assist her, but she was stubborn. The result was tragic."

Don Lazaro bent to fill an old coffee can with feed from a burlap sack leaning against a post in the middle of the stable. He dumped the feed into the mare's trough and set the can back on the wooden shelf next to the stall.

"As for the guns, I would gladly order that they be put away if they were not a necessity, Dr. Harrison. Occasionally guerrillas and *bandidos* pass through the province, bad men who would very much like to use La Esmerelda as a staging ground to smuggle cocaine into the United States. We are too remote to call the *policía* when there is trouble. I am the *policía* here."

"I see."

"Pray do not imagine I relish the authority, Doctor. Some things are forced upon one."

Don Lazaro opened the door and flipped a light switch, motioning for Bailey to go in ahead of him. She passed near enough to don Lazaro to feel the heat of his body, an involuntary thrill running through her.

"Will this be suitable for your work?"

The veterinary infirmary had a freshly painted concrete floor and banks of bright fluorescent lights overhead. A long, stainless-steel table stood in the middle of the room. There was a double sink, also steel, against one wall, a propane-powered stove on one side of it, a refrigerator on the other. The appliances were scrubbed spotlessly clean, like the rest of the room. Shelves along one wall contained big jars of medicine, bandages, and other veterinary supplies.

"This will do nicely."

"If there is anything else you require for your field laboratory, you have only to ask. The entire resources of La Esmerelda are at your disposal."

"You have gone to great lengths to care for your horses, don Lazaro. There should be a clinic in Paradisio stocked this well."

She looked up into don Lazaro's puzzled eyes. "Has a single child in Paradisio been inoculated against smallpox and diphtheria?"

"You do not understand the Zona. They would never allow an outsider to treat them."

"Then arrange to have an Indian learn to become a nurse-practitioner, the way you paid to have some become teachers. I'm not talking about brain surgery, don Lazaro. Giving a child a DPT shot is something even one of the prostitutes in your hotel could learn to do."

Don Lazaro looked down at her without flinching. "The idea has merit," he said finally.

"I don't mean to be rude, don Lazaro, but as a physician it's my responsibility to point such things out."

"We shall have to discuss it further at another time."

"Good enough," Bailey said. "I'd like to take blood samples from the servants and ranch hands at La Esmerelda tomorrow. I didn't have much success with it back in Paradisio. The Indians seem to be pathologically afraid of needles."

"The Zona are very brave. It was not your needle they feared."

"Then what?"

"You unknowingly violated local taboo, Dr. Harrison. You wanted their blood. To a Zona, the blood is where the soul resides."

"Wonderful."

"Old beliefs die hard in this corner of the world, Doctor."

"I need those samples, don Lazaro. You don't have any idea how dangerous this virus could turn out to be."

"I think I do, Dr. Harrison. Let me talk to my people. I will make them understand."

"You can convince them I'm not trying to steal their souls?"

"I will prove it to them by example. Tomorrow, before you do anything else, Dr. Harrison, you must collect a sample of *my* blood."

Nueve

ROBERTO SAT CROSS-LEGGED on the ground, staring into the fire, mouth slack, head tilted at an odd angle. A strand of hair pulled loose from his ponytail fell across his face. His forehead was smudged with soot, as if he'd been to Ash Wednesday Mass. There was dried vomit on his black T-shirt.

Naked figures danced in the fire, iridescent bodies of red and gold. Roberto controlled them with his thoughts, directing the tiny burning bodies to run and whirl, to burn low and leap high, writhing in ecstatic pain.

A jaguar had led him to the power place.

At midday, Roberto found jaguar footprints near Bone Lake. The jaguar was his spirit animal, so whenever he encountered one, it was never *just* a jaguar.

Roberto followed the tracks all afternoon, high up the saddle-back ridge to a rocky summit overlooking a sunken valley with a sluggish river against the far rim. The ridge was the only way up or down. At the summit was a large, flat table of bare rock. That's where the tracks ended. The spirit animal had climbed to the power place and vanished into the air.

Roberto felt the eternal wind blow past him as he stood

on the power spot, the jaguar's breath coming through the secret door to the other world. Power had brought him there for a purpose. He built a fire, ate a handful of mushrooms from the leather pouch, and sat down to wait.

The rain came. The sorcerer used his power to hold an invisible dome of dryness and warmth over himself and the fire until the storm cried itself out. The sky cleared. The stars came out. Roberto continued to sit on the power spot, waiting, thinking.

Perhaps he wanted don Lazaro's death too much.

Any kind of yearning was a sign of weakness, don Paulo had said, and weakness was dangerous to a sorcerer, since it repelled power the way water repelled oil. The only thing that attracted power was power. The trick to becoming a sorcerer was to start out with no power, but to accumulate it, a little at a time, until you were strong enough to pass freely between the worlds.

Roberto took Father Juan's head from the burlap bag and put it in front of the fire. Most of the flesh was rotted away, though a few wisps of gray hair clung stubbornly to the pate. Unlike the bleached specimens he had handled in anthropology class, Father Juan's skull was a mottled dirty gray and smelled awful.

The dancing flames arranged themselves in the image of the *gringa* doctor. She hovered in the fire, her naked body floating above Father Juan's skull so that her feet seemed to dance lightly upon the grizzled bone.

Another blasphemy was going to occur at Zonatitucan, unless Roberto stopped it.

A branch snapped in the darkness.

Roberto's eyes searched the night, but after looking

into the fire so long he saw nothing but the fire's after-image. He reached out with his senses, as don Paulo had taught him, feeling for a presence. Something was there, something coming his way.

Roberto grabbed for Father Juan's skull, but the grinning death's-head seemed to leap away to the other side of the world. Roberto's arm extended until it was a thousand miles long, his hand the jaguar's breath, running swiftly and silently through the night.

"*¡Hola!*"

The greeting rumbled out of the darkness like an earthquake, making the rock beneath Roberto tremble, kicking up sparks in the fire.

Roberto stood and lurched forward, overwhelmed by hallucinations. The ground opened in front of him. He tried to look down, but the Underworld's molten red glare was impossible to face for longer than a second. Shielding his face from the apocalypse, he stumbled around the campfire, managing to get to the other side without setting himself on fire.

Bile was rising in Roberto's throat. He was going to vomit again. The mushrooms always made him sick. He somehow managed to force his stomach back down. Gritting his teeth, he made himself turn to stone inside—strong, unafraid, merciless, a Zona warrior.

A shadow came to life, moving along the edge of the light.

"I didn't know it was you, Roberto. I was on my way back to camp, saw the fire, and thought I should check it out. You know how don Lazaro is about trespassers."

Roberto realized it was Ignatio, the foreman for a crew of forestry rangers who selected mature trees to cut down, marking each with an *X* in Day-Glo orange spray paint.

"Are you all right, Roberto?" Ignatio peered at him from across the fire. "You look a little *malo*."

Roberto swayed back and forth, becoming suspicious. The guardian could adopt any form it chose. Maybe this was not really Ignatio.

"This isn't a good place to sit and get quietly drunk, *hombre*."

"I'm not drunk."

Had he said that? Had anybody said that? Maybe Roberto had only thought about saying that.

"Why don't you come with me back to camp? In the morning Julio will make you breakfast."

Ignatio reached for Roberto's arm to steady him on his feet. Roberto watched his fist shoot out—it seemed to have a will of its own—and smash Ignatio's face. The blow caught the other man flat-footed. He careened backward, hitting the ground on one shoulder, rolling over.

The skin on Ignatio's face instantly blackened, becoming bloated, suppurated. Muscles and sinews broke through, here and there bits of raw bone extruding through the putrefying skin.

"Why did you . . ."

"You're already dead and rotting in the grave," Roberto said, his voice seeming to come from a long ways away, from a dark and distant star.

Ignatio's veins quivered and stretched, his dead heart struggling to force congealed blood and corrupt gas through his body. One of the veins exploded with a pop, then another. White corpse worms slithered from the ruptured blood vessels, the mucus they excreted leaving bright trails through the darker jelly of Ignatio's decomposing flesh.

Ignatio opened his mouth to speak, but the dead man's tongue had been transformed into a frog—Chuwen, the god of the grave, warning him about the *gringa*.

Ignatio tried to stand, but Roberto kicked him in the ribs. Ignoring the groans, Roberto turned to look for his machete. The blade, dull from chopping vines, went only halfway through Ignatio's neck, becoming stuck in the spine. Roberto had to put his boot against Ignatio's shoulder for leverage to pull it free.

Ignatio made a noise like a pig being slaughtered, blood spewing from his throat. He seemed to be trying to get away, but he couldn't control his body's coarse spasms.

The machete came down a second time, finishing the job.

Roberto used his sheath knife to cut out the heart. He ate part of it; it helped to settle his stomach. He put the rest of the heart on a rock in front of the fire as an offering.

Roberto sat down again on the power spot and looked up at the stars. It was still early. The guardian might yet come.

Diez

THE SOUND WAS intermittent and annoying, like a mosquito in a dark room.

Where would it end now that it had started?

Alvaro Marquez was awaiting Lazaro on the veranda. Generations of Marquez men had served Lazaro, descendants of the Indians who built Zonatitucan, their bloodlines remaining pure in the remote province. The Indian's hearing was nearly as acute as Lazaro's, his perceptions so powerful that he sometimes seemed to share his master's preternatural abilities.

"I will prepare for the new visitor," Alvaro said.

Lazaro frowned and said nothing.

A blue Land Rover materialized on the ridge above the hacienda, still nearly five kilometers away. The truck hesitated briefly, then began its steep descent, perspective making it appear to tip almost vertical, a metal fly climbing down a green wall shimmering in the afternoon heat.

For years Lazaro had known that someone would eventually turn up, searching for Zonatitucan.

Dr. Janis Levy's visit had ended very badly.

Dr. Harrison was a surprise. Lazaro had not expected someone else would come so soon after the *policía* carried away poor Janis's mortal remains. He also had not guessed it would be a physician, instead of another archaeologist.

And now this, a third intruder.

Lazaro walked around to the west side of the veranda and flung himself down into an oversize rattan chair.

There was also Roberto to consider. His preoccupation with the past had become a dangerous obsession. Something had happened to him in America, something that filled his heart with anger. Roberto had become irrational and unpredictable. Not even Lazaro knew what Roberto might do next.

Lazaro made a steeple of his fingers, frowning at the slowly approaching vehicle.

There was no stopping the flood once the dike began to crumble, he thought. A few innocent satellite photographs of the rain forest had set in motion something that even Lazaro, with all his experience and guile, might not be able to stop. The powerful evil he'd held in check for five hundred years seemed destined to be loosed upon the world.

He was a rather short middle-aged man whose barrel chest and high, serious forehead made him appear taller than he really was. His chestnut-colored hair was a long, tangled leonine mane pushed back behind his ears, falling against his shoulders. He had a prominent brow that was deeply furrowed with horizontal lines. His deep-set eyes were filled with fierce energy, his mouth a downward-turning slash cut into a strong jaw that seemed best suited to frowning. The overall impression was formidable, even forbidding.

The stranger wore an odd combination of formal clothing and bush gear, as if he'd dashed out of a bank office and into the rain forest with time to only partly change his attire. Beneath an olive-drab bush jacket was a starched white shirt, pearl-gray tie, and blue silk vest. A gold chain looped from a buttonhole to the left vest pocket. He wore his trousers tucked into the tops of knee-high black leather Wellington boots.

"Buenos días, señor."

The stranger turned from the book whose spine he was examining, a collection of Franz Kafka's writing. The man's face was so darkly passionate that Lazaro expected an outburst. Instead, the stranger smiled disarmingly and came forward with his right hand extended.

"I must apologize for my uninvited intrusion into your privacy." He spoke with a German accent. "My name is Ludwig Samsa."

"Welcome to La Esmcrclda, Herr Samsa. I am Lazaro Ruiz Cortinez. May I offer you coffee?"

"Thank you, don Lazaro."

The German sat on the couch across from Lazaro, leaning back into the corner, his right arm thrown up across the backrest, confident, at home in the world.

Lazaro focused on the German's expanse of forehead, gently probing his mind. He met with startlingly solid resistance. Unlike the thoughts of most people, who possess only a weak will, Herr Samsa's thoughts could not be easily read.

"You must be wondering what brings me to your corner of the world, don Lazaro."

Lazaro nodded slightly.

"I am an entomologist. I spend most of my time lecturing in Berlin, but I have taken a sabbatical to come to the rain forest to pursue my particular field of interest—butterflies."

"The rain forest is home to many rare and unusual species, Herr Samsa. Is it any particular butterfly that interests you, or is it butterflies in general?"

"The giant blue morpho."

"You will find many examples in the forest around La Esmerelda. Yesterday morning I saw a morpho this big." Lazaro held his hands out flat, the thumbs touching, to illustrate the enormous specimen.

"The very grail I seek!"

Alvaro materialized in the room, noiselessly deposited two bone china cups and saucers on the table between the two men, and slipped back out again without a word.

"You will find many specimens of *Morpho cypris* flying low along the forest trails near here in the morning, Herr Samsa, before returning to their roosts."

Lazaro watched the German over his cup as he took a sip of strong black coffee.

"Forgive me for saying so, don Lazaro, but I'm afraid you are mistaken. *Morpho cypris* lives high in the canopy. You are thinking of *Morpho peleides*, which is more commonly found flying in the open places low to the ground."

"How stupid of me. Of course, you are right."

The German matched his smile, seeming to know Lazaro was testing him.

"I have a confession to make, don Lazaro. The real thing that brought me to La Esmerelda is something even more rare than the giant blue morpho."

Lazaro raised an eyebrow.

"I came here because of your piano! Entomology is my profession, but music is my passion. I have not touched a keyboard in the two months since I left Europe. A man in Punta Cahulta told me you had a Steinway transported all the way across the Cordillera Talamanca. When I heard that, I decided to repair here immediately and throw myself on your mercy. I beg you to indulge me. I am like a man who is dying of thirst, though it is not water I need but . . ." The German paused and gave Lazaro a strange look. ". . . music."

"I am sorry to disappoint you, Herr Samsa, but the piano is very badly out of tune. It is the climate. The humidity is impossible. The man in San Vito who tunes it for me, a retired music teacher, will not be here again until the end of the month. I'm afraid you have come here for nothing."

"But that is even better! I worked my way through college as a piano tuner. I can repay your favor with a small service."

A flash of lightning filled the windows with an instant of brilliant blue light. The explosion of thunder that followed shook the coffee cups in their saucers, echoing against the mountains surrounding Zonatitucan, coming back to visit them a second time. The rain started, pounding down so hard that it might have been signaling the end of the world.

"Only if you consent to be my guest, Herr Samsa," Lazaro said, holding the German's eyes. "We do not have nearly enough visitors at La Esmerelda."

The German bowed his head to show assent, looking back at Lazaro with a smile that could have meant anything.

Once

IT WAS ALMOST like a picnic, don Merino thought, giddy with fever.

He stood in the kitchen area of his two-room house on the mountain above Paradisio, gathering random provisions, this and that, whatever he could lay his hands on that seemed right. He put some rice into the old flour sack, along with fruit, sugar cubes, a stub of a candle, and a hawk's feather he'd found in front of his house.

Don Merino opened the rum bottle and took a deep drink, gathering his strength. The doctor in San Juan had warned him not to drink, but what the hell did it matter? Rum was the only medicine that brought him any relief.

"A chicken would be good," don Merino mumbled to himself. Too bad he didn't have a chicken.

He put the rum into the bag with the rest of the provisions and clapped a sweat-stained campesino hat securely on his head. With the sack slung over his shoulder, he headed down the trail, hobbling with his cane like a character in a sinister fairy tale.

To die peacefully in his own bed—that was the only thing that mattered to don Merino now, even if he died alone, hiding in the rain forest from the *policía* and the partners he'd cheated in Mexico City.

He walked a little ways and sat on a log to rest, fishing the rum out of the sack for another drink, his hands shaking. The day was hot, the trail difficult. Going down the mountain was hard enough. Getting back up would be far worse.

When don Merino reached the clearing it was almost noon. He set his bag down on the altar.

"A chicken would be good," he said to himself again.

Don Merino had heard they used animals in their ceremonies, chickens and sometimes goats, cutting their throats, collecting the blood in wooden bowls.

He arranged the modest offering on the altar and spit a mouthful of rum over everything, the way they said the voodoo mambos did it in the islands. He knew it wouldn't be right, but the important thing was to show respect. If the Indians knew he respected them, then maybe they'd leave him alone to die peacefully in his own bed.

He'd heard them in the clearing at night, chanting in front of the altar in the incomprehensible Zona dialect, their lanterns flickering will-o'-the-wisps among the trees. The shrieks and screams made his skin crawl. He knew the bloodstains on the stone altar were not from chickens.

When don Merino finished, he turned away and crossed himself with his bony right hand, the blue veins standing out against the almost translucent yellowish skin. He was a Catholic and didn't want to go to Hell for worshiping at a pagan altar. It was just that he wanted to die peacefully, in his own bed. Certainly God would understand his intention and that he was too sick to leave Paradisio.

Don Merino fortified himself with another slug of rum. The flour sack was empty now except for the bottle, but it still seemed heavy. The dying man began to inch his way back up the mountain a few steps at a time, leaning heavily on his cane, regretting that he didn't have a chicken to leave at the altar.

Doce

✦

LUDWIG STOOD WITH hands clasped behind his back, gazing across the darkened garden.

Beads of rain shimmered on the leaves, pearls delicately balanced on jade petals. Above the graceful silhouettes of trees, queued against the southern horizon like ballerinas awaiting their turn onstage, the Milky Way was a diagonal sash of diamonds draped across the silken sky. Tropical night-blooming flowers filled the air with scent, but the perfume of Dr. Bailey Harrison's blood was sweeter still.

Ludwig improvised a melody in his mind, a tune so dreamy it was almost sad. The late-afternoon thunderstorm had been a symphony. Now the night's lyric stillness was a nocturne—quiet, reflective, pensive, a mood somewhere between romance and regret.

"One of the things I like best about being far from civilization is the brilliant night sky. I wish you could see the stars from the Amazon basin or the Himalayas. It is a vision only a poet could describe."

Dr. Harrison stood close to Ludwig, looking up at the sky, sharing it with him.

"Even with the lights of the hacienda behind us, you can see the nebula in Orion." He pointed. "The bright star above the nebula—Orion's shoulder—is Betelgeuse."

"Perhaps you both would care for some port."

Don Lazaro had come silently into the library. He'd been standing there for nearly a minute, watching them on the veranda through the open French door. Dr. Harrison had not heard him, though Ludwig had sensed their host's presence even before he'd come into the room.

Dr. Harrison sat on one end of the couch as don Lazaro's servant served the port. Ludwig chose the opposite end, moving the pillow so he could sit with his back straight. Don Lazaro lowered his angular frame into a wing-backed chair situated with the fireplace behind it. He resembled Mephistopheles, Ludwig thought, with the flames flickering behind him, his fingertips forming an arch beneath his chin.

Dr. Harrison took a tiny sip of port.

"How did you develop an interest in entomology?" she asked.

"I have been enthralled with the process of metamorphosis ever since I was a child. A worm—a repulsive, lowly, slithering thing—withdraws into a cocoon and is transformed into a creature of sublime grace and beauty. This has always seemed to me to be nature at its most magical."

Ludwig glanced at don Lazaro, who was close to scowling.

"You must not encourage me to ramble about my parochial interests, Dr. Harrison. I turn into the most unbelievable bore when I start talking about order Lepidoptera."

"Not at all," she protested. "I find it fascinating."

"Earlier I promised you music. Allow me to enjoy don Lazaro's excellent piano while it is freshly tuned."

"I suppose that would be an acceptable compromise," Dr. Harrison said with a smile.

Dr. Harrison's warmth contrasted with don Lazaro's coldness. He'd become distant and withdrawn during supper. Dr. Harrison and Ludwig had conducted a long supper-table discussion about viruses, a subject about which don Lazaro knew little. His mind was elsewhere throughout most of the meal.

Ludwig went to the piano and pulled out the bench. He opened his hands over the keys, flexing and relaxing them, limbering the muscles and tendons. The ivory keys were cool to his fingertips. To have a gift, to lose it beyond hope of ever regaining it, only to get it back so unexpectedly—this was the true miracle of his life as a vampire.

"Is there anything in particular you would like to hear, Dr. Harrison?" Ludwig asked, eyes closed, fingers poised, like a mystic awaiting a vision of rapture. He was trembling slightly, though it was visible only by looking very closely at his wrists.

"I adore Chopin."

"Then for you, dear Doctor, Chopin . . ."

Ludwig played for nearly a half hour, following Chopin's ghost as it led him brilliantly from one piece to another. And then, suddenly, the spirit was gone and with it the music.

"Bravo," Dr. Harrison whispered.

Ludwig could feel her eyes on him. He sensed her opening to him, the protective chrysalis of a serious and ambitious professional drawing apart, revealing the heart of the woman within.

"Perhaps some Liszt," don Lazaro said. "If it is not too technically demanding, of course."

"The first song is in your honor, don Lazaro."

Ludwig began with the *Mephisto Waltz*, his hands treating the impossible sixty-fourth-note runs as if they were quarter notes in a beginner's practice book. He played in a trance, his head fallen forward and eyes closed, his hands moving effortlessly, fluidly, up and down the eighty-eight keys.

Ludwig segued through the Liszt oeuvre, pieces requiring nearly inhuman reaches that not a dozen pianists in the world could perform adequately. But Ludwig was more than human and his playing more than adequate. The music poured from his hands as if it was his soul touching the keys. He improvised complex counterpoints and harmonies as he went, transforming the music into something not even the pyrotechnic Liszt could have equaled.

When he'd finished, Ludwig sat bent over the keyboard, exhausted body and spirit, a jar from which everything had been emptied. His long hair was damp with perspiration, his breath coming in short, shallow gasps.

Dr. Harrison came to the piano and put her hand gently on his shoulder. He felt a strange yet familiar yearning stir deep within his ancient breast.

"That was indescribably beautiful."

"I am so very gratified that you think so, Dr. Harrison."

"Please, call me Bailey."

The diamond-hard chrysalis around Ludwig's heart cracked open, emotions stirring to life in him that had spent more than a century in dusty sleep. The moment's intimacy made Ludwig forget don Lazaro, and Lazaro's role in the increasingly complicated affair. Lazaro sat watching them, glowering in his chair in front of the fire like a fallen angel brooding over Paradise lost.

"Bailey," Ludwig said, trying out the name against his ear.

The sound was filled with brightness and air. He heard a violin in his head, the melody as joyful and innocent as a child at play. He would put this spontaneous creation down on paper, dedicating the string quartet to a woman who was so lovely, so intelligent, so much an inspiration to the composer.

Lazaro coughed dryly.

"I have mountains of work to do in the morning," Bailey said, seeming to suddenly remember who she was and why she was there. "I need to excuse myself and get a good night's sleep."

"Of course . . . Bailey."

Ludwig accompanied her to the door.

"Thank you again for the music," she said. "I don't think I've ever heard anything so beautiful. I hope you'll play for me—for us—again."

"It will be my pleasure," Ludwig said, and bowed.

"Good night, don Lazaro."

Lazaro nodded but said nothing.

Ludwig returned to his seat when she was gone, filled

with the unexpected sweetness of the moment. It made him so happy that for a few minutes he was able to ignore don Lazaro, who was glaring at him with anger and jealousy. These were unfamiliar emotions for don Lazaro, Ludwig saw, looking into his host's mind. How quickly love can unmake a gentleman!

"And so," Ludwig said finally, leaning back against the couch, crossing his legs.

Don Lazaro tried to force his way into Ludwig's thoughts.

Ludwig smiled to himself and removed the pocket watch from his vest pocket. It was set for Venice time. Ludwig kept a palazzo on the Grand Canal. He spent most of his time there, when he wasn't working for the *Illuminati*.

Veins stood out in don Lazaro's temples. There was no longer any subtlety in his approach. His mouth was set in a determined line, his brows sharply drawn, hooding his eyes as he tried to penetrate the German's closely guarded mind.

Ludwig snapped the watch shut and looked up at don Lazaro, shaking his head. Don Lazaro could never touch his thoughts. His powers were weak compared to Ludwig's.

"Who *are* you?" don Lazaro demanded, realizing his telepathic efforts were futile. "And *what* are you?"

Ludwig said nothing.

"I had not thought it possible, but it seems . . ." Don Lazaro could not believe the conclusion he had reached.

"It seems that we have more in common than interests in music and the lovely Dr. Harrison," don Lazaro said.

Ludwig maintained his serene smile and his silence. Perhaps it would be best to tell don Lazaro nothing. After all, Ludwig thought, he was probably going to have to kill the other vampire.

Trece

✦

"I THOUGHT YOU might like coffee and a sandwich," Lazaro said, coming into the makeshift lab with the tray. "You missed lunch."

"Thanks," Bailey said.

She barely glanced up from her work. On the table was a rack of plastic vials containing a few cc's of blood. She transferred a crimson drop onto a slide and put it into the microscope.

"You were able to get all the samples you needed?"

"Mmmm," she answered, adjusting the instrument, her attention on what she saw in the magnified blood.

Bailey wore her hair swept up on her head so that it wouldn't get in the way, revealing the delicate curve of her naked neck, its tanned skin covered with a light, almost imperceptible golden down.

A lady used to be admired for the milky whiteness of her skin, Lazaro thought, and a body kept carefully soft and plump by as little physical exercise as possible. Modern women—you called them ladies at your peril, Lazaro had read—were tanned and lean from running, cycling, even lifting weights.

Bailey wore a starched white lab coat over a T-shirt and blue jeans. The Nike running shoes seemed to go with the black Timex Ironman runner's watch on her left wrist. Lazaro frowned at the rubber gloves. The white latex fit her hands like a second skin, like the pale hands of the dead.

"You're not going to eat?"

"What?" Bailey looked over her shoulder at Lazaro. She'd already forgotten he was there.

"Your mind would be sharper if you took a break for a few minutes. You've been bent over that microscope since breakfast."

Bailey straightened, flexing her back.

"Why don't you set your work aside long enough to come outside into the garden and have a cup of coffee with me? When you get tired, you begin to make mistakes."

Bailey smiled at Lazaro and sighed. She began to peel off the gloves.

"I guess a break wouldn't hurt," she said. "A short break," she added.

"You are certain that a virus killed Dr. Levy?"

They were sitting on an iron bench under a banyan tree, the tray on a table in front of them. Bailey had eaten half the sandwich and was drinking a second cup of coffee.

"The DNA fragments in Dr. Levy's remains indicate that's the case."

"Fragments?"

"DNA breaks down after death."

"So you can only infer she was infected."

"If a bomb explodes in a building, Lazaro, you don't need to see the bomb to know what happened."

"Then a virus is like a bomb?"

"In a manner of speaking. A virus injects its genetic code into a host cell, taking over the cell's functions. The host cell becomes a slave factory dedicated to producing more viruses. The viruses multiply, swelling the infected cell until it can't hold any more. The cell then ruptures and dies, spewing the viruses into neighboring cells and the bloodstream, spreading the infection."

"It sounds predatory."

"Without a doubt. Viruses are microscopic vampires that prey on healthy cells to survive."

Lazaro stared at Bailey, struck by something that had never occurred to him before—an explanation for who he was, for what he was.

"And viruses are deadly?"

"Some, especially the Level Four bugs."

"I do not understand. What is Level Four?"

"Biohazards are categorized according to lethality. A disease like AIDS, which has infected at least sixty million people and will probably kill them without a medical breakthrough, is classified Biosafety Level Two because it isn't easily transmitted. Level Four is reserved for the worst viruses, diseases like anthrax, Ebola, and Marburg that are extremely lethal as well as extremely infectious. There are no vaccinations against Level Four agents and no treatments once you become infected. You die horribly. Ebola Zaire rots you from the inside out, turning its victims into puddles of goo that ooze blood and putrescence from every bodily orifice. You even bleed from your *eyes*. The skin comes off your tongue. Your internal organs rot from the inside out."

Bailey laughed with embarrassment.

"If you'd seen what some of these bugs can do, you'd want to fight them as much as I do."

"Something like this killed Dr. Levy?"

"I think so. The fortunate thing may turn out to be that she died in the rain forest."

"How can you say that?"

"Think about what could have happened if Dr. Levy had gotten on a plane, coughing during the flight, spraying a fine, viral aerosol throughout the airliner. The other passengers, never imagining they are infected, get onto other flights, returning to homes in other cities, in other countries. Within the course of a few hours, a hot agent that has spent forever living in an obscure beetle in a Costa Rican rain forest is on its way around the globe."

"Does that ever happen?"

"You bet. There have been a couple of good Ebola scares in the United States from lab monkeys imported for research. Mostly, though, it's relatively innocuous stuff, like influenza. That could change, now that so many of the world's rain forests are being cut down."

"What does that have to do with disease?"

"Rain forests are God's own factory of life and death. Who knows what's lurking out there, waiting to be picked up by some unsuspecting logger—or archaeologist? Combine what's happening in the rain forests with the speed of travel today, and you've got a recipe for an epidemic of horrific proportions. One of these days we're going to have a firestorm, a Level Four meltdown on a worldwide scale."

Bailey put down her cup and gently touched Lazaro's arm.

"Are you all right, Lazaro? You have the most stricken look on your face."

"You spoke of the virus injecting its genetic code into the cell it infects. Can a virus change you?"

"I'm not sure I understand the question."

"Can a virus put its genetic code into you, turning you into something different, a hybrid, part human and part whatever the virus is?"

"I've never heard of it happening."

"But it's not impossible?"

"I suppose it's theoretically possible."

Lazaro got to his feet and began to pace. "I am very concerned about the risk you would be taking if you go deeper into the rain forest, chasing this sickness."

"So am I. I'm going to take every precaution."

"Will it be enough?"

"It'll have to be," Bailey answered, reaching for her coffee cup, finishing what was in it. "My best bet is to find an animal, maybe a howler monkey that is sick, and come up with a living specimen of the virus so I can see what we're really up against. You're sure no one lives near the ruins?"

"Nobody lives in Zonatitucan valley. The Indians believe it is haunted."

"They're probably right. If there is something in that

valley that kills visitors, it seems perfectly natural that the Indians have a mythical explanation to help keep people from going there to become infected."

"I don't want you to visit the ruins. Stay here and do your research at La Esmerelda. Surely that will be adequate."

"I have to go. I have a job to do."

"Would it make a difference if I told you I have personal reasons for asking you to not risk your life by going into the rain forest?"

"What personal reasons?"

Lazaro turned toward Bailey, wanting to kiss her but knowing it was not the right moment.

"Oh," Bailey said, seeing it in his eyes, the color rising in her cheeks.

"Though our friendship is only beginning, I cannot bear thinking I might lose you."

"But the health of millions of people depends on me doing my job, Lazaro. If you really care about me, you'll understand why I've got to do everything I can to find out what killed Janis Levy. We both know the answer is out there, in the rain forest."

Lazaro looked to the edge of the rain forest, the line where his carefully tended gardens stopped and the wildness began. She was right. Through the rain forest, beyond the volcano with its lazily rising plume of steam, down into the valley that held the lost city of Zonatitucan—that was where the answer waited.

"The pieces of the puzzle all fit, Lazaro. Dr. Levy, the city in the rain forest the Indians seemingly abandoned, the legends about haunted ruins—it all points to a hot agent. The virus is waiting for me there."

"But so is danger."

"I am not afraid. I know the risks and how to minimize them."

"And if I refuse to let you visit the site?"

"How could you do that?"

"Zonatitucan is on my land. So is the place where Dr. Levy's body was recovered. What if I decided that the danger is too great for me to permit you to visit these places?"

"Then you will learn that I am a very determined woman," Bailey said, her voice suddenly cool.

"And you will learn that I am a very determined man."

"I'll visit the ruins with or without your permission. Ludwig will help me. He knows the rain forest."

"Ludwig be damned!" Lazaro almost shouted.

They were suddenly both on their feet, toe-to-toe, glaring at each other.

"I forbid you to visit Zonatitucan."

"I am not one of your servants," Bailey said, her voice rising. "You can't forbid me to do anything."

"You will be trespassing. My men will keep you out."

"I'll go to the government."

"For all the good it will do you."

"You bas—" The word caught in Bailey's throat. Too angry to speak, she stormed past Lazaro toward the stables.

There were only two choices. He could relent and agree to help Bailey. Or he could stand fast and refuse to let her visit the city of the dead, alienating the woman he was falling in love with—and the German, who had his own reasons for wanting Bailey's research to proceed.

Whichever choice he made, Lazaro thought, it seemed destined to be wrong.

Catorce

"DO YOU THINK Dr. Harrison is all right?"
Vincent blew smoke rings across the bar toward
Father Xavier's table.

"What are you getting at, Father?"

"I was just thinking about her out at La Esmerelda."

"Dr. Harrison can take care of herself."

"That's what Dr. Levy thought."

"If you're talking about that germ—"

"Virus," Father Xavier said, correcting him.

"If you're talking about that *virus*, Dr. Harrison knows
how to stay healthy. But I will say this: If you go looking
for trouble, it usually finds you, mon."

"That is true, unfortunately." Father Xavier glanced out
the cantina door, into the darkness he seemed to regard as
actively malevolent.

"You worried about the virus, Father, or the man?"

"Don Lazaro is a gentleman," Father Xavier snapped,
quick to defend his parish's benefactor.

"One fine-looking man. And rich."

"Dr. Harrison didn't come to Costa Rica to find
romance."

"No, but maybe she'll find some anyway."

"I doubt it," the priest sniffed.

Vincent grinned, knowing he'd backed the priest into a logic corner. He loved to debate Father Xavier—their disputations were usually about the Bible—although sometimes the ganja Vincent smoked made it difficult to hold on to the threads of his own arguments.

"If don Lazaro is a gentleman, and Dr. Harrison is both a lady and someone who knows how to keep herself away from sickness, then what do you have to worry about?" Vincent asked, springing the trap.

"I don't know," Father Xavier admitted, staring at his beer.

"I do."

Father Xavier looked up sharply.

"You're a priest. Worrying about people's virtue is what you do for a living."

"No, Vincent, I'm afraid it's more than that this time."

"So you *did* see the way Dr. Harrison looked don Lazaro up and down," Vincent crowed.

"That's not what I meant," Father Xavier said with an impatient gesture. "Listen to me, Vincent. This is important. Haven't you noticed that something peculiar is going on in Paradisio?"

Vincent's eyes narrowed. "What do you mean, peculiar?"

"Things are happening off in the fringes we don't hear about because we're considered to be outsiders. There are two worlds here, the ordinary one we're allowed to see, and one that the Indians keep for themselves, a parallel reality we can only catch glimpses of from time to time."

"That's the beer in your head talking, Father."

"Don't you ever get the feeling that here is a place where a lot of things happen that people never talk about?"

"There's nothing special about that," Vincent said, the cigarette dangling from his bottom lip. "Wherever you go, things are happening people don't want you to know about. People stealing, people cheating, people lying, people sleeping with their neighbors' wives. People working the edges, getting what they can get while the getting is good."

Vincent stabbed the cigarette out in the ashtray.

"Dealers selling dope. Cops busting dealers, stealing their money and their stash, turning around, selling it themselves. The rich ripping off the poor. The poor ripping off the rich. Preachers getting down with the women in the choir, turning them into their babies' mamas."

Father Xavier stared at Vincent with his mouth open.

"It's life in Babylon, mon," Vincent said. "It's all part of Jah's mysterious plan. It's been that way since we left the Garden of Eden. It will stay that way until the Lion of Judah sets us free."

"This isn't Babylon, Vincent. It's Paradisio, Costa Rica."

"All the world is Babylon, Father."

"And evil . . ."

"Yah, mon. This is Babylon."

"This place is evil!" the priest shouted.

Vincent and Father Xavier stared at each other, each equally startled by the outburst. The night's silence settled back over the cantina, oppressive rather than peaceful.

Vincent came across the room, pulled out a chair, and

sat down next to Father Xavier. He leaned forward on his elbows, whispering though they were the only people in the cantina.

"Take my advice, Father. Forget what you think you know and keep your heart pure. Jah will take care of you if you pray."

"God has forsaken this place, Vincent," the priest said in an emotional whisper. "This is a province for the damned."

"Whatever is happening here has been happening here for a long, long time," Vincent said. "It was here before us. It will be here long after we're gone."

"Then you do know what I'm talking about!"

"I am not blind," Vincent whispered, as if afraid the night would hear.

"Out in the rain forest—it's probably happening right now! No wonder this town is so quiet at night. They're all *out there*."

"Let it be, Father. Indian magic, voodoo, witchcraft, sorcery—it doesn't matter what you call it, and it's better if you don't call it anything at all. Let it be."

"But Dr. Harrison!"

"What about her?"

"She's gone with don Lazaro into the very heart of darkness. She has no idea what she's dealing with."

"Don't you think don Lazaro will take care of her, Father Xavier?"

"What if he is part of it?"

Vincent just stared.

"Forget it," Father Xavier said, backtracking. "I was thinking out loud." He drained off the last of the beer.

"Take my advice and let it be," Vincent said, pushing the wooden chair backward with his legs.

"I have an obligation," Father Xavier sputtered. "I have taken vows."

"Don't forget what happened to Father Juan."

"What are you talking about?"

Vincent tapped a cigarette on the table three times, tamping down the tobacco, then stuck it in his mouth.

"Father Juan started noticing things, funny things like you have, and decided to make it his business. Next thing you know, he disappeared."

"Do you think there's a connection between the pagan rituals and Father Juan's disappearance?"

"Don't you?" Vincent lit the match with his thumbnail, watching it flare before bringing it to the tip of the cigarette. "That's what happens to people who get involved in things they shouldn't in the rain forest. They disappear."

Vincent exhaled a long plume of blue smoke that smelled of tobacco and marijuana mixed together.

"Remember what happened to Father Juan. I don't want anything to happen to you, Father Xavier. You're the best customer I've got."

Quince

❖

"IWANT YOU to leave La Esmerelda."

Ludwig toyed with the gold chain threaded through the buttonhole on his vest as he looked out over the garden. The magnificent gardens were a point in Lazaro's favor. They indicated he had a soul.

"What you want is not of particular interest to me, Lazaro."

"You will leave *now!*"

The rage in Lazaro's face was a disappointment. It was embarrassing to see such a lack of self-control. To allow one's mind to become clouded with anger—it was the biggest mistake a vampire could make.

"You must help Dr. Harrison continue her research," Ludwig said, returning to the topic they had been discussing before Lazaro lost his temper.

Lazaro's lips became a tight, thin line. They barely moved when he spoke. "How dare you come uninvited into my house and presume to tell me what to do?"

Ludwig smiled, rubbing the golden links of the braided watch chain between his thumb and forefinger. The chain was a good-luck piece, a gift from his friend and teacher, Mozart.

"Because at this particular crossroads you need someone to tell you what to do."

"I will make you leave, Samsa, if that is what you
want."

"Do not humiliate yourself by trying."

Ludwig looked back out over the garden. The peaceful
vista had a soothing effect on him. He was pleasantly
surprised that he hadn't already had to kill Lazaro.

"Dr. Harrison has important work to do," Ludwig said,
without looking back at his host. "You must take her into
the rain forest so that she can continue her research."

"I refuse to put Bailey's life at risk."

"Tell me something, Lazaro. Hasn't your curiosity
ever led you to search for the explanation behind the
strange metamorphosis that transformed you into a vampire? Surely you are too intelligent to believe super-
natural agencies were responsible for making you into
the creature you have become. Or do you honestly
believe God made you a monster to punish you for the
cruel role you played so many centuries ago?"

"You know nothing of my sins."

"You are mistaken, *mein Herr*. I know who you are,
and I can surmise what you did." Ludwig turned and
smiled at his rival. "You pretend to be a descendant of
the conquistador Lazaro Ruiz Cortinez. We both know
you *are* Lazaro Ruiz Cortinez."

Ludwig's words struck him like a lash.

"Do not bother to ask how I know, Lazaro. I know
everything."

Lazaro dropped into the chair, overwhelmed by
memories and guilt.

"Which is how I know that it is imperative for Bailey

to continue her work," Ludwig said, sitting across from Lazaro. "Do you have any idea how close she is to unlocking the secret of what we are?"

"What *we* are," Lazaro said, rousing himself from his depression. "I can't tell you how strange it is to realize that there are others like me. I had thought I was the last of the race. To think there are others like me, others who understand what it is like—this eternal existence that gives us everything and yet nothing, this *horror* . . ."

"It is a lonely path, for those without friends and allies. Without my brothers and sisters in the *Illuminati*, I would have gone mad long ago."

"The *Illuminati*?"

"A benevolent *Vampiri* society dedicated to cultivating wisdom and harmony in the world. There are others, too— vampires who do not walk with us, the dark side of our race, a sinister brood we try to keep in check. Our original assumption was that you were one of them, though now I see that your character leans toward the benign."

"Damn me with faint praise, Herr Samsa."

"Pray forgive me," the German vampire said with a crisp bow from where he sat. "A few of the rough edges of my mortal personality remain."

"I have never done anything but strive to do what is right," Lazaro said, sounding self-righteous.

"The issue is whether what you think is right is in fact quite wrong," Ludwig said, giving Lazaro a frankly appraising stare.

"Have you appointed yourself my judge?" Lazaro demanded, angry again.

"The *Illuminati* made me your judge, jury, and executioner, if need be. The final role is one I will not be required to play, if you decide to embrace our quest for wisdom."

"You're threatening me."

"I do not merely threaten, don Lazaro," Ludwig said darkly. "It is crucial that Dr. Harrison complete her work in the rain forest. Either with your help or without it."

"Regardless of the danger to her?"

"It strikes me that you are chief among the dangers the good doctor faces."

"You mock me, Samsa."

"I speak only the truth."

"Bailey has nothing to fear from me."

"Your lack of self-awareness is appalling, Lazaro. I could teach you much, were your runaway pride to allow you to become my student."

"I doubt you could teach me anything."

"I'm tempted to prove otherwise," Ludwig said, his eyes disappearing beneath his frowning brow. "But let us leave that subject for the present. Of far greater importance is Dr. Harrison's research into the virus that is at the root of our metamorphosis."

"Then the virus she is hunting—it is what turned us into *vampiros*?"

"*Ja*. It modifies human DNA, transforming ordinary mortals into something quite extraordinary. We know little about it, beyond the fact that it is weak, that three successive infections are required before the virus can do its strange work. That is why there are so few like us."

"So it is science, not ritual."

"Ritual, *mein Herr*?"

"The three 'kisses' that bring on the sickness of the gods in Zona ritual. I had believed them to be necessary ingredients in the Indian sorcery. It seems there is a much more reasonable explanation."

"It is presently up to Dr. Harrison to illuminate the 'reasonable explanations' science can offer into our shared condition. We understand but little of the virus's functions. Bailey is brilliant, in her quiet way. The *Illuminati* has decided to nurture her work. Sometimes human goals and *Vampiri* goals are in harmony. This is such an occasion."

"You would let Dr. Harrison tell the world about us?"

Ludwig shook his head, his brow deeply furrowed again, his eyebrows standing out like stone ridges.

"Then we are back to where we started. I will not allow her to come to harm."

"You mistake my meaning," the German said. "The *Illuminati* do not kill innocent mortals. That is the *Illuminati*'s most sacred law. There are ways to arrange things so that sensitive information does not become general knowledge in the mortal world. The *Illuminati* fortune is helpful in these matters. Our order's wealth is without limit. Dr. Harrison will hardly be the first human researcher to enjoy our confidence—and sponsorship."

Lazaro stood up and walked to the fireplace. He picked up the poker and jabbed the logs, sending a flock of sparks flying up the chimney.

"I am still reluctant to put Dr. Harrison's life at risk. I am not in the habit of expressing my emotions, Samsa, so let me just say that I care for her."

"As do I," Ludwig said.

For a long moment the two vampires stared at each other, Lazaro clenching a poker in his hand, Ludwig possessing powers that made him dangerous even without a weapon.

"Think of it this way, Lazaro. If Bailey can survive staying in an isolated house with two vampires, the odds are good that she can survive a research expedition into the rain forest—especially if those two vampires assist and protect her."

"But there are other risks, things you do not know about. It is not just the virus—or the Hunger in us both—that concerns me."

"Do not presume you understand the limits of my understanding, Lazaro. Or my resourcefulness. I have been in many complicated situations in my travels for the *Illuminati*."

"Can you guarantee her safety, Samsa?"

"There are no guarantees in life. Not for mortals. Not even for vampires." Ludwig smiled. "By the way, I had thought you would have figured out by now that my name is not Samsa. Do you really still not know who I am?"

Lazaro shook his head.

"When we first met I had been examining your books. Pity poor Gregor Samsa, who woke up one day in Kafka's *Metamorphosis* to discover he had been transformed into a cockroach. And pity us. We woke up one day to discover that we had been transformed into vampires, miraculous creatures capable of great good and of even greater evil. I also thought that telling you my name was Samsa dovetailed nicely with my story about being interested in butterfly metamorphosis."

"Yes, very clever," Lazaro said without amusement.

"You know me quite well, Lazaro, although only

through my work as a composer. Permit me to introduce myself. . . ." The German stood and made a sweeping bow. "Ludwig van Beethoven, at your service."

Dieciséis

BAILEY SAW AN elaborate iconography of death wherever she looked.

Skulls, serpents, bats, jaguar-headed warriors carrying bundles of severed heads by the hair—these were the images that held the most significance to Zonatitucan's vanished inhabitants. The bat clearly occupied a central place in the city's pantheon; its image was repeated again and again in the gruesome illustrations sculpted into the Pyramid of the Moon and other temples.

Zonatitucan's ruins were neatly laid out along a broad central plaza, the city designed to focus the eye toward the biggest and most elaborate structure, the Pyramid of the Moon, which hugged the rain forest on the eastern border of the complex of crumbling stone buildings.

Bailey had expected Zonatitucan to be decorated with images of the sun, sheaves of grain, totems of rain and river gods, the archetypal givers-of-life common to most prescientific civilizations. However, the Zona had drawn the energy for their civilization from a pre-ternaturally dark corner of the human psyche, their

111

mythology welling up out of a place in the soul that was as wild and untamed as the rain forest surrounding the city.

Staring up at the Pyramid of the Moon, Bailey was looking at the ruins of a culture based entirely upon the veneration of death.

Bailey was glad the builders of Zonatitucan had vanished. She would not have wanted to meet them.

Bailey looked over her shoulder at the sound of approaching footsteps, nervous without knowing why, possessed by an intense sensation of déjà vu.

"Do you know what it is that strikes me the most about this place?" Lazaro asked, his voice low, as if it would have been sacrilegious to speak in his normal voice. "The quiet. The profound and resonant quiet. It seems to me to be the silence of eternity."

Bailey sensed it, too—stillness like a hungry vacuum drawing everything into itself, overpowering, overawing, consuming.

"Think of the plaza as it must have been when it teemed with people. This was the capital of a powerful civilization, a city-state that imported its grain from estates far beyond its own valley, which is too small to have fed a city this size. If you use your imagination, you can hear the citizens' voices as they go about their business, bartering for corn and for pottery, shells, precious stones, and slaves brought back from remote trading missions as far north as Mexico City."

Lazaro's whisper caused a vivid image to take form within Bailey's mind. The plants and vines disappeared from the plaza, and the duotone color scheme of green and brown was repainted with a brighter and more varied palette. It was as if she were dreaming with her eyes open.

"Then come the shouts of the criers, telling the people to make way for the priests," Lazaro said.

Bailey *saw* it: the people crowding back from the center of the plaza, their conversations falling away to an expectant hush.

"The procession emerges from the Temple of the Feathered Serpent God—there, across the plaza—for the slow, solemn procession up the *Avenida de los Muertos*. The priests' feet, clad in sandals decorated with disks of gold and silver, tread in time to the beating of the sacred drums in the sunken courtyard. After the priests come the soldiers, a phalanx surrounding the prisoners captured in battle. The prisoners' arms are bound cruelly behind their backs, their naked bodies painted blue. The captives all share the same distant look in their eyes. They know what is going to happen to them, but they do not care. They have been drugged. The procession reaches the Pyramid of the Moon and begins to climb the stairway to the altar at the top, where their priest-king, the Great Zona, waits to begin the sacrifices."

The ghosts Bailey had been watching vanished from the Avenue of the Dead. The vision of a crowded, busy city evaporated into the dusk, leaving behind the hulking ruin of temples overgrown with creeper vines and staghorn ferns. Her eyes fell on a bas-relief image carved into the lichen-mottled stone. It was either a man or a god in elaborate Aztec-style ceremonial garb. A necklace of human skulls was spread across his broad chest, his headdress incorporating the outline of a bat within an explosion of feathers and interlocking geometric designs.

"Human sacrifices?"

"Of course," Lazaro replied. "They were the fuel that fired a rich civilization. The architectural wonders, the profound understanding of astronomy, the elaborate religious ceremonies—all of it was fueled by human blood."

"No wonder the Indians think this place is haunted," Bailey said.

"Indeed," Lazaro said. "In a very real sense, Zonatitucan *is* haunted."

An almost palpable atmosphere of mystery clung to the Pyramid of the Moon, with its macabre ornamentation. The temple symbolized a power that had coalesced in the rain forest a millennium earlier, then disappeared back into the nothingness of time, leaving behind only the ruins as a monument to the enigma of its builders.

"How strange that an entire civilization could simply disappear."

"Maybe it hasn't."

Bailey's eyes grew wide.

"The Zona are still here. Jorge, Eduard, Alvaro—the Indians are all descendants of the people who built this city."

Bailey nodded. "The conquistadors never made it this far."

"There is no record of it. Costa Rica had no gold. The

conquistadors were interested in gold and nothing else. The same cannot be said of the priests who traveled with them. To the priests, the treasure to be pillaged in the New World was locked within the Indians' souls. They came to conquer pagan religions, to convert the heathen idolaters to Christianity."

"Maybe it wasn't such a bad idea," Bailey said, looking up at the altar atop the pyramid. "How many human beings lost their lives there, sacrificed to savage gods?"

Lazaro started to say something but changed his mind and looked away.

"The Zona escaped the conquistadors only to have a virus conquer them."

"You find viruses lurking everywhere."

"They *are* lurking everywhere, Lazaro. Especially in a rain forest."

"I suppose," he said dismissively.

"During the Black Death, *Yersinia pestis*, a rod-shaped bacterium too tiny to see with the naked eye, wiped out half of Europe. It upset the entire political structure of the fourteenth century, driving people out of their walled cities and into the countryside." Bailey looked up at the Pyramid of the Moon, frowning. "It's going to happen again, Lazaro. Until science finds a way to stop it, it's going to happen again and again, as it has throughout the vast sweep of human history."

"Because of this?" Lazaro said, sweeping his hand at the ruins surrounding them.

"Maybe not here, not now. But it will happen again. All of our knowledge is still not enough to keep us safe from the threat of plague."

"Can you defeat the virus that infected Dr. Levy?"

"There are vaccinations and treatments for most diseases. I don't know whether there's anything that can be done to stop what killed Janis Levy. If not, there's always containment, which is all that can be done with the hemorrhagic fevers, anthrax, and the other Level Four killers. This biosphere's natural containment may be why we didn't see evidence of the virus hiding in this valley until Dr. Levy's visit. The mountain range creates an ideal barrier, keeping the virus in and the people out."

The sun slipped into the chasm between the two mountains behind them then, two shadows sweeping in on the city like curtains closing on an enormous stage. A shaft of golden light hit the pyramid's stairs and began to climb.

"My God, do you think that is intentional?" Bailey asked in a hushed voice.

Lazaro nodded solemnly. "The city was laid out along celestial meridians. The architects of Zonatitucan had a sophisticated understanding of astronomy."

The light reached the stone altar at the summit of the Pyramid of the Moon, transforming the stone there from muddy brown to deep red—the color of rubies, the color of blood.

"Lazaro!"

A young man stepped out from a stone portico where he had evidently been watching Bailey and Lazaro. Bailey recognized him from the cantina. It was the young man who had so rudely refused to speak to her. Roberto, Vincent had called him.

Bailey heard a commotion coming from camp, the sound of something being knocked over and angry voices. Jorge Larrea Ballesteros came running with his machine gun, Lazaro's other two men with pistols they must have kept concealed beneath their shirts. There was no sign of Ludwig, who had gone off in search of morpho butterflies in the dusk.

Lazaro motioned for his men to stop before they could interpose themselves between him and Roberto. He spoke to Roberto in what Bailey recognized as the Zona dialect. There was nothing in his tone to tell Bailey that Lazaro felt the least threatened.

Now it was Roberto's turn to talk—a furious burst of words, the verbal equivalent of automatic weapons' fire.

"Lazaro?"

He turned his head toward Bailey without taking his eyes off Roberto. The same relaxed expression remained on his face. Whatever the confrontation was about, Lazaro was staying cool.

"What's wrong?"

"I told Roberto he is trespassing. His answer was that *we* are the ones who are trespassing. He said these sacred ruins belong to his people and that we defile them with our presence."

"You must understand why we're here, Roberto," Bailey said, appealing directly to the young man.

Roberto spat on the ground, then slowly raised his hand until his finger was pointed at Bailey.

"It is your presence Roberto objects to most," Lazaro told her. "It seems I have lived here long enough to have earned a certain degree of acceptance."

"This place is dangerous," Bailey said, speaking again to Roberto. "There's a good chance a virus here could kill us all."

"I welcome death," Roberto said.

"Good-bye, Roberto," Lazaro said.

"*¡Bastardo!*"

"Two years at Harvard and that's the most eloquent denunciation you can make?"

"*¡Bastardo!*"

Bailey noticed that Ludwig had silently come up on them. He stood apart, watching Roberto and Lazaro with curious detachment.

"Roberto was my favorite," Lazaro said, "my golden child. I treated him like a young god, but he grew up to treat me like a devil."

Bailey felt Roberto's cold eyes on her now, burning her, stabbing her. There was suddenly a frightening pressure in her chest, as if Roberto's hands had closed around her heart and were squeezing it. She moved her lips to cry out, but no sound came. She felt as if her heart was being crushed.

"Roberto!" Lazaro said sharply.

Roberto turned away without another word, walking toward the rain forest.

"You've had a bad scare, but you will be all right," Lazaro said, putting his arm protectively around Bailey.

She had been gasping for breath, but Lazaro's touch made the fear leave her. The sensation that her heart was being crushed disappeared. Her breathing began to slow.

"Do not worry about Roberto," Lazaro said, his voice a low murmur in her ear. "I will not allow him to interfere with your work."

They began to walk back to camp, Lazaro's arm still around her—protecting her, soothing her, filling her with desire she could not ignore no matter how hard she tried.

Diecisiete

✦

"MUCHAS GRACIAS, MUCHACHO!"
Father Xavier gave the surprised boy a peso. He was not in the habit of tipping the child for delivering the mail the weekly supply truck dropped off at the Hotel Paradisio, but this was a special occasion.

He was in the church, preparing for Sunday Mass. His first impulse was to rip open the envelope, but it seemed unfitting. Instead, he finished his work as quickly as he could, closed up the church, and hurried across the rutted street to his house.

A letter from Margarita Alvarez Corona—one of the few blessings afforded him in Paradisio.

Xavier poured a glass of sun tea and carried it onto the front porch, lowering himself into the creaking rocker his predecessor had left behind. He put the envelope on the railing and looked at it tenderly, savoring the sweetness of the memories it evoked, these recollections his most prized possessions.

Margarita Alvarez Corona.

The breeze moved a little, stirring the fragrance of wildflowers in the air, a scent not unlike the perfume in Margarita's hair. He remembered with great detail her smile, her delicate ears, the soft down on her arms in the lamplight, the touch of her skin beneath his fingertips. . . .

How exquisite to remember it all, if also painful.

Their indiscretion—it hardly seemed a mortal sin—had cost Xavier his parish in Mexico City. Yet it had been worth all that and more. A poet had said it best. Sitting alone on his porch in Paradisio, Xavier whispered the words to himself, a verse he had once whispered to Margarita.

> The awful daring of a moment's surrender
> Which an age of prudence can never retract
> By this, and this only, we have existed. . . .

The letter was encased in an eggshell-white envelope from an expensive stationery shop in Mexico City, delicately inscribed in India ink. He wrote her every week; she wrote back less frequently, busy with her life now that she had finished university and started work as a teacher. It had been—Xavier counted in his mind—five weeks since her last letter. An eternity!

The address on the envelope, written in her familiar delicate hand—even this touched Xavier's sensitive heart. His Margarita, his little bird. He would repent, but he would never forget, never regret, their love.

Margarita's letters were the only thing that made life bearable. Xavier hated his exile in Paradisio, where his only friends were a fugitive swindler dying of cancer and a Jamaican running from drug trouble. The rain-forest Indians were distant and unresponsive pagans who crept away in the night to participate in unspeakable ceremonies. They had killed his predecessor—at least according to the half-loco, marijuana-addled Vincent. All of this was made worse by the arrival of Dr. Harrison, who insisted that a deadly virus lurked in the rain forest amid the serpents and tarantulas, waiting to bring them horrible deaths, bleeding from the eyes, bleeding from the fingernails—agonies worse than any martyr ever suffered.

Xavier took out his penknife. He inserted the blade into the envelope and slit it neatly along the top, carefully removing the letter and unfolding it.

Father Xavier, the letter began.

He looked up, seeing the white clouds boiling over the mountains. Soon they would turn black and hurl down lightning and rain.

Father?

He read the greeting again and frowned. Not *Dearest Xavier,* not *Beloved Xavier* or the other salutations Margarita had used in the love letters she'd written him in his banishment, but *Father Xavier.*

The letter began as usual, relating the latest news about their friends in Mexico City. It touched several times on a man named Dominick, a talented young architect they had met at a party. Her tone changed in these passages, a subtle but obvious indication that she held Dominick in special regard. The bomb, when it was finally detonated deep in Xavier's heart, was not entirely unexpected.

I enjoy Dominick's company so much that I hardly realized that we were spending most of our time together, that something was happening between us, not because we planned it, but simply because it was happening naturally, easily, the way it once did between us.

Xavier leaned forward and put his head in his hand.

Still, it was something of a surprise when Dominick declared that he loved me—and yet it was no surprise at all, because I already knew it in my heart, even as I knew that I had come to love him, too.

"Dear God," Xavier groaned.

This does not change or diminish what we felt for each other, or what we shared. But that is over now. The situation, we both agreed, is impossible. You are in Paradisio, I am in Mexico City. Besides, you are married to the church. Our being together, as wonderful as it was, was a sin for which God will one day make us both pay.

"I am already paying," Xavier said to the mute sheets of paper in his hand.

Our lives must go forward, not as one life, but separately. I know this, and I know you know it. That is why I'm sure you will not hate me for telling you that I've agreed to marry Dominick and move with him to Miami, where his company has opened a new office.

Xavier began to rapidly blink. He felt as if his heart was being wrenched from his chest.

By the time you read this, I will be Dominick's wife. I pray that you will know that what I am doing is best for both of us. And while I can no longer continue to write to you and consider myself faithful to my new husband, I will always cherish what we once shared.

The letter was signed simply, *Margarita*.

Xavier dropped the letter and buried his face in his hands.

The clouds continued to build, blotting out the sun. The wind came up and blew the letter off the porch.

Xavier was still sitting in the rocker with his face in his hands when the evening rains came. He only realized the letter was gone when he stood up to go into the house, the pages blown away into the rain forest by the storm.

What did it matter?

He did not want to read Margarita's final letter a second time.

Dieciocho

✧

"COGNAC?"
Beethoven looked up from the campfire and nodded.

Lazaro's servant poured two fingers of the brandy into a tulip-shaped snifter and presented it to the German. Beethoven cradled the glass in his hand to warm the liqueur, the concave stem between his second and ring fingers, the bowl against his palm. The cognac was a rich amber hue when he held it up to the firelight. He brought the glass to his nose and breathed in deeply, nodding approval.

"Old, rich, and powerful—like us," Beethoven said, speaking German so the Indians wouldn't understand. Bailey had already retired to her tent for the night.

Lazaro did not speak Beethoven's native language, but he nevertheless understood what the other vampire had said. Though the spoken words were lost to him, the same words occurred simultaneously in Spanish within Lazaro's own head, a private telepathic translation.

"You've gone to considerable lengths to make us comfortable in camp," Beethoven said. "For that I thank you."

"When you live so far from the rest of the world, you learn that a few civilizing pleasures are the only things that separate you from savagery."

Beethoven took a small sip.

"Very good indeed," he said, pronouncing judgment on the liqueur. "It is a pity you and I can relish only the taste. There are times I would welcome the release drink used to bring. Our *Vampiri* bodies metabolize poisons too quickly for them to affect us, yet I would not complain if the sweet poison in this glass could disable me just a little tonight."

"You liked your liquor, then?" Lazaro asked, amused.

"*Ja.* In truth, the men in my family liked wine too much. Myself, I was in pain much of the time. Kidney stones, stomach trouble, migraine headaches—ach, there seemed no end to my mortal misery. Doctors were useless to me, so I treated myself, prescribing liberal doses of the only medicine that brought me any relief. And, of course, I became profoundly depressed when I lost my hearing. I did not present a very friendly face to the world."

"But you hear well now?"

"Praise be to *Gott*, my hearing is completely restored," Beethoven said. "That is the true miracle of my life, and I relive it every time I sit down to the piano." Beethoven raised his glass. "To our health, one thing we no longer need to worry about."

"To our health," Lazaro echoed.

Tell me about Roberto.

The telepathic question caught Lazaro off his guard.

"Let me worry about him," Lazaro said after a moment. "I know how to handle him."

"Ignoring problems does not make them go away, Lazaro."

"I know what I'm doing."

"Do you?"

"I am more than two hundred years older than you," Lazaro said. "I do not need your counsel to know how to best captain my ship through life's perils."

Beethoven began to laugh, in part because the naive and inexperienced vampire *was* two centuries his senior, but also because of the stilted court French Lazaro had used to keep his servants from understanding the meaning behind his words.

"It is hardly a laughing matter."

"You are quite right, Lazaro. I humbly apologize. I have no wish to intrude in your personal affairs."

"Very well, then."

"But he must not interfere with Bailey's work."

"I give you my personal assurance that he won't. He has no real power here. His words are filled with sound and fury, but like an actor reciting lines upon the stage, they signify nothing."

"Good," Beethoven said, speaking German. "Because if he threatens Bailey, I will kill him."

The Indians did not understand, but Lazaro got the message perfectly.

Diecinueve

✧

THERE WAS ONLY a self-inflating air pad beneath Bailey's sleeping bags, but it felt like the softest feather bed in the best hotel in the world.

She stretched out on her back and replayed the long day's events in her mind. Trekking through the rain forest. The steep trail up the mountains between the twin volcanoes, El Perro and Monte Aguila. And finally Zonatitucan, the ruins impressive yet vaguely menacing in the twilight.

And Lazaro.

Her thoughts kept returning to Lazaro, as if drawn by some intractable force. He'd been impressive on the *Avenida de los Muertos*, turning aside Roberto's threats without seeming angry or the least bit afraid. She admired Lazaro's confidence and control, qualities she cultivated in her own character.

Bailey shifted on the sleeping bag.

At La Esmerelda, Lazaro had said that he cared for her. It was obvious that Ludwig did, too. Bailey resolved—and not for the first time—that she wouldn't allow personal matters to interfere with the job she had come to the rain forest to do.

Between the rains and darkness, there had been time to see only a little of the city. After the Pyramid of the Moon, Lazaro had shown her the Pyramid of the Feathered Serpent and its surrounding *ciudadela,* the Jaguar Temple, the Storm God's Pyramid, and a handful of other structures whose names Bailey was too tired to recall while lying outside the door of sleep.

She'd tried to talk to Lazaro about Roberto, but he had been unwilling to discuss it. The nerve was too raw, the hurt too deep. It was sad that his protégé had grown up to hate him. Roberto seemed to consider anyone who wasn't an Indian to be an intruder in the rain forest. There might be some logic to that, but hardly enough to justify hatred, Bailey thought.

The trees above her tent rustled with a brief commotion—a monkey whose curiosity about their camp had finally overcome his timidity. In the morning she would set out traps for primates and small rodents. Monkeys were intelligent and could be difficult to trap. The servant Jorge might have to shoot several. Bailey didn't like seeing animals injured, but monkeys were expendable in the war against disease, while people weren't.

Bailey had to find the virus that killed Janis Levy. . . .

Her mind began to lose focus. Lazaro, Roberto, monkeys, the mysterious virus—all began to slide across one another as if she were viewing the subjects of her thoughts through a kaleidoscope. A minute later she had drifted into an exhausted, dreamless sleep.

"Stop it!" Bailey whispered.

She was more asleep than awake, her eyes closed, mistakenly thinking she was home in Atlanta with one of her cats, Ajax or Comet, licking her foot.

Bailey jerked her leg.

The annoying sensation stopped.

Bailey descended back into unconsciousness and began to dream of Roberto.

The two of them were alone in the rain forest at night. They were on a mountain above Paradisio, in a clearing that surrounded a rectangle of stone inscribed with the same hieroglyphics she had seen in Zonatitucan. Roberto's body was illuminated by a strange glow that seemed to emanate from his flesh. When he turned to face Bailey, anger suffused his aura with flashes of red and black.

Roberto lifted his right hand and slowly turned it palm up—a signal.

The trees began to change, metamorphosing like butterflies, only in this case it was a transformation from the lovely to the hideous. The bark on the tree trunks flowed vertically, melting, the wrinkled lines arranging themselves into hostile faces—the faces of rain-forest demons Roberto had captured with his sorcery. Branches became gnarled wooden claws dressed in leaves that trembled as they elongated, reaching toward Bailey.

Roberto's aura was almost perfectly black now, yet it glowed with impossible brilliance, like the darkness visible in Milton's vision of Hell.

The tropical paradise was a real-life version of the Garden of Eden, except that the serpent had wrested control of the myth. A primordial evil walked amid the rain forest's perpetual shadows—an evil whose power Roberto wished to command.

The tickling sensation on her foot began again. Bailey moved her legs in her sleep, but it wouldn't go away, even in the midst of the nightmare.

It was then that Bailey noticed Roberto was looking at her with fear in his face.

"No!" Roberto cried.

The sinister trees bent and swayed all around them as if battered by a windless tempest from the starry night sky.

Roberto was no longer looking at Bailey's face but at the ground at her feet.

Bailey moved her foot again, jerking it. The unpleasant tickling stopped, but only for a moment before beginning again with a new vigor.

"Wake up!" Roberto cried to Bailey, his eyes frantic. "Wake up, Dr. Harrison!"

It was not the warning, but the realization that Roberto was somehow really *in* her dream, that made Bailey sit straight up, her head brushing against the tent's nylon ceiling.

"Jesus!" Bailey whispered to herself, trying to shake off the nightmare.

The moon had risen over Zonatitucan, its silver light shining through the tent's mesh door. Bailey pushed the button on her runner's watch. Almost twelve-thirty. The zippered netting was open a few inches in the corner of the door. Either she'd been too tired earlier to notice, or else she hadn't set the aluminum pull tab to keep the tension in the nylon walls from working it open.

The tickling, licking sensation against her foot began again.

Bailey looked down at her feet, eyes wide.

The vampire bat was tiny enough to fit in the palm of

Bailey's hand. It lay on its belly on her naked foot, which stuck out at an angle from her unzipped sleeping bag. The bat had opened a vein on the instep of her left foot several inches below the ankle. Pushing against the thumbed wings that were also its arms, the bat raised its furry head to look up at Bailey. The creature had little white teeth that looked extremely delicate, yet sharp, like porcelain stilettos. Its eyes regarded Bailey without fear, two glittering black pearls.

Bailey jerked her foot—an autonomic spasm of fear.

The bat held on to her foot and hissed angrily, drawing back its lips to fully expose the wicked teeth in its mouth, a miniature vision of Hell. It lowered its head again, a long, glistening tongue snaking out of its mouth to lap at the uncongealed blood that continued to trickle from the open wound.

Bailey began to scream.

Veinte

✧

BAILEY WOKE TO the quick panic of knowing she was sicker than she'd ever been in her life, sick enough to die.

She'd traveled from the United States to Costa Rica to search for a virus that had already killed Dr. Janis Levy and that had in all probability wiped out the entire population of Zonatitucan.

She had found it.

She tried to analyze her symptoms, to inventory them in order to do a rough self-diagnosis, but she couldn't get past thinking about the fever burning her up from the inside out. Her T-shirt and underpants were soaked completely through, her hair damply matted against her head. Her temperature had to be dangerously high, 105°, she guessed, maybe 106°. She felt as if molten lead were circulating sluggishly through her veins, pouring dull fire into every cell in her body.

Bailey dimly perceived that the weight pressing down on her chest, threatening to smother her, was the sweat-sodden sleeping bag. She tried to throw it off, but it clung doggedly to her arm, wrestling with her. She struggled briefly then fell back, exhausted, defeated by an inanimate adversary, trapped within the suffocating cocoon.

Bailey would have cried, if she'd had the strength.

She drifted in and out of consciousness, cognizant of only the misery. Her joints throbbed with dull pain, as if her knees, elbows, and shoulders had been covered with a pillow then beaten with an iron pipe. Her teeth vibrated in their sockets, her ears buzzed, and her hands felt swollen to twice their normal size—all symptoms of the fever.

Of course! Bailey thought during a brief moment of lucidity.

The awful memory of the ratlike creature feeding on her ankle, lapping her blood with its pink tongue, made her realize that the vampire bats living in the Zonatitucan valley were the vector for the infectious virus.

Her working thesis had been that the monkey population transmitted the virus to humans, a primate-to-primate species jump, which was fairly common. But the missing part of the equation linking the deadly virus to Dr. Levy—and now Bailey—were the tiny rain-forest bats. The bat colony in Zonatitucan carried the lethal disease.

Bailey rubbed one foot against the other. She felt the bandage held firm against her ankle with the surgical tape she'd used to bind the dressing after sterilizing the wound. She'd tried to wash the bite clean with disinfectant, but she realized even at the time that it was a futile effort. That damage had already been done, the infection entering her bloodstream through the open wound as efficiently as if it had been injected into her in a laboratory experiment.

Delirium reclaimed its hold, filling Bailey's mind with vivid hallucinations. She could *feel* the virus moving through her system now, crawling inside her arteries like ants, penetrating her capillaries, puncturing cell walls, methodically violating them one at a time, serpentine alien DNA strands corkscrewing their way into the nuclei of her cells. It was the cytological equivalent of being raped— again and again, cell by cell, microscopic assailants penetrating her genetic code with their poison seed.

There were antibiotics in the medical tent, syringes she'd prepared in advance with massive doses of amoxicillin. But even a powerful intravenous drip would be useless against a virus.

"Lazaro . . ." Bailey's whisper was faint even to her own ears.

Someone opened the door, cool air flooding into the stifling tent. Lazaro lifted her gently, cradling her in his arms. It was impossible for Bailey to open her eyes. The light hurt too much. It was morning. The night had slipped away, a long feverish tangle of broken images.

"Lazaro . . ."

Her lips moved, but perhaps she heard her voice only within her own mind. Bailey was aware of his presence. He was near her, with her, and that at least was a comfort. Knowing Lazaro was watching over her allowed Bailey to relax enough to sink into a dreamless sleep.

When Bailey opened her eyes, she was being carried on a litter, feet first.

They should not take her back to La Esmerelda. They were only putting the people at the hacienda at risk. The hot agent should remain contained by the ring of mountains that circled the ruined city, the natural barrier that had kept the contagion—and the bats that carried it—from spreading the infection.

Bailey wanted to explain this to Lazaro, to warn him, but she didn't have the strength to speak. Indeed, she was barely able to think. The thoughts forming dimly within her febrile mind were like the outlines of shapes half glimpsed through a deep, concealing fog. The billowing gray mists drew near, blocking Bailey's vision, filling her head with a darkening grayness, leaving room only for the labored sound of her own slow-beating heart.

Bailey woke up in her bed in her room at La Esmerelda.

She lay with her eyes closed, listening to angry voices. She was too weak to make herself look at the men, who, judging from the volume of their voices, were sitting just a few feet from the edge of her bed. Lazaro and Father Xavier, the priest from Paradisio, were arguing about something. About her. Bailey drifted off for a few minutes. When she woke up again, Father Xavier was talking to Lazaro about his soul, telling Lazaro that he understood his anguish.

Why had they come into her room to have this personal conversation?

She felt herself sink deeper into the semiconscious delirium.

Father Xavier's voice metamorphosed into Ludwig's as she floated darkly along, a rudderless boat adrift on a river of fever. They were in the library, murmuring in low tones, the conversation tense, both men choosing words with utmost care. Bailey knew she was either dreaming or hallucinating. How could she hear Lazaro and Ludwig if they were whispering to each other in the library, in the far wing of the hacienda?

The sound of a luna moth flying through the garden captured Bailey's unanchored attention. Bailey listened to it land on the broad leaf of a rubber plant in an unpainted clay jar on the veranda outside her room. She heard it twitch its antennae and slowly open and close its wings, throwing off a delicate golden dust that floated through the air to settle gently on the shiny leaf with a pitter-patter softer than the hush of snowflakes floating to the ground.

The virus was opening Bailey to a completely new paradigm of reality—or else she was completely out of her head, she told herself.

The luna moth whispered to Bailey, telling her there was magic in the rain forest, magic that was inside her now, part of her. The truth was far more complex than she had imagined, the moth said, knowledge too subtle for words to define. She would have to get beyond language and logic if she was to understand, the moth whispered. The only way she could understand was to experience the truth directly.

How? Bailey asked, shaping the word with her lips without making a sound.

Do not think, the moth said, but observe everything and try to remember.

Alvaro had come into the room earlier in the evening and opened the French doors so that the refreshing night air would cool the room. A light breeze moved through the gardens, lifting the gossamer curtains by degrees, stirring them like the sails of a dream come to carry Bailey beyond her suffering. The bed began to glide across the floor, through the open doors, and across the garden, following the golden moth toward the rain forest.

Bailey heard Umberto, one of Lazaro's men, making love to Lucina, the cook's helper, in her room. Bailey wanted to return to the hacienda, to Lazaro, but the moth would not be turned from the course it had charted. They moved toward the trees, rising higher to clear them, the bottom of the bed brushing softly across the topmost leaves.

In the rain forest below, a jaguar crouched in the darkness, stalking its prey, its mind intent upon a single act. There was danger in the forest, the moth told Bailey. Good and evil coexisted in a delicate balance, for that was the way of the world. Bailey soon would have to decide for herself which power to adopt as her ally. When her eyes were truly open, she would have to choose.

To the north, standing on the escarpment overlooking La Esmerelda, was Roberto, staring down at the soft lights of the hacienda, the hatred in him deepening with each sharp breath he drew into his lungs.

Roberto knew that the magic had touched Bailey, the moth told her.

He would kill her, if he got the chance.

Veintiuno

THE ROOM WAS large and formal, with heavy antique furniture and rich oil paintings on the walls. The venetian blinds were lowered against the noonday sun, the varnished wooden slats opened at a downward-slanting angle, splaying narrow bars of golden light across the floor in the dimly lighted room.

"*Buenos días*, Father."

The master of La Esmerelda rose up from behind his desk. Don Lazaro was thin to the point of emaciation, yet there was nothing frail about his appearance. Quite to the contrary, there was power and confidence in his movements. Perhaps don Lazaro was not sepulchral so much as serpentine, Father Xavier thought. The sunken eyes, the hollow cheeks, the long, angular frame—a physiology undiluted by so much as a single ounce of fat, the human equivalent of one of the jaguars that lived out in the rain forest.

Don Lazaro's hand was hot to the touch, his grasp firm nearly to the point of pain.

"Thank you for making time to see me today, don Lazaro."

Father Xavier looked for signs of fever in don Lazaro's

eyes, but the only thing he saw there was hunger. Or what *seemed* to be hunger, Father Xavier told himself, knowing he had to be mistaken. Don Lazaro was far too wealthy to have ever known hunger.

Don Lazaro nodded to indicate the priest should take one of the two stiff-backed chairs facing the desk. The door was closed behind them by don Lazaro's servant as he left the room. Apparently Father Xavier was not to be offered lunch or even coffee after the long journey to La Esmerelda in the parish's rattletrap Jeep. These small discourtesies were impossible to miss.

"I've come to see Dr. Harrison."

"Oh?"

"I understand she is quite ill."

Don Lazaro stared at Father Xavier so long that the priest thought he wasn't going to reply but continue to rudely stare at him.

"Where did you hear that?" don Lazaro finally said, ending the uncomfortable silence.

"I cannot betray a confidence, don Lazaro," Father Xavier said with a small smile. He did not care to admit that he'd overheard two Indian women whispering about the *gringa* having "the sickness."

"I assure you she is being well cared for."

"I would not believe that it could be otherwise. Tell me, has Dr. Harrison contracted the virus she came to the rain forest to find? I pray that is not the case."

"Of course not," don Lazaro answered, a little sharply. "She has a touch of malaria, nothing more."

"Gracias a Dios."

It was *only* malaria. Father Xavier was almost as happy for himself as he was for the good doctor, since he'd intended to pray with her even if she was sick with the disease that killed Dr. Levy.

"I would like to pay my respects to her," Father Xavier said.

"You are not a doctor," don Lazaro said, as if pointing out something that had not occurred to Father Xavier.

"No, I am not, although I honestly don't know what that has to do with it, don Lazaro. My concern is for the health of Dr. Harrison's soul."

Don Lazaro laughed bitterly and slumped in his leather chair.

"A soul is no laughing matter, don Lazaro. Not hers. And certainly not yours."

Don Lazaro glared at the priest, dropping any pretense at polite discourse.

"This might be an appropriate time for me to observe that I have yet to have the pleasure of seeing you in church in Paradisio, don Lazaro."

Lazaro rocked gently back in his chair, looking at the inlaid skull mask on his desk, pointedly ignoring the priest's question.

"Perhaps you prefer to worship at private services."

Don Lazaro's eyes moved sideways to meet Father Xavier's, the priest feeling an almost physical wave of hostility emanating from his opposite. Don Lazaro seemed to be looking straight through him, reading his innermost thoughts, his most guarded secrets—his broken heart. Father Xavier began to feel slightly sick to the stomach. He unconsciously covered his abdomen with his hands, as if to shield himself from the stare don Lazaro used to pin him against his chair.

"I am not interested in discussing religion with you, Father."

"Have you lost your faith, don Lazaro?"

"I have no faith," the master of La Esmerelda said, his voice hollow, disembodied.

Father Xavier breathed deeply through his mouth, trying to calm his stomach. He usually enjoyed matching wits with sophisticated unbelievers; philosophical debates over cocktails had been one of his favorite pastimes in Mexico City. Now, however, his only concern was to keep himself from vomiting. "But . . ."

"I have seen too much of how the church operates. One need look no further than the indigenous Indian population throughout Central America. The church and the conquistadors made quite a team, each equally rapacious and greedy. The Indians had an advanced culture before we—before the Spanish—arrived and systematically wiped it out."

"It sounds as if you have made a study of the subject," Father Xavier managed, speaking with his eyes closed.

"You do not look at all well, Father. Would you like a glass of water? Cognac perhaps? I can offer you mescal, if that is more to your liking."

"I'll be all right," Father Xavier said, opening his eyes. "But tell me, don Lazaro, if you have no faith, why do your generous gifts make it possible to keep the church open in Paradisio?"

"Noblesse oblige, Father. Look around you. This is not Mexico City," he said with heavy sarcasm that seemed intended to sting the priest. "There are no museums, galleries, or universities in Paradisio. The church and my school are the sole objects of charity here in the rain forest."

"Then why do you insist that the Indians attend Mass?"

"Where did you get such a preposterous idea?"

"Please." Father Xavier held up his hand as if to fend off prevarication. "The peasants fill the church every Sunday. They come to Communion. Their children learn the catechism."

The priest took another deep breath.

"Yet they do not believe. The Indians remain virtual strangers to me. I have always known that they come to Mass because you tell them to, the same way they send their children to the excellent school you sponsor, as if learning to read Greek and appreciate Mozart is of any use to them here in the wilderness."

"I have nothing whatsoever to do with the people going to church," don Lazaro said, turning away in his chair with an angry wave of the hand. "I do not tell them to attend church, but I do not tell them *not* to attend, either. They are free to do as they will."

Don Lazaro stood up from his chair and began to pace, the footsteps of his knee-high riding boots muffled against the antique Persian rug surrounding his desk.

"Quite to the contrary, I have made every effort to help the Zona learn to reason these matters out for themselves, thinking that they would choose logic and reason over superstition. Unfortunately, the people here are drawn to whatever gods and powers present themselves. I've tried to lead them out of the darkness, but it's been hopeless, utterly hopeless."

"I know something of the dark night of the soul, don

Lazaro. Let me ease the spiritual anguish I sense within your soul."

"You know *nothing*, priest," don Lazaro said with withering contempt.

"I know that God loves you."

Don Lazaro's eyes filled with such fury that Father Xavier thought don Lazaro would move to strike him, but instead he remained where he was, staring down at Father Xavier, trembling with anger.

"You are more deluded than you can possibly imagine, priest."

"I think I would like to see Dr. Harrison now," Father Xavier said, getting to his feet, his voice shaking despite his best effort to appear unaffected by don Lazaro's irrational anger.

"You are not welcome at La Esmerelda," don Lazaro said. "I want you to leave immediately."

Father Xavier's hand came up to his chest, unconsciously touching the silver crucifix he wore around his neck, struggling to hold don Lazaro's stare.

"Now!" Lazaro commanded.

"I'll go," Father Xavier said at last, losing his nerve. "Tell Dr. Harrison I came to La Esmerelda to pay my respects. I will pray for her."

Father Xavier felt don Lazaro's eyes burning into his back as he walked toward the door.

Praying for Dr. Harrison—it was the only thing he could do for her.

Veintidós

✧

THE HOUSE WAS deathly still.

Aside from the occasional rustle and hiss from the fireplace, the only sounds were his breathing and heartbeat—and her sweet breathing, and her heartbeat, sweeter still.

The blood coursed through the vampire's ancient heart in slow and deep strokes, like the heavy tolling of a cathedral bell, six chimes to the minute. Her still-mortal heart beat nearly ten times faster, not as strong as Beethoven's but with all the limber suppleness of youth.

The others had departed, disappearing into the night, leaving the two of them alone in the hacienda—Ludwig van Beethoven and Dr. Bailey Harrison.

The flames flickered red, blue, and yellow. Fire was a paradox. It could warm, but it could also burn. Life was filled with paradoxes. What made you great could just as easily destroy you, unless you were careful and wise. And lucky. There was an element of luck in everything—in love, in music, in living the strange life of a vampire. Not really knowing how things were going to work kept life interesting after so many centuries.

He pictured Bailey in bed, beautiful even while burn-

145

ing up with fever from what the servants ominously referred to as "the sickness."

Temptation played an important role in *Vampiri* life— endless temptation to misuse one's power to get mortals to do whatever one wished. It was not always easy to choose the right path. Not even Beethoven was infallible.

Or entirely beyond the reach of temptation.

The fire crackled in the grate, as if mocking him.

Beethoven closed his eyes and directed his thoughts outward, rising up from his body, passing down the darkened corridor, slipping through the bedroom door as easily as smoke passes through the screen in a window. Bailey's face was intelligent and purposeful despite her troubled repose. But equally apparent were the fullness of her lips, the delicate arching of her eyebrows above her sleeping eyes, the promising softness of her breasts.

The fire sighed, bringing Beethoven falling back into his physical body.

A bit of resin boiled out of the end of a log, the golden amber instantly igniting in a flare of light. The fire brightened momentarily in the darkened room, starkly illuminating highlights, making the shadows darker, deeper.

Beethoven listened to the blood whispering through Bailey's body, the fanning rhythm of valves opening and closing in her heart.

The mantel clock, a Hamilton in a case that curved like the hip of a woman lying on her side, chimed the first of the eleven times it would ring to mark the hour.

Beethoven stood suddenly and went down the hall, moving so quickly and quietly in his preternatural stealth that no mortal passing him in the corridor would have noticed his presence. In the next moment he was standing over Bailey.

Her lightweight cotton nightgown rose and fell, the sound of her breath sweet music to his ears, the perfume of her blood far sweeter still.

Why did she dream of Lazaro instead of him?

Beethoven was far too enlightened to be jealous. It was only the Hunger moving in, he thought, enticing him with its wild song.

The carotid artery in her neck throbbed with each heartbeat, making Beethoven's upper jaw ache with the familiar dull pain. He had but to open his mouth and the incisors would come down from their cavities and lock into place with the dull click of bone snapping against bone.

Bailey sighed in her sleep, turning her head to one side. Deep in her subconscious, she knew what he wanted—and she offered herself to him, unable to deny him his pleasure. Beethoven's will was irresistible. He could have her, if he wanted to take her.

He stood there a full five minutes, allowing the temptation to pull him and the Hunger to push him, savoring the delicious possibilities. Mozart and the others in the *Illuminati* would have disapproved of his little game— seeing how long he could stand at the brink of this precipice without losing his balance.

No one would know if he gave in to this urge—least of all, the woman. Like a skilled craftsman he would leave no trace of his handiwork, erasing from her memory the ecstatic explosion of pleasure she would experience if he chose to give in to temptation and sink his teeth deep into her neck.

But had Lazaro already satisfied himself with her? She had become infected with the virus at Zonatitucan, from the bat's bite. What if Lazaro had also taken advantage? Thrice given the kiss of blood and there would be nothing anyone could do to stop the transformation from taking hold.

Bailey moaned softly in her sleep.

Joining the *Vampiri* might aid Bailey in her work, vastly expanding her already capacious intellectual powers. But it might just as easily drive her mad, as it did so many who made the change, turning her into a bloodthirsty killer. Beethoven was far too conservative a vampire to wittingly transmit the gift without obtaining the *Illuminati*'s carefully considered consent.

The vampire gently touched Bailey's feverish cheek with his fingers. She sighed, and the tension went out of her sleeping face, her discomfort eased a bit through the power of his suggestion.

The vampire began to back out of the room, sensing his way around a chair behind him without bothering to see it with his eyes.

Her work was too important to the *Illuminati*. Beethoven could not allow himself—or Lazaro—to jeopardize it. There were others who could satisfy his need.

Beethoven let himself out the front door, suddenly feeling a need to put distance between himself and the beautiful doctor.

He strode through the garden, eyes downcast, intent upon something only he could see. It was easy enough to see where the people from the hacienda had melted into the rain forest. Their footprints on the grass shimmered like phosphorus to the vampire's eye. A trail started at the garden's edge, its mouth hidden behind a stand of ferns that were taller than a man's head.

Beethoven followed the path. Anything to distract him from thinking about Bailey—anything to keep temptation and the Hunger from joining forces to overpower him.

The ground was soft beneath his feet. He could have traveled much faster, but he felt no urgency to catch up with the others. It was pleasant to be in the rain forest. The darkness was alive with sounds, the complex music of the night. The path had started out in the direction of the mountains and continued that way without detour. After only a quarter hour of walking, the path became steep.

He was on the way to Zonatitucan, only this path was a much more direct route to the ruins than the roundabout way Lazaro had taken them a few days earlier. Despite Lazaro's claim to the contrary, Beethoven knew there was a second pass through the mountains, one that allowed the city to be reached after only an hour of walking from La Esmerelda.

The trees fell away as the vampire climbed higher, the full moon making the night bright as the trail zigzagged between boulders, winding its way upward among the rock scrabble toward the declivity between two peaks. A meteor streaked across the sky from east to west as he reached the summit. Far below on the other side, the ruined city was spread out across the center of the almost perfect bowl formed by the mountains, like a matchbox cupped in a giant's hands. The Pyramid of the Moon rose above the other structures, an arrow pointing toward the heavens.

A crowd of perhaps two hundred people gathered in the plaza at the temple's base. Three people were climbing the steep stone stairs up the pyramid—two men gripping the arms of the young woman between them. A single figure waited atop the pyramid, torches bathing his face in flickering light. As the trio reached the summit, the figure raised his arms, offering his dark benediction to the secret ceremony.

A scowl darkened Beethoven's face. He had known many vampires, some of them geniuses and saints, others depraved criminals with unimaginably twisted minds. Still, he had never witnessed anything like *this*.

Lazaro took the hands of the woman offered to him in sacrifice and led her toward his altar.

Don Lazaro Ruiz Cortinez, the conquistador who first visited Zonatitucan five hundred years earlier, had transformed himself into Lazaro the God.

Veintitres

$\diamondsuit$

VINCENT LOOKED UP from the two-year-old copy of *Playboy* opened in front of him on the bar, expecting to see a customer. The cantina's half doors swung a little, but there was no one there.

The wind. It must have been the wind.

Vincent reached for his beer and saw the beaded curtain connecting the cantina with the hotel move, as if someone had ducked his head through, then pulled it back again.

He went to the curtain and looked through, looking for one of the girls, probably Juanita down to scout his ashtray for roaches to get high. The hotel lobby, lighted by the single dim lamp on the registration desk, was deserted. There had been only one customer that night, a cowboy who had gone upstairs with Simone and left afterward.

Vincent absently scratched his dreadlocks and returned to the cantina, looking slowly around, certain that he was not alone but unable to find anything to substantiate the impression.

"Voodoo," he muttered, crossing himself.

Or maybe it was the ganja. He'd never smoked much

before coming to Paradisio, where there wasn't anything better to do with his head. Maybe he ought to lay off it awhile. The weed of wisdom was making him paranoid.

Simone lay on her back in bed in the darkness, feeling a little sad, the way she always did after a customer finished and left her alone. She thought about the money locked in the metal box beneath her underwear in the drawer, counting it in her head. Almost enough to leave Paradisio. Maybe she'd go to Miami, where she had a cousin in Little Havana.

Footsteps came down the hall and stopped outside her door. A key turned in the outside lock.

Vincent.

He didn't pay for sex, but at least she wouldn't have to be alone. She threw back the single sheet covering her body, slid to one side of the wet spot, and spread her legs. Vincent liked her that way—pretending to want it.

The door opened and closed. He came into the room so quickly that Simone didn't actually see him. He stood next to the bed looking down at her, a mute silhouette in the darkness. Simone could feel the hot waves of desire rolling off him, infecting her with a longing she had not known since she'd started selling her body.

"Fuck me hard—really hard," Simone said.

She heard the breath catch in his throat. It turned him on to hear her talk that way. He leaned forward to touch her shoulder, the light of the full moon that came through her one window falling across his face.

It was not Vincent.

*   *   *

Vincent yawned and flipped out the centerfold.

Miss January was outstanding. Magnificent breasts—forties, according to her vital statistics—and platinum hair. Vincent eyed her closely, his lips pursed, wondering if they were real. He decided they were.

Vincent looked up from the magazine at the empty cantina. It was nearly one in the morning. Time to lock up, head upstairs, and visit Simone, the new girl. He was getting up when a feeling of incredible sleepiness came suddenly over him. He sat back down on the bar stool, tipped back his head, and released a long, comfortable yawn. Maybe if he leaned forward on the bar stool and put his head against his folded arms for a few moments, it would be just long enough to stop his eyes from burning.

For the first time since he'd come to Paradisio to run the cantina and hotel, Vincent fell asleep in the bar.

Simone sat up in bed and grabbed at the crumpled sheet, gathering it over her breasts, watching the silent *gringo* with the shock of wild hair. His deep-set eyes were a little frightening; they seemed to glow in the darkness with a light all their own.

"You scared me to death," Simone said, still breathless but recovering enough to give the stranger a nervous smile. "I thought you were someone else."

The man grabbed the sheet and threw it across the cramped room almost before she knew it, his eyes roaming over her body, touching it the way his hands soon would.

"I'm used to meeting my friends downstairs. Since

Vincent gave you the key, I assume the two of you have taken care of the details."

The man said nothing, and Simone began to feel afraid again. She hoped Vincent had explained that she didn't do the rough stuff. There was another girl for that, if that's what he was into.

"Why don't you take off your shirt. I'll rub your—"

His lips were suddenly on hers, kissing her deeply as he forced her backward against the pillow. She returned his kisses with passion nearly equal to his, thrusting herself against him and moaning. Simone tore open his shirt, the popped buttons flying around the room.

The man pulled away, standing, peeling off his torn and buttonless shirt, dropping it on the floor. He smiled down at her, observing her reaction as she watched the two-inch-long blood fangs come down from their recessed cavities in his upper jaw and lock into place with the dull, audible snap of cartilage.

Simone knew that she should scream, that she should do everything she could to get out of the room, to escape from the monster come to visit her in the dead of night.

She did nothing.

Everything was mixed up inside, her wires crossed, the circuits within her brain that registered horror and arousal somehow interchanged. Simone lay writhing on the bed, burning up with desire, wanting only to be back in the demon's powerful embrace.

"Hurry!" she pleaded.

Simone's mind raced ahead, seeing what was about to happen because he wanted her to see it—the pain, the pleasure, the way she could satisfy the Hunger boiling in his immortal veins, and in doing so partake in the bliss that only angels and vampires could know. He was going to make love to her, but he was also going to open her jugular and drink her steaming blood as it sprayed into his mouth. He could take her life, too, in an instant, if he wanted.

"Do what you want," she whispered, giving herself to the vampire completely—her body, her blood, her life if he chose to take it.

The vampire sat down beside her and put his hand gently on her neck, his fingers over her jugular. At first she felt her pulse beating against his fingertips, but after a moment she could hear the powerful rhythm of his heart resonating with her own body. Her heartbeat skipped twice and began to slow, the rate decreasing until at last her heartbeat was in concert with his.

His shadow loomed over Simone as his body covered hers. At the moment he entered her the way a man enters a woman, he likewise buried his teeth into her neck. She felt a stabbing pain in the side of her neck, followed by an awful sensation that was somewhere between strangling and drowning. Panic was about to overtake her when the bliss hit like a lethal jolt of electricity.

Simone gasped and raked her fingernails across the vampire's back.

It was as if every moment of sexual ecstasy she had ever known, or would ever know, was exploding inside her. But it did not end. Instead of a few moments of climax followed by a slow, comfortable fade, the prolonged orgasm continued to build in her, leaping from one plateau of pleasure to the next, until it was nearly more than her body could stand. She began to tremble, her breath coming in short, sharp gasps, her nervous system possessed by an ecstasy infinitely more powerful than any a mere mortal could give her.

What did it matter if her blood was flowing out, firing the furnace of the vampire's ancient heart, feeding the mysterious restorative essence of life eternal to bones that had walked the streets in Napoleon's time?

Simone's trembling built until she was thrashing about beneath the vampire. Her body was fast becoming cold and numb, but it hardly mattered.

Simone lay back with her eyes rolled up in her head, deliriously drunk on *Vampiri* rapture, ready to die if only it would prolong the exquisite pleasure a few moments longer.

Veinticuatro

✧

BAILEY SMILED AT Lazaro. The effort consumed most of her energy.

"I've had the strangest dreams."

"From the fever," Lazaro said, drawing up a chair beside the bed, frowning at the food tray Alvaro had parked across her lap. "Is that all you are going to eat?"

"I had a little fruit. Maybe I'll try more later."

Lazaro speared a piece of mango on the fork, lifting it to Bailey's mouth as if feeding a child. "Come on, now. Have a bite for me."

"I detest mango."

Lazaro slid the mango off the fork with his finger and stabbed a melon ball. Bailey allowed Lazaro to put the fruit into her mouth. She chewed with her eyes closed, savoring the delicious sweetness. Lazaro was waiting with more when she finished.

"Please, no. My stomach can't handle it."

Lazaro regarded her skeptically.

"I know what I'm talking about," she insisted. "I'm a doctor." Bailey shut her eyes, too easily exhausted. "How long have I been sick?"

"The entire fortnight since our visit to Zonatitucan."

"Two weeks?" Bailey came up off the pillow a few inches then fell back. She felt Lazaro's hand cover hers where it lay against the sheet—strong, reassuring, warm.

"We were able to get a little water and broth down you. Still, you've lost weight."

Bailey lifted her free hand to her face, running her fingers over cheekbones that stood out sharply against paper-thin skin. Her hand slipped down her neck, feeling the sharp definition of her clavicle, then falling limp and useless at her side. She should have been on a glucose IV during the past two weeks. The medications were in her supplies. Of course, there was no one at La Esmerelda besides her who knew how to set up an intravenous feeding.

"And the others?"

"Only you have been ill. Do not worry. Bringing you to La Esmerelda has not caused the virus to spread."

"Thank God for that."

Lazaro's hand tightened on hers.

"I do not know what I would do if I lost you."

She smiled up at Lazaro, sensing the bond between them, hearing it in his voice. Bailey had found more than a virus in the rain forest. She'd discovered something precious and unexpected, something some people searched for their entire lives.

She was still smiling when she fell asleep a few minutes later, Lazaro's hand covering hers.

It was daylight when Bailey awoke.

Lazaro was still sitting beside the bed, watching her,

greeting her with a smile that made her wish she was strong enough to take him in her arms. The sunlight surrounded him with a brilliant aura, making it almost impossible for her to look directly into the golden penumbra. Lazaro, dressed shirt to boot in his usual black, was a dark angel, come to watch over her while she slept.

"Good morning," she said, lifting her hand to shield her eyes, still sensitive to the light.

Lazaro was on his feet instantly to draw closed the heavy curtains.

Bailey pushed herself up a little on her pillows. She was definitely stronger today. She was going to make it, she thought. She was going to live. But then her doctor's mind went to work, sobering her.

"You took a terrible chance bringing me back here."

"Surely you do not think I could have left you in Zonatitucan."

"No," Bailey said in a quiet voice.

She studied the backs of her hands, seeing the blood vessels running through her desiccated flesh, blue lines beneath skin that had become pale during her two-week convalescence.

"Is this how it was with Dr. Levy?"

Lazaro nodded. "She, too, became ill after her first visit to the city. The symptoms were the same."

"But she died."

"Yes, but that was later, after she'd gone back by herself, although I tried to convince her against it. She must have become infected again. Perhaps she was weaker the second time. Or perhaps the virus is not so deadly as you thought and is only dangerous if there are multiple infections."

"The virus may have mutated into a less lethal form. Genetics predispose some viruses to rapid mutation. That's why it's so difficult to come up with flu vaccines. By the time the labs devise a way to battle a strain, it's already become something else, something the vaccine can't touch."

"Are you planning to go back to the ruins?"

The look on Lazaro's face was so filled with concern that Bailey almost wished she could do something besides tell him the truth. "I have to. I need to go back and collect specimens from the bats."

"And the danger?"

"There is always danger in life, Lazaro."

"No one knows that better than I," Lazaro said, his face grim, his voice defiant, almost angry.

After a long silence he pushed back the chair and went to stand by the window. He stared at the soft folds of the deep blue velvet drape, lost in his thoughts, haunted by them.

"There is so much about this place, and about me, that you do not understand. Perhaps if I told you the true story of this place, you would understand why it is imperative that you never return to Zonatitucan. No, it is even worse than that. You must leave La Esmerelda as soon as you are strong enough to travel. You must flee the rain forest as if not only your life but your soul were in the worst imaginable danger."

Lazaro had waited many centuries for someone like Bailey, but now that she had finally come into his life he had no choice but to send her away before it was too late. The pain was almost more than he could bear. He felt as if his beating heart were being torn from his chest, what the Zona did with their sacrifices.

"The real horror is not the virus you came to find. The real horror is me. It is me you have to fear most of all, for I have become the living incarnation of an unspeakable evil."

Lazaro turned to tell the rest of it to her face, to see the fear and disgust mirrored in the eyes of the woman he loved.

Bailey, weak from the virus, had fallen back asleep.

Lazaro went quickly to the bed and stood looking down on her. She'd heard nothing of the tortured preamble to his confession. It had come to nothing—like his entire lost and meaningless life.

Lazaro trembled with frustration, but most of all with desire and the Hunger.

Staring at Bailey, so lovely and helpless, the vampire realized that not even he himself knew what he was going to do next.

Veinticinco

✧

MARIA THERESE WAS careful not to let the screen door slam when she came out of the one-room servant's cabin. She stood on the veranda, silhouetted against the glow of the hurricane lamp burning on the table inside, a slim young woman of eighteen, with thick, flowing hair and full breasts. Glancing first right and then left, she started down the stairs, the second step groaning from the weight of her bare foot. Jumping past the final step, she hurried up the road a little ways at a half run, anxious to put darkness between herself and Carlomango Cordoba's house.

Lazaro closed his eyes as she went by, breathing in the aroma of perfume, sex, and blood eddying in the air behind the young woman. He detected no guilt in her, no sense of regret for her wickedness, for her sin.

Lazaro was one of the few people at La Esmerelda who weren't surprised when she married Anonimo instead of Carlomango. Maria Therese had a taste for expensive things. Anonimo may have been twenty years her senior, but he was a man of substance at La Esmerelda, Lazaro's ranch foreman, with his own Toyota pickup and one of the few houses on the plantation with electricity.

Maria Therese had not given up the handsome young Carlo. She continued to make love to him, but discreetly, only on nights that Anonimo was in San José, picking up a shipment of supplies.

Maria Therese stopped along the dark, narrow road, a passage barely wide enough for a single vehicle to pass between the trees and ferns. She listened hard in the night, straining to know if someone was following her, sensing that someone, or something, was. What if it was a jaguar, come down off the mountains in hope of catching a dog or pig? Or Anonimo, returned from San José a day early, come to look for his missing wife with his Colt revolver in his hand?

Lazaro plunged silently into the forest, moving around the obstacles with a preternatural ease and speed it would have been impossible for any mortal to match. He stepped back onto the road as Maria Therese hurried toward the house she shared with Anonimo, her safe haven.

She nearly collided with Lazaro in the darkness.

"Something's following me," she cried, throwing a frightened glance back up the dark road.

"You are safe now," Lazaro said, putting a hand on her back. "I will see that you come to no harm."

The door to the house where Anonimo and Maria Therese lived was unlocked. There were no locks on the doors of any of the houses at La Esmerelda.

Maria Therese reached for the chain to switch on the electric lamp.

"Leave the light off, please."

She turned slowly toward Lazaro, beginning to smile. "I can satisfy you in many ways, don Lazaro," Maria Therese said boldly.

Lazaro's only reply was the hungry look in his eyes.

She unfastened the buttons holding the cotton dress closed, pulling it back from her shoulders, letting it fall to the floor. She was naked beneath the dress, her golden-brown body still glistening with a light sheen of perspiration.

Lazaro did not move. The hunger in him was not of the usual sort—it wasn't the Hunger. If he took her, it would not be because he needed to but because he *wanted* to.

Maria Therese stepped out of the dress and lay down on it on the rug, her knees bent, her arms open.

"What you want is here." She lifted her chin a little, turning it to show him her neck, then thrust her hips upward, more wanton than Lazaro had realized. Maria Therese was of an age and inclination that made passion the center pole of her being. She knew the vampire would give her an experience beyond anything she could ever know with a mortal lover.

Maria Therese's lust was infectious. The Hunger flamed up inside of Lazaro, the pounding of his heart a deafening roar in his ears, dissolving what remained of his control. He threw himself on the supine woman.

Maria Therese returned his kisses with desperate passion, pushing her tongue deep into his mouth, cutting herself against Lazaro's distending blood teeth. Their mouths were suddenly filled with Maria Therese's honeyed blood, making Lazaro moan with pleasure.

A part of his mind floated above the room, looking down on Maria Therese where she lay beneath him, pinned to the rug like a butterfly on a kill board. He watched her eyes when she saw his glittering ivory fangs, which could tear human flesh faster than any surgeon's scalpel. She was not afraid. She knew the pleasure the vampire's kiss would bring and the prestige of becoming one of the master's chosen ones.

Their lovemaking was reaching its mutual crescendo when Lazaro drove his teeth deep into the willing young woman's neck, puncturing her jugular, feeling an orgasmic explosion inside him as the first gush of rich blood splashed against his throat.

Maria Therese gasped and clutched at his arms, trying to push him away yet trying to pull him closer, both at the same time. He drank her blood greedily, drawing it into his mouth with ugly wet sucking sounds, swallowing great gulps when a few tender sips would have served as well.

Maria Therese's body began to convulse.

Lazaro knew he should stop himself, but still he continued to drink, intoxicated with the inexpressible sense of power that came flooding into him with each swallow of Maria Therese's blood.

Reveling in sensual abandon, for the first time in his long existence as a vampire Lazaro did not concern himself with whether the woman beneath him lived or died. He had always known in his heart that vampires—once the artifice was stripped away—were at their most elemental essence predatory killers.

Maria Therese's body was still beneath his now, her heartbeat an irregular flutter, a dying moth beating its wings against a lamp chimney.

An inner voice begged Lazaro to stop, but he refused

to listen to the angel of his better nature. Just a little more blood and he would be satisfied. . . .

Only one thing could have made the experience more delicious, Lazaro thought, drunk with blood. He closed his eyes and imagined that the woman impaled beneath him was Bailey.

Veintiseis

✧

ROBERTO GOYA DE MONTEZUMA squatted on his haunches in front of the fire with his paperback edition of *Constant's Astrological Tables*.

Not all aspects of European culture were corrupt and useless, Roberto thought, opening the book. Since consulting the heavens was an essential part of a Zona sorcerer's work, *Constant's* was a useful resource for witchery. Roberto flipped through the well-thumbed pages, tilting the book to take advantage of the flickering firelight. He found the page and ran his finger down the long column of numbers.

Mercury was in retrograde.

"Interesting," he said to himself.

Unpredictable things happened whenever the planet appeared to move backward through the night sky. Well-laid plans unraveled and extraordinary coincidences occurred. Retrogrades were also a perfect time for looking into the past—which in a sense was what Roberto was most interested in, both personally and for his growing circle of followers.

Roberto closed the book and returned it to the rear pocket of his jeans. It would be an excellent night to visit

Zonatitucan, to climb the Pyramid of the Moon, to call the Zona gods into himself, inviting them to make him one of them.

Of course, his adversary Lazaro would never allow that. . . .

There was a rustling in the trees just beyond the fire-light. Roberto stood, searching the darkness. It was a jag-uar, he thought, the illusive ghost of the cloud forest, curious about the firelight. ~~~~ alesce amid the trees, a mass of vaguely menacing energy drawing together just beyond the light.

Roberto was mistaken. It was not a jaguar.

The guardian had arrived.

Roberto extinguished the fire and followed the guardian for nearly an hour, to a place in the forest where a large boulder protruded from the ground, a titanic, half-buried egg rising higher than the trees. Roberto *felt* the power of the place—the peculiar tingling in the air, as if lightning were about to strike. The guardian had led him to a gateway to the shadow world.

There were no footholds on the rock's smooth surface, no way to climb it without ropes and pitons. Roberto closed his eyes, extending his personal power upward. He felt a trembling sensation in his solar plexus, a weird tugging as if he were about to vomit. The feeling passed, and Roberto opened his eyes. He was standing on top of the rock.

Roberto sat cross-legged in the exact center of the power spot, as the guardian directed, his body west, the direction of the Underworld, the lines of the earth and the lines of the sky intersecting within the sorcerer's body. Power welled up out of the earth, concentrating itself in him.

The guardian indicated Roberto should focus himself toward La Esmerelda.

The young sorcerer shut his eyes. The familiar feeling of weightlessness came over him, his soul breaking free from his body like a ship slipping its mooring lines. Roberto looked down and saw his physical body sitting on the rock, an empty shell awaiting his return.

Roberto rotated slowly in the air and began to float toward La Esmerelda, moving faster until everything became a blur. He closed his eyes and thought of his destination and was instantly there, standing beside Dr. Bailey Harrison's bed, looking down on her.

For an Anglo, she was attractive, Roberto had to admit, watching her sleep. But Dr. Harrison had lost weight and no longer possessed the sort of robust healthiness Roberto associated with American women. She was almost wraith-like from the sickness of the gods.

Roberto felt his aura darken and throw off angry red flashes of malice in the sleeping woman's direction, making her toss and turn in her sleep. Roberto hated Dr. Harrison for trespassing at Zonatitucan, but he hated her even more because the holy fever had touched her. He was about to pull the pillow from beneath her head to smother her when the guardian caught his attention.

Lazaro would return to La Esmerelda and stop Roberto before he could finish the job, the guardian warned, communicating with its peculiar wordless language. Did the young sorcerer believe he had gathered enough personal power to face the vampire's rage?

Roberto reluctantly backed away from Dr. Harrison, drifting through the wall, following the guardian toward his next destination.

* * *

The longhaired German sat alone in the library, staring at a book of T. S. Eliot's poetry without actually reading *The Wasteland*. There was something peculiar about the foreigner, something more than met the eye. Roberto *saw* this but was unable to unlock the enigma he represented: the German had a secret, something he kept carefully concealed from the world.

Roberto should have taken care of the German—and Dr. Harrison as well—when they first came to the rain forest. Once Lazaro was out of the way, Roberto would permit no foreigners to come into their land. Keeping out the foreigners, the *extranjeros*, would keep the Zona pure.

The German closed the book and turned slowly until he was staring straight at Roberto, the deep frown making his eyebrows stand out like ridges on his prominent brow. Roberto knew it was impossible for mortal eyes to see his astral body floating invisibly in the room—though the German did indeed seem to be studying him with severe disapproval.

The German pursed his lips as if to blow out a candle.

Roberto felt himself being pushed backward, his spirit being driven from the room. Roberto knew the German couldn't be responsible for this strange phenomenon; the *extranjero* couldn't possibly have the power. Roberto did everything he could to remain in the room, but whatever force was pushing him backward was too strong for him to resist. Roberto was blown through the hacienda roof, rising higher and higher into the night sky, expelled from La Esmerelda.

He could think of no possible explanation for the way he'd been driven from the hacienda—unless the German was himself a sorcerer. Perhaps he was an Old World witch, a necromancer who commanded the power to summon and manipulate the spirits that lived within the earth, and on it, and in the air above. Roberto decided to reconsider his instinctive hatred for the *extranjero*. The German might be, like *Constant's Astrological Tables*, one of those rare useful aspects of the corrupt European culture. If Roberto and the German pooled their power, they might be able to crush Lazaro. The *extranjero* witch was a potential ally.

Roberto looked down at the rain forest until he found the guardian, waiting for him in front of Anonimo's house. Anonimo was one of Lazaro's employees, a lackey who had refused to join the others at Roberto's ceremonies, although his beautiful young wife had secretly become one of Roberto's acolytes. The guardian called Roberto down to the house, indicating that he should look in through the side window.

The sorcerer drifted over the veranda flooring and looked in through the glass.

What he saw surprised him so much that it made it impossible to maintain himself on the spirit plane, slamming him back into his physical body.

"Oompf!"

Roberto flipped over, turning a backward somersault. He scrambled to his feet, ignoring the fact that he'd bloodied his left elbow against the rock.

"The hypocrite!" Roberto screamed with outrage, turning to the guardian. "Lazaro has always made an elaborate pretense of taking blood only when the phases of the moon correspond with the ritual. You saw him there tonight, lying on top of Maria Therese, his teeth deep in her throat while he had his way with her. This is an abomination!"

The guardian glowered. Roberto had missed the point entirely. He had failed to comprehend what the guardian had tried to show him at Anonimo's house.

"The fool!" Roberto cried, suddenly understanding what the guardian was trying to show him. "He has put the first sickness of the gods in her, lingering too long over his pleasure."

The guardian hunched up in the darkness, the way it did when it was excited.

"Yes, yes, of course you're right!" Roberto crowed. "Lazaro won't bother to watch over Maria Therese the way he does the *gringa*. Especially not while he's drunk with the power of his excess. It's there for the taking!"

A ripple of agreement went through the guardian's shadowy outline.

Roberto continued to stand where he was, thinking about his sudden reversal of fortune. With Mercury in retrograde, extraordinary coincidences did indeed occur.

Roberto suddenly looked up at the guardian, startled.

"You're right. What am I waiting for? Come on!"

The guardian followed Roberto down off the vertical rock and into the forest. The sorcerer was getting very close to finding his destiny, and the guardian was there to serve as his guide.

The moon had come up by the time Roberto had walked to Anonimo's house, a thumbnail of light rising up over the trees, three nights into its third quarter. It was two-forty-five in the morning, Roberto estimated.

The guardian gave Roberto no sign that he should hesitate, so he bounded up the stairs and pulled open the door without knocking. Maria Therese was on her back on the floor on the braided rag rug in the center of the living room in a semidelirious stupor, her dress crumpled beneath her.

Roberto lit a holy candle on the mantel out of deference to the guardian's aversion to electric lights and put it on the floor next to the naked woman. The florid bruise on the side of Maria Therese's neck circumscribed the raised, purplish areolae of two still-gaping wounds where the vampire had punctured her jugular to suck her blood. The wounds appeared to crawl in the flickering candlelight. When Roberto got down on one knee to examine Maria Therese's neck, he saw that the wounds *were* crawling. Her body was repairing itself at a miraculous pace. Helped by the divine essences from the vampire's own mouth, the fast-healing tissue seemed to move as it drew closed around the wounds. By dawn, if Maria Therese survived the blood loss, the bites would be nothing more than two vaguely sore spots; by noon, they would not be even that. And whether or not she remembered—that would be a function of what Lazaro wanted her to remember. If he chose, she would be able to recall nothing of the incident. Such was the power of the gods.

Roberto lowered his mouth to Maria Therese's neck. Her skin was hot beneath his lips. He ignored the shudder of revulsion that went through his body when his tongue slid over the identical depressions in her neck. Roberto's mouth filled with a heady admixture of dried blood, perspiration, and something vaguely metallic—perhaps the iron in her blood, he thought, perhaps some immortal residue of the vampire's saliva.

Maria Therese, insensate, began to moan.

She thinks that I am *he*, Roberto thought, wondering whether to be gratified or insulted, as he began to suck at the puncture wounds in Maria Therese's neck.

The woman's eyes opened as her sounds of pleasure became terrified animal sounds. Roberto's efforts to get blood from the partly healed wounds became more insistent, but it was nearly futile. Aside from a weak trickle that resulted from ruptured capillaries in the woman's neck, Lazaro had left the well astonishingly dry.

Roberto jumped to his feet and kicked Maria Therese in the side of the head, the force of the blow rolling her onto one side. The guardian hovered ominously in the doorway, advising Roberto to calm down and to find a simple solution to a simple problem.

Roberto put his foot on Maria Therese's shoulder and rolled her onto her back again. The angry bruise rising on her head was nearly as ugly as the purple-and-yellow sore on her neck. Maria Therese's eyelids fluttered as the irises came down and focused on him—the terror returning as soon as she remembered where she was and what was happening.

"The most amazing coincidences occur when Mercury is in retrograde," Roberto said in a perfectly calm voice. "There is something I have been trying to possess for a very long time. And now, it seems, you are quite unexpectedly able to help me get it."

Roberto got down on his knees, roughly shoving her arm out of the way so that it pointed over her head, flattening her left breast against her chest, her lower ribs standing out against her golden skin. Roberto raised his own hands and held them chest high, his fingers spread wide and slightly curved, as if he were gripping an imaginary ball. He drew in a slow, deep breath. Even with practice, the technique was extremely difficult to get right.

Maria Therese knew what was coming next. She had attended Roberto's renegade ceremonies to raise Zona power. She managed to scream just before Roberto drove his hands downward in a powerful thrusting motion, his fingers penetrating the flesh of her breast, going all the way into the pericardial sac, the fibrous membrane surrounding the heart.

Maria Therese gasped and arched her back, clawing madly at her attacker.

Ignoring her struggles, Roberto withdrew his hands far enough to get his fingers around two ribs. Grabbing the ribs like two slippery bars he hoped to pry apart, Roberto began to pull in opposite directions. A vein popped, spraying Roberto with blood, followed by the ragged snap of bone and cartilage breaking inside the woman's chest.

Maria Therese's jaw locked open in a silent scream, her eyes on the young sorcerer as her arms fell limply back against the rug with two dull thuds.

Roberto looked down into the gaping hole in the woman's chest, ignoring the blood splattering him, the gore smearing his arms halfway to his elbows.

"Trophy of power!" Roberto cried, unable to contain his exultation.

Maria Therese's heart was completely exposed now.

Roberto took the heart in his hands, slipping his fingers around the twitching and slippery organ.

Maria Therese's breath came in loud, rasping wheezes, her fingers clawing blindly at the braided rug. Her eyes registered inexpressible and uniquely mortal horror as she stared helplessly up at Roberto.

"Accept this offering and make me a god!" Roberto said, his face uplifted.

He braced himself and began to pull. The heart tore free from the superior vena cava, a spray of blood splattering Roberto in the face. He opened his mouth, swallowing what he could of the blood and the seed of immortality it carried. Putting all his strength into it now, he felt the arteries stretching like rubber hoses as they struggled to maintain possession of the organ that gave them life. With a sharp, wet snapping, the blood vessels finally tore from their valves, freeing the heart from its mortal bonds.

The raw flesh was tough and chewy, but Roberto managed to tear off a chunk with his teeth and swallow it whole, as the ritual required. He held the heart up to his lips then and drank from the torn pulmonary artery, squeezing the ventricles as if forcing juice from a succulent melon.

Maria Therese was completely still now, a silent scream frozen on her face that would remain until worms consumed her flesh. Her eyes stared at nothing. Her legs were drawn up at a provocative angle, her fingers still holding the rug balled up inside her dead hands as if in passion.

After pausing to lick a dribble of hot blood trickling down the inside of his left hand, Roberto brought the heart to his lips again. Crushing the organ against his mouth with both hands, he forced the remaining blood from the heart's chambers into his mouth, more blood than he could swallow—the blood overflowing his mouth, streaming down his chin, a red rain falling on the front of his already-soaked shirt.

He could already feel the power seeping into him, the stolen kiss of immortality that would help turn him into a god.

Veintisiete

✦

THERE WAS NO one there—not one person, not even the whores.

Xavier looked out across the empty church and sagged, the remaining confidence draining out of him like Communion wine from a spilled chalice. The empty church seemed a perfect reflection of his own emptiness. He was a shepherd without a flock, a spiritual leader without followers, a ridiculous figure who put on a cleric's robe each day to hide his own moral bankruptcy.

He sank into the front pew, slouching against the uncomfortable mahogany backrest, his spine bowed. What did it matter if he didn't say Mass that morning? Who would know? Who would care?

Ending up in Paradisio had been his own fault. He'd been a willing participant in his fall from grace. He was a pariah for his sins, sent to do penance in a subtropical hell where not even the most impoverished peasants had any real faith in the Church's teachings.

What was the point of continuing the charade?

To his nominative parishioners, the holy mystery of the rituals Father Xavier performed during Mass were minor acts of magic that paled beside the unspeakable

178

rites they attended at night in the rain forest. Xavier remembered what don Lazaro had said about the peasants. The people were not interested in logic, as don Lazaro wished—or in faith, as Xavier had prayed—but in the old superstitions of the forest.

Don Lazaro's words came back to Xavier.

"The people here are drawn to whatever gods and powers present themselves. I've tried to lead them out of the darkness, but it's been hopeless, utterly hopeless."

Utterly hopeless—yes, it was.

Xavier leaned forward in an attitude of prayer. He was not praying, however, but surrendering to despair. He felt beyond prayer. God had abandoned him, he thought, casting him into an underworld ruled by a beast whose signs were the feathered serpents, skulls, and other aspects of the demonic.

Father Xavier knew what he *should* do. A courageous priest would do battle against the evil that lived amid the tangle of vines and jaguars, the sinister force Christianity had failed to defeat in five hundred years of battle.

Xavier was not courageous.

Xavier was not a priest so much as a man dressed up in a priest's collar, someone going through empty motions, hollow gestures, a dancing puppet whose strings were held by his bishop.

Xavier could not convince the Indians to believe when he was no longer certain that he himself believed.

Veintiocho

✦

"YOUR COFFEE, DON Lazaro."

Lazaro barely acknowledged his servant.

"There is also one of Obdulia's croissants. She asked me to tell you that it is still warm from the oven."

Lazaro lifted his right hand several inches and let it fall back to the arm of the rattan chair, dismissing Alvaro. The servant stepped backward through the door leading into Lazaro's rooms from the veranda and was gone.

The sky was growing light as the morning rain fell from a charcoal-gray sky. The rain was unusually heavy, even for La Esmerelda. Water gathered in small pools in the garden, reflecting the regular flashes of lightning, the puddles trembling with each volley of thunder. There was so much running off the roof over the veranda that it would become as solid as sheets of glass for several seconds at a time. Beyond the wooden railing that divided the dry and wet worlds, the garden was like a shimmering underwater mirage.

Lazaro glanced at the coffee without moving more than his eyes, seeing the steam drift up from the cup. Inside the house behind him, a door opened and closed.

180

Someone turned on a water tap. He heard the sounds of servants going about their morning routines.

There were no dawns at La Esmerelda; the days began and ended with deluges. Lazaro had not seen the sun come up and go down for longer than he could remember. Instead, there was the rain, always the rain, marking the beginnings and ends in the rain forest.

Lazaro leaned back and shut his eyes, suddenly very weary of it all. He had come far and yet he had gotten nowhere. Perhaps he had fulfilled his obligations and could now leave the rain forest, returning to the real world with Bailey. He wished to God he knew whether he dared leave, yet was far past seeking divine guidance—five hundred years and a dozen lifetimes past it.

The lines deepened in the corners of Lazaro's closed eyes.

The vampire could hardly believe he'd surrendered to his most animalistic desires. Playing his role with the Indians was one thing, but he could never forgive himself for his degrading behavior with Lucina and Maria Therese. He considered his soul irretrievably lost, but until recently he'd had his honor. Whatever happened now—no matter how impeccable his behavior from this day forward—he had lost something he could never get back.

Lazaro almost imperceptibly shook his head from side to side.

Where would it end, now that he had permitted the fiend to take control? He had raised the floodgates to dark passions he might never again be able to dam up. The chrysalis had begun to open, revealing not a butterfly but something misshapen, a malignant and inexpressibly malevolent being Lazaro had spent five centuries keeping carefully chained up in the deepest dungeon of his soul.

Bailey's image seemed to hover in the rain when he opened his eyes, an apparition he could not banish, lovely and at the same time tormenting. A year ago Lazaro never would have doubted his ability to control himself. But no longer. Dr. Janis Levy's visit to the rain forest had marked the commencement of a downward spiral Lazaro feared would not end until he had completed the transformation from man to monster.

More than anything else, Lazaro feared for Bailey. Already once kissed, as the Indians said, the first dangerous step was taken. Which would be worse: for Bailey to share his curse, or to become its victim?

Lazaro could no longer hide from his darkest desires, now that he had given in to them with Maria Therese. How easy it would be for him to lose control completely with the beautiful *gringa*.

The Hunger and love—perhaps the most dangerous combination of all.

The roar of thunder made the decking shake beneath his chair.

If only the eternal rain could wash away his sins, calling forth a flowering goodness from the depth of his ancient and shadow-filled soul, instead of this howling lust for Dr. Bailey Harrison's blood!

Maybe the time had come to end it all.

Lazaro had never before contemplated seeking such a resolution to his life, but perhaps it was time to halt an existence he considered, despite its outward trappings of wealth and refinement, a failure. Though he was immortal, Lazaro had never doubted he would one day come to the end of his road. If time itself would end, then so must end the life of the vampire. He was certain an act of extreme violence was all it would take.

But what would happen to Bailey?

Lazaro knew he could never go into the ultimate darkness, leaving her behind. He mostly trusted Beethoven, but not entirely; and there was Roberto to consider. Roberto would make it impossible for her to stay in the rain forest and continue her work. Of course, the greatest threat to Bailey was Bailey herself. Her scientific curiosity would lead her back to the ruined city, where she would be certain to suffer the same ignoble fate that had befallen him. What would become of her then, without him or even the Zona way to guide her?

There was one other possibility, though so remote that Lazaro was too realistic to put much hope in it. If Bailey could identify the virus that had changed him into the monster he had become, perhaps she could also find a cure. Lazaro would have gone back to being mortal in the blink of an eye. He and Bailey would at least have the chance of a life together then, growing old together, the way God had intended it to be for a man and a woman, ready for natural death when it came to take them.

Maybe he and Bailey could even have a family, if she could cure him of his grotesque condition and reverse its effect. Lazaro had always wanted a son. The only real happiness the vampire had known during the past five centuries had been those few fleeting years when Roberto was a child and had trusted and loved him.

He picked up the coffee cup and held it without bringing it to his lips, as if he'd instantly forgotten he was holding it. Bailey was the key, his one chance to become human again, and to love. He would have to be strong to resist the Hunger, but he knew how to be strong. Surely five hundred years of restraint counted for something.

The sound of the storm seemed to part around a woman's shrill scream. It came from the far side of the garden, from the direction of Anonimo's house.

The china cup dropped to the wooden flooring and shattered, splattering coffee on Lazaro's trousers as he jumped to his feet. He ran through the rain toward the hysterical screaming. Servants from the hacienda were behind him, running with him toward the screams, and others came racing down intersecting paths. Lazaro reached the lane that fronted Anonimo's house. Jorge Larrea Ballesteros was sprinting down the road from the bunkhouse, the machine gun slung over his shoulder held tight against his chest as he ran, getting there a little ahead of Lazaro.

Lucina, Obdulia's helper and Maria Therese's closest friend, was standing outside the front door, tears streaming down her face, her mouth open in a continuous scream. Lazaro took the steps in a single bound, the expression on Lucina's face changing from shock to terror in a heartbeat. The girl threw herself away from Lazaro as if expecting him to attack her, even with a dozen people standing behind them in the rain. She knew the bystanders would just watch, unable or unwilling to help as Lazaro sank his teeth into her neck.

Lazaro had long suspected the Indians' respect was only fear disguised. Now there would be no reason for them to disguise their terror. For years, perhaps generations to come, they would look at him only with fear, he thought bitterly.

Steeling himself against witnessing the final, unmistakable evidence of his descent to bestiality, Lazaro stepped quickly into Anonimo's small living room.

There was something terribly familiar about what had been done to the poor young woman's body. It had been many years since Lazaro had seen such savagery, yet he remembered vividly—as if he could ever forget!—coming to Zonatitucan and seeing what the Zona priests did atop the Pyramid of the Moon.

Lazaro became gradually aware that others had crowded into the room with him, their clothing soaking wet, like his, rain streaming from the black hair plastered against their skulls. Lazaro turned to Jorge. The tendons in the back of the man's hands stood out more plainly against his skin as his fingers tensed around the machine gun.

There was a jostling at the door as Beethoven pushed into the room. The German made his way to the body, looked at it briefly, then shot Lazaro an accusatory stare.

Lazaro barely moved his head from side to side. He should have felt some small measure of relief to realize that he hadn't been responsible for Maria Therese's death, but the scene was too sickening for Lazaro to experience anything but visceral revulsion.

"Roberto," Lazaro said in a low voice.

A ripple of fear spread through the room at the sorcerer's name. Roberto had not been spoken of openly at La Esmerelda since the day he returned from America and called Lazaro a foreign devil who had stolen his people's birthright. Lazaro was aware of his former protégé's activities, though he refused to believe Roberto could convince many of the Indians to follow him. Roberto was a fanatic. The others were deeply traditional, but in a calmer, conservative way, he thought.

Lazaro looked back at Maria Therese.

This went beyond sorcery, beyond Roberto's deluded ideas about resurrecting Zona culture. Maria Therese's murder and mutilation were the work of a deeply disturbed mind. How had Lazaro failed to recognize sickness within the brilliant boy's troubled soul? Lazaro was angry at himself for failing to see it, for missing the opportunity to get help for Roberto before it had come to this. Perhaps there was still time. There were doctors who treated infirmities of the mind. Perhaps Beethoven could suggest a clinic. In spite of Roberto's horrific crime, Lazaro still loved his adopted son.

"See that she is taken care of," Lazaro told Jorge.

The man nodded.

"When Anonimo returns from San José, bring him to me before he sees anyone. Let me tell him about Maria Therese. Say nothing. Do I make myself perfectly clear?"

Jorge nodded a second time.

Lazaro took one more look at Maria Therese. He shared responsibility for this crime. If Lazaro had not taken the young woman, Roberto never would have bothered her. Lazaro knew what Roberto had been after. It was obvious he had gotten it.

Lazaro turned and walked out, restraining himself from an impulse to rip the door off its hinges and smash it into a million pieces before he stalked down the steps and into the rain.

"Lazaro."

Beethoven broke away from the crowd and caught up with him. They walked through the downpour without speaking, their shoes squishing against the wet gravel path.

"Lazaro," Beethoven said again. "We need to make sure nothing like this happens again."

"I'm taking Bailey away from here," Lazaro said, as if he hadn't heard. "It's not safe for her at La Esmerelda."

"Her work will help unlock the mystery of our race. She must continue her research. The *Illuminati* insist on it."

"The *Illuminati* can all go hang," Lazaro snapped. "I want Bailey out of here. I love . . ." Lazaro's voice broke. He hesitated, having to gather himself together before he could proceed. They stood facing one another, boot-to-boot in the driving rain.

"I love Bailey," Lazaro said. "I will not let anything hurt her."

"Then focus your concern on Roberto. His insane scheme to join with the *Vampiri* is the real danger. Surely you realize where that could lead. Roberto intends to hurl his people headlong into the ghastly pit of their bloody past."

"Roberto needs help."

"What Roberto needs is to be *stopped*," Beethoven said harshly, leveling his finger at Lazaro's heart. "You took responsibility for Roberto Goya de Montezuma. I'm holding you responsible for that poor girl's murder and any other crime Roberto commits. It's up to you to bring a halt to this immediately. And if he harms Bailey—"

"That will never happen," Lazaro vowed, interrupting.

"If he harms Bailey," the German vampire continued, "I will kill you with my bare hands."

Beethoven turned sharply away, leaving Lazaro to look after him, rain running down his face.

Veintinueve

✧

VINCENT HELD THE match to the tip of his cigarette, squinting through the smoke at the table where two drunk cowboys whooped with laughter. The cowboys laughed until they were out of breath, pounding their hands on the table, slapping their legs as if the antique joke the bigger cowboy had told was the funniest thing either man had ever heard.

The two whores at the table with the cowboys smiled politely at their hosts. Vincent caught the women's eyes and glanced upward briefly, the signal that it was getting time to corral their customers upstairs. If the cowboys got too drunk, they'd pass out at the table before the *prostitutas* could earn their pay.

One of the cowboys fell over backward in his chair, which started the drunks roaring with laughter again. The whores grinned but shot Vincent covertly apologetic looks. Vincent raised his eyes, indicating *Upstairs*.

The cowboys had come to Paradisio from the far corner of the ranch to get a new Toyota pickup don Lazaro had bought them. Vincent did a quick tally of their liquor tab in his head. It was going to be a long trip back to the logging camp in the morning with the hangovers the men were going to have.

Father Xavier was alone in his corner. The priest no longer bothered to bring a book to read, visiting the cantina now for the express purpose of getting drunk. Vincent found Xavier's newfound love of drink distasteful. He didn't like having to hoist the priest up on his shaky legs and show him to the door before he could lock up and go to bed.

Vincent stabbed his cigarette into the overflowing ashtray on the bar and lit another. A depressed priest getting drunk every night in the cantina was not exactly a prescription for good business. Maybe Vincent could find a leper to sit outside the door, a scabrous beggar to scare off what little business he had.

"Vincenzo!"

It was easy to tell when Father Xavier was drunk. He started calling Vincent *Vincenzo*.

"Another mescal, *por favor*."

Vincent started to tell the priest he'd had enough, but his saloon keeper's ethic stopped him. Father Xavier's money was as good as anybody's. He noticed the priest was still carrying a gun, the weapon bulging in his back pocket. Vincent didn't blame him. They'd all heard about the murder of the young Indian woman at La Esmerelda. Vincent had expected the *policía* to show up any day, but they had yet to arrive. Don Lazaro was apparently dealing with the crime in his own way. Not that it would surprise Vincent if his employer chose to hush it all up.

The outline of a man appeared in the cantina door.

Yanira had been leaning on her elbows against the bar, her breasts straining against the cotton blouse, her nipples hard and distinct. She put on her whore's smile and walked forward to meet Roberto. Roberto allowed Yanira to take his arm, which struck Vincent as odd. It was the first time he had ever seen Roberto show any interest in the whores.

"Tequila," Roberto said without actually looking at Vincent, addressing him in a superior manner. Roberto took his drink and Yanira to the table in the corner opposite Father Xavier. He pulled out the chair for her, his manners as elegant as don Lazaro's.

"¡Asesino!"

Anonimo came into the cantina with a machete high in his right hand. Anonimo's woman had been the one killed at La Esmerelda. He looked at Roberto with murderous hatred and said it again: *"Murderer!"*

Vincent had heard it whispered that Roberto's split with don Lazaro was over the younger man's involvement with sorcery. Maria Therese's murder—her heart had been cut out, one of the cowboys had said—certainly sounded like witchcraft to Vincent. No one had mentioned Roberto's name in connection with the crime to Vincent, but it seemed to make sense.

Anonimo grabbed the edge of the table where Roberto sat with Yanira and threw it to one side. Roberto looked up at Anonimo, his expression calm, even peaceful, as Yanira screamed and scrambled to get out of the way. Vincent didn't bother to reach for his shotgun. Roberto didn't deserve Vincent's help, if he was the one who'd gutted Anonimo's beautiful young wife like a pig in a butcher shop.

Roberto jumped up and knocked the machete out of Anonimo's hand, moving faster than seemed possible. Anonimo was facedown on the floor in the next instant, Roberto astride him, lifting the older man's head by the hair. Roberto brought his right hand slowly around in front of Anonimo's face, showing the middle-aged man the knife that had materialized in his hand as if by magic.

"Stop!" Father Xavier cried, lurching to his feet, belatedly deciding to become involved.

Vincent brought the sawed-off shotgun up from behind the bar and, holding it with one hand, leveled it at Roberto. Roberto just grinned, tossing his head to throw his ponytail back over his shoulder as he pressed the knife against Anonimo's neck, knowing Vincent couldn't shoot him without hitting Anonimo.

There was fever in Roberto's eyes. Roberto was ill, Vincent thought, burning up with fever.

Vincent allowed the shotgun barrel to fall a few inches. Maybe Roberto had the same fever that killed the woman archaeologist, the disease Dr. Harrison had come to Paradisio to find. For the first time since the confrontation started, Vincent was afraid. He didn't want to get sick and die.

"For the love of God, let him up," Father Xavier said.

Roberto smiled at the priest and drew the blade slowly across Anonimo's neck, from left to right, with a single long, deliberate motion. Anonimo made a horrible retching noise, but what spilled across the floor was not vomit but blood—a great expanding pool of red that flowed across the unvarnished wooden flooring in the cantina with surprising speed. Roberto pulled Anonimo's head back farther still, releasing the blood at an even faster rate. A sickening smile opened in the middle of the man's neck. His other mouth, his real mouth, hung open and slack. His eyes were already blank, the glassy stare of the dead.

Vincent braced his forearm against the bar and pulled both triggers on the sawed-off shotgun.

The firing pins clicked loudly against the shells.

The weapon did not fire.

Roberto turned his smiling face toward Vincent. It was witchery that had made the shotgun misfire, Vincent knew, the dread touch of Roberto's sorcery crawling through him like an icy chill. The sound of falling chairs and running feet told Vincent the two cowboys and their whores were running from the cantina.

Vincent dropped the shotgun on the bar and reached for the billy club he kept for settling run-of-the-mill disputes. Vincent had an instinctive dread of knife fights, which had a way of ending with the winner being as cut up as the loser.

Roberto didn't come for Vincent. Instead, he grabbed Yanira by the wrist before she could react. Her eyes stayed on the bloody blade in Roberto's right hand. She did not resist as he dragged her toward the doorway.

Vincent ran to the end of the bar with the club, following them out the door, not wanting to let Roberto take

Yanira but far too experienced in the ways of violence to run headlong into a waiting knife.

There was no sign of Roberto and Yanira in the street. The night had swallowed them whole.

Treinta

"**W**HEN DO THE *policía* arrive, don Lazaro?"

"I have not notified them."

"What?"

"I have not sent for the *policía*."

"And why not?" Father Xavier demanded, his voice rising.

Don Lazaro did not respond.

The priest came up off the couch where he and Vincent sat in don Lazaro's library at La Esmerelda. Vincent lightly put his hand on Father Xavier's arm. The priest pulled free, too upset to be restrained or to restrain himself.

"Are you out of your mind, don Lazaro?" Father Xavier said, nearly yelling. "Two people have been butchered. And they're just the ones we know about. I shudder to think how many others there are like them."

Alvaro, don Lazaro's servant, put down the tray of coffee he'd brought into the room and stepped between don Lazaro's chair and Father Xavier. Alvaro was the smaller of the two men by more than a head, but Vincent had no doubt the Indian could make short work of the priest.

"Keep your goon away from me."

"Alvaro is my butler, Father Xavier. None of my security personnel are present. This is just a friendly conversation. Perhaps you should sit back down so that we might continue in a calm and rational fashion."

"If you had made some token effort after Maria Therese was killed, the second of these two extraordinarily vicious murders might have been prevented," the priest said, perching on the edge of the couch.

"As I understand the unfortunate encounter, it was Anonimo who attacked Roberto."

"Roberto easily disarmed the older man and got him down on the floor, sitting on his back, slitting his throat as I begged him to spare Anonimo's life. Did your informant tell you Roberto grinned at me as he killed Anonimo? If there was any doubt that Roberto killed Maria Therese, what he did in the cantina erases it."

"What Father Xavier says is essentially true," Vincent said, interrupting to brake the priest's fast-accelerating hysteria. "Roberto killed Anonimo in cold blood."

"You must send for the *policía*, don Lazaro," Father Xavier said, waving his hands. "Justice for Maria Therese and Anonimo demands it. The safety of the people demands it. God in His Heaven demands it. Roberto must be stopped before he kills again."

"I rather think you are overdramatizing, Father," the vampire coolly replied. "As for linking Roberto to Maria Therese's death, what evidence have you beyond Anonimo's implied accusation?"

"Have you taken leave of your senses? I understand you have a relationship with this troubled young man, don Lazaro, but even you must see that Roberto has become a dangerous psychopath. The time has come to face the facts. I cannot imagine how the seed of such wickedness came to be planted in Roberto, but it has taken flower. Satan has marked him, claiming him heart, mind, body, and soul."

"Satan?" don Lazaro asked with a crooked smile.

"I have seen the evidence with my own eyes in the rain forest. Do not think that I have failed to recognize what is going on here. The mark of the Beast can be seen in the ashes and offerings left at the secret altar in the rain forest outside Paradisio. We are facing something much more sinister here than the brutal attacks of a killer, don Lazaro. Here, in the midst of this vast and isolated wilderness, we are confronted with nothing less than Evil itself."

Vincent scowled at Father Xavier for bringing witchery into the conversation. He wished he'd never let the priest talk him into coming with him to see don Lazaro. It was becoming increasingly difficult for him to follow his policy of staying away from black magic. It was everywhere, even in don Lazaro's luxurious estate. In fact, La Esmerelda might even be the most bewitched place of all.

"Is it a psychopath or Satan we must fear?" don Lazaro asked sarcastically. "I'm afraid you've lost me, Father. And is it the *policía* I should summon? Perhaps an exorcist is more what the situation requires."

Father Xavier turned to don Lazaro's German house guest, who had been sitting quietly to one side, following the conversation with his eyes. "Herr Samsa, maybe you can make don Lazaro understand his duty."

"You would lecture me on duty?" don Lazaro demanded, his voice rising.

"I am truly sorry, Father Xavier," the German said, ignoring his host's interjection as he sat forward from his chair within the shadows. "While I hardly share don Lazaro's apparent attitude that this subject is fit for jest, this is not my parish, so to speak."

"Then I will summon the *policía* myself," Father Xavier said. "Certainly you will not deny my request to use your radio, don Lazaro."

"Of course not, Father Xavier. But unfortunately, the radio is broken."

"And I am the pope."

"I beg your pardon?" don Lazaro asked sharply, anger flashing in his eyes.

"Excuse me, don Lazaro," Vincent interrupted, trying to salvage something of the quickly degenerating meeting. "I mean no disrespect. You know I have no love of the *policía*, but this can't continue."

"You can be assured that I will deal with Roberto," don Lazaro said ambiguously, giving Vincent a look that said he wasn't going to elaborate.

"Good. Then I need to make only one thing clear between us."

Don Lazaro showed polite interest, giving Vincent courtesy that he for some reason withheld from the priest.

"If Roberto shows up again at the cantina, I'll kill him," Vincent said in a businesslike voice. "I'll kill him in the blink of an eye, without giving him a warning or a chance to defend himself or run away. He's not going to carve up me or any of my girls the way he did Maria Therese and Anonimo."

Don Lazaro gave Vincent a baleful look but nodded. "I

will instruct my men to search the rain forest for the woman Roberto took away from the cantina. I do not recommend you venture into the forest to look for her yourself."

"If I thought Yanira was still alive, I'd have to ignore your advice, don Lazaro."

"You would be wise to leave this in the hands of don Lazaro's security personnel," the German advised, not looking as if he had any more faith than Vincent that the prostitute Roberto had kidnapped would be saved. "They know the rain forest and will have the best chance of tracking them."

Vincent exhaled an enormous sigh. "I liked Yanira a lot," the Rastafarian said, close to losing his well-cultivated cool. "She may be a whore, but that doesn't give Roberto the right to do whatever he wants to her."

"Certainly not," don Lazaro agreed.

Vincent looked away from his employer. Someday Vincent would be a wealthy and powerful man; then, he would be the one who called the shots. As for the present, there wasn't anything he could do to make things right.

"How is Dr. Harrison?" Father Xavier said.

"Much better. She is resting now," don Lazaro lied. "She shouldn't be disturbed."

Vincent stood. "Come on," he said to Father Xavier. "We said what we came here to say."

Father Xavier walked with Vincent to the door and stopped, looking back.

"I hope to God you know what you're doing, don Lazaro," the priest said, his face white, his voice shaking.

Don Lazaro sat up in his chair, his eyes seeming to

stab Father Xavier. "Do any of us really know what we're doing?" don Lazaro demanded.

Father Xavier and don Lazaro stared at each other until Vincent tapped the priest on the shoulder and led him from the room.

Did any of them really know what they were doing?

Not bloody likely, Vincent thought.

Treinta y Uno

✦

BAILEY LOOKED UP from her microscope and smiled when Lazaro came into the makeshift lab.

"I apologize for interrupting your work."

"That's okay," she said, stretching before she pushed her stool away from the counter. "Did I hear a truck earlier?"

"Two men from town came out to speak with me. They have returned to Paradisio. How is your research coming along?"

"I think I've actually done about everything I can without the resources at my disposal back at the Centers for Disease Control in Atlanta."

Lazaro's smile disappeared. "Then you're thinking of leaving?"

Bailey blinked rapidly and nodded. "I can't begin to thank you enough for your hospitality and for taking care of me when I got sick."

"It was the least I could do."

"And also for obtaining the specimens for me. Both bats were, as you know, riddled with the virus."

"You were too weak to go back into the rain forest. I wanted you to be able to continue your work as you regained your strength. You know how interested I am in your research."

"You and Ludwig have become my biggest supporters."

"What have you learned?"

"I've discovered some anomalies in the bats' blood that can only be described as bizarre."

"How so?"

"I've found signs indicating both extreme strength and extreme weakness. It's as if the animals were both healthy and sick at the same time—which is impossible, at least within the boundaries of ordinary biology."

"Then perhaps something extraordinary is responsible."

"To say the least," Bailey replied, accepting Lazaro's arm and allowing him to lead her out of the lab and toward their favorite bench in the garden.

"The hemoglobin in the blood is unusually potent. Their blood is able to transport a significantly greater amount of oxygen than usual, making your little vampire bats extremely efficient and strong creatures."

"But?" Lazaro said, anticipating her new tack.

"But there is also evidence of an unusual early breakdown of the red corpuscles—a sort of premature cell death that resembles sickle-cell anemia."

They sat on the bench, their bodies close enough for their legs and arms to touch. Bailey's proximity filled Lazaro with the Hunger, which he ignored, as well as desire of a different sort that he made no effort to repress.

"I would have expected the animals to have been sick, at least judging from the condition of their blood. I suppose there's the possibility that they are able to transform the blood they consume in a way that overcomes the pathological weakness inherent in their own blood. Some genetic modification may have taken place as part of the action of the retrovirus. I'd need more specimens to investigate this theory. What I'd have to do is devise a series of tests to see how the animals metabolize the blood they drink."

Bailey paused and put her hand gently on Lazaro's shoulder.

"And, of course, I'd need live specimens to take back to Atlanta, though it would be terribly dangerous to take infected animals from the isolated valley where they have lived for eons. It would be much safer to do the research here, if the equipment were available."

"Then have whatever you need shipped here, Bailey. You know you are welcome to stay at La Esmerelda for as long as you like."

"That's an offer I find difficult to reject," she said, looking deep into Lazaro's eyes. "Unfortunately, I doubt I could convince my boss to send an electron microscope and the rest of my gear out of the country. The transportation costs alone would give him a stroke."

"Then allow me to sponsor your research."

"It's wonderful of you to offer, Lazaro, but you have no idea how much that could be. It would cost close to half a million dollars to set up a lab with everything I'd need."

"No matter," Lazaro said with a shrug. "I have more money than I could possibly spend in a dozen lifetimes. It would be a tremendous honor to help you unlock this profound scientific mystery."

"Is your curiosity purely intellectual, or do you have a personal interest?"

Bailey did not resist when Lazaro gathered her into

his arms. She looked up at him, ready for his answer, for his lips.

"I assure you that my interest is both intellectual *and* personal," Lazaro whispered, "intensely, passionately personal."

Bailey closed her eyes, waiting for Lazaro to kiss her.

Treinta y Dos

IT WAS COOL and damp, the temple's interior more like a cave than a man-made structure. Air rustled through the debris on the floor in dank drafts that moved at irregular intervals through the living darkness, shepherding the sound of slithering insects and water dripping upon wet stone.

It was here the long-departed Zona warriors had spent their final night of life as mortal beings.

The room had once been splendidly appointed, a sacred place where the brave heroes and their beautiful consorts sat upon golden thrones covered with jaguar fur while meditating on the life about to end, and the life to begin. A splendid new existence awaited each of them on the other side of the door, on the other side of the awesome transformation they were about to undergo.

Roberto pulled a rectangle of folded mesh from his backpack, then a roll of silver duct tape. The orange polypropylene netting was used at La Esmerelda to keep birds out of the fruit trees. It would serve equally well for other purposes.

Standing on his toes, the sorcerer began to tape the mesh over the doorway opening onto the plaza. Humidity and time had rotted away all traces of the entry's wooden door centuries earlier. All dwellings in Zonatitucan once had doors and window shutters that were closed tightly each night as dusk fell. Only those who had distinguished themselves in battle and their consorts were permitted to be outside at night, when they might accept the gods' kiss and join with the immortals. The others remained locked in their houses after dark, during the time when only gods and heroes walked in Zonatitucan, worshiping at secret rites conducted atop the Pyramid of the Moon.

Roberto knew himself to be the only man alive who understood the significance of the room he occupied in the squat temple across the plaza from the base of the Pyramid of the Moon's great staircase. He alone could read Zonatitucan's hieroglyphics describing the law and the solemn rituals and incantations. Roberto Goya de Montezuma—successor to the last Great Zona priest-king, the heir to an entire civilization, ruler of the coming new age, savior whose return to the rain forest had been foretold a thousand years earlier in hieroglyphics inscribed in the sacrificial altar atop the Pyramid of the Moon.

The young sorcerer stood back from the doorway and examined his handiwork. The mesh would still allow air to circulate into the dank room; the sacred bats, however, would bounce their shrill little cries off the mesh and veer away without entering. Roberto intended to follow the sacred forms precisely. His time would not come until the following night, the momentous deed occurring as it always had, the anointed one standing atop the great pyramid to make his sacrifice, the gods in their heavens looking down on the rebirth of the newest incarnation of the Great Zona.

Roberto had twice been kissed by the gods. Tomorrow night the third blessing would make him an immortal.

Roberto grinned to himself, thinking back on the first kiss, a secret known only to himself and the guardian. It had been the night Lazaro brought the *gringa*, Dr. Bailey Harrison, to Zonatitucan. The guardian had instructed Roberto to linger before he exited the valley. Roberto followed the guardian's advice and was bitten by a bat flying out of a ruin on the edge of the city in search of its nightly meal. The guardian had been right about Lazaro. Besotted with the beautiful American doctor, Roberto's greatest enemy had been too distracted to realize the victory Roberto had claimed.

Lazaro himself had indirectly given Roberto the second kiss, via Maria Therese.

Now nothing, not even Lazaro, could stop Roberto. He would repeat the archaic ritual the next night atop the Pyramid of the Moon, inaugurating the new millennium. Later, he would transform worthy warriors from among his growing band of followers; they would strike out beyond the valley and the rain forest, regaining the lands the Zona empire had possessed during its golden age, before Lazaro the conquistador came. And that would be only the beginning.

Yanira was behind Roberto, silently watching him put up the netting. He had cut down two trees, dragged them into the room, and lashed them together with rope to make a ten-foot-high X. Yanira was tied to this impromptu cross by her wrists. On the floor before her was a stone table carved in the shape of a skull, the skull's stony eye sockets staring up as if awakened from a centuries-long sleep to observe the arrival of the sacrifice whose fresh blood would summon the ghosts of a sleeping vampire army.

Roberto brought his backpack from the door and removed the shoe box filled with burned-down candle remnants stolen from Father Xavier's church. There were dozens of stubby wax fingers, mostly white, with a few red ones left over from Advent. When he had the candles arrayed on the stone skull, he waved one hand through the air above them. The candles burst into flame, filling the room with cheerless flickering light.

Yanira screamed at this minor feat of sorcery, struggling vainly against her bonds. Roberto came to her. He gently laid the back of his hand against her cheek, rubbing it up and down. Yanira tried to pull away, a useless gesture. There would be no easy escape from the sorcerer.

"Tonight is too soon," Roberto said, "though I truly wish that this wasn't the case."

Roberto turned his head sharply, listening as the guardian spoke to him from the plaza.

"I *know*," Roberto said. "Do you think I've come this far to become impatient and throw it all away?"

Yanira trembled as she watched the dark form drift through the netting and come into the room, a shadow with substance and an unmistakable menace.

"The stars will not be in the proper position until tomorrow," Roberto said, talking again to Yanira. He held up his paperback copy of *Constant's Astrological Tables* as evidence that he knew of what he spoke. "There is a proper form that must be obeyed. The stars, the moon, the planets—everything will be in order tomorrow at moonrise."

Roberto put down the book and began to caress the woman's breast. He had hardly started to unbutton her blouse when her breasts spilled out, large and brown, her nipples the color of light chocolate.

"Ah," Roberto said, touching the naked flesh, feeling its softness against the palm of his hand. "It would be better if you were a virgin instead of a whore. In olden times, we brought captives back from the wars, prisoners from the north, slaves taken after we crushed our enemies' armies in battle and carried off their women. A virgin was preferred for the most sacred rites, but perhaps it is enough that you are not one of us. It would be unseemly to sacrifice a Zona woman. There are so few of them—of us—remaining in the world."

Roberto thrust his fingers into the waist of her skirt, ripping it away from her. He roughly pushed her underpants down and stepped back to admire her.

"You are beautiful for a whore, but there is something I desire far more than your body. My change is only two-thirds complete, yet already I crave the rich red wine of immortality that runs through your veins."

Yanira Rojas's eyes opened wide as she tried to turn her face away from Roberto, as if even that much escape was worth the effort.

"Perhaps I am only imagining it," Roberto said, closing his eyes, "but I would almost swear I can smell the aroma of your Nicaraguan blood as it courses through your veins. It is sweet, like clover honey, yet rich and stout, like good strong coffee."

A flash of lightning filled the room with a second of

weird blue illumination, followed by the roar of thunder and the full-bore start of the evening rain.

Roberto picked up a coil of rope as the thunder echoed from the stone temple walls, tying an end around one of Yanira's ankles. He looped the rope high up and farther out on the makeshift pillory and slowly drew up the rope, lifting the woman's leg until her ankle was as high as her shoulder. She balanced on one foot, her leg up as high as it could naturally stretch. Roberto paused then gave the rope one final, cruel pull.

Yanira groaned and stood on the toes of her supporting foot, tears running down her cheeks.

Roberto stood there, enjoying her discomfort for many minutes before he lowered the rope and turned to rummage through his backpack.

"The Zona slaves wore rings to mark their station," Roberto said, his back to her. "I don't mean the kind of ring you put on your finger."

When he turned, Yanira saw the big curved upholstery needle in his hand and shrieked.

"Scream all you wish. There's no one to hear you but the guardian and the ghosts of Zonatitucan. Besides, I find that my enjoyment increases proportionally to your fear."

Roberto bent and licked her left nipple, feeling it become hard against his tongue.

"This will hurt a little, I think," he said, putting the cork from a wine bottle against the nipple and carefully positioning the needle. Yanira abruptly fell into a stunned silence. Roberto hesitated, in no hurry, looking into his prisoner's imploring eyes. He moved his right hand slightly, seeing her flinch when he pricked her sensitive skin. The flame on one of the red candles, burned down to its nub, guttered in the melted wax and went out in a hiss and plume of smoke that raised the smell of paraffin in the room.

"Now, I want you to hold perfectly still. . . ."

Roberto jabbed the needle through the soft flesh and into the cork with a single quick thrust.

Yanira's wail was followed by a volley of thunder that seemed to shake the temple's foundations.

"You must be careful not to move," Roberto advised. "As much as this hurts, it will only be worse if you jerk around so that the needle tears open your flesh."

"*¡Bastardo!*"

"That's right," Roberto said. "Hate me. Hate and fear—they are the food that nourishes my growing power."

Roberto's hands trembled as he slowly withdrew the needle, lifting it to his eyes, turning it in the candlelight to study the way the glittering crimson shaded the sharp silver shaft. He brought the needle to his tongue and licked it clean, his eyes closed, savoring the taste of Yanira's blood.

Roberto opened his eyes and saw that Yanira had fainted. Her body hung slack against her bonds, the ropes creaking from the additional weight. A glistening trickle of blood ran down Yanira's breast, following the soft curve of her flesh, gathering in a growing circle of crimson that threatened to obey the summons of gravity and break free and become a long, scarlet teardrop.

Roberto dropped to his knees before the woman like a man praying before an altar. He slowly began to lick the blood from her breast. He started where it was most plentiful, pausing to probe the fold beneath her breast with his tongue before moving slowly toward the source. As his lips fastened at last around the bleeding nipple, he moaned and his body shook with a long and powerful climax of his unnatural pleasure.

Blood, the life, the way of the Zona *vampiro* warrior-gods!

A powerful gust of wind ripped at the mesh netting over the doorway, blowing a spray of cold rain into the room. Lightning flashed and thunder roared as the howling storm lifted itself to a level of fury unusual even in the rain forest. It was as if Zonatitucan's savage ancient gods were roaring their approval for the long-delayed arrival of a new acolyte to their forgotten religion.

Roberto, transported by the pleasure this small taste of blood brought him—appetizer for the great endless feasts to come—scarcely noticed.

Treinta y Tres

✧

L AZARO PULLED BACK the draperies and threw open the French doors. The night air washed into the room like a long, cool wave of water.

"Lazaro?"

The vampire wrapped his robe tightly around his slim, hard body, knotting the belt in front. Bailey was lying with her hand against the pillow when he turned around, watching him closely. There was concern hiding behind the softness of her smile.

Lazaro sat down on the edge of his bed and took her hand between his. He already knew what she was going to say. It was sad, but inevitable. The greater issue, however, was what it would do to her feelings for him. Would she still love him if she knew the truth? Even if she did, they would have to overcome almost insurmountable obstacles to be together. Lazaro often wished he was an ordinary mortal, but never so much as at that moment.

"There is something I need to tell you about my research, Lazaro."

Lazaro waited for her to find the words. He'd made no real effort to conceal the truth. His honor would not allow him to lie to his beloved. He had given her a sword and given it to her freely; she could either put the weapon aside and love him, or plunge it deep into his heart.

"When we were talking earlier, I did not tell you everything that I've learned in my work. Do you remember the sample of your blood I drew?"

Lazaro looked at her, imagining her facing him with the sword in her hands as he sat unarmed and ready, willing to accept whatever fate she assigned him.

"The same unusual characteristics I found in the bats' blood are present in yours," Bailey said, sitting up in bed, modestly holding the sheet to cover her breasts. "You're infected with the virus."

"Indeed," he said simply.

"You should be a very sick man."

"But I am as strong as a bull," Lazaro protested. "Stronger."

"I think you might be a carrier," Bailey said, blurting out the words like a death sentence.

"A *what*?"

"A carrier is a person who is infected with a disease without actually becoming sick from it. They can, however, unknowingly pass the infection on to other persons."

"It sounds as if it could be dangerous," Lazaro said.

"Carriers can be extremely dangerous. There was a famous typhoid carrier during the nineteenth century who was a walking plague, leaving sickness and death behind her wherever she went."

"Are there no present-day typhoid carriers?"

"Vaccinations have brought the disease into check."

"Perhaps there will one day be a vaccination against the virus infecting me."

There were suddenly tears in Bailey's eyes. "Perhaps," she managed to say.

"Maybe there will even be a cure."

All Bailey could do was nod.

"I am deeply moved at your concern for my well-being," Lazaro said, caressing her hand. "And by your bravery. If I am a carrier, is it not possible that I might infect you?"

"I'm in love with you, Lazaro. Besides, I think the infection I recovered from may have given me at least a degree of immunity."

"You must not worry about my welfare," Lazaro said, gently wiping away her tears. "I do not think the virus will make me sick."

"You don't know that."

"Yes, I do. I have carried it in my blood for many years. It will not kill me."

Bailey tipped her head and gave Lazaro a curious look. "Are you telling me that you've known all along that you were infected?"

"Yes. I remember very well how it happened."

"And why haven't you told me before?"

"Please do not become angry. I had no reason to think I would infect you." Lazaro looked away, shamed by his own duplicity. "I thought you would be afraid of me if you knew the truth."

"Tell me."

Lazaro looked up and saw the frank curiosity in her eyes.

"Tell me everything," she said. "I want to know. It's what I came to the rain forest to learn about."

Lazaro stood and walked to the window, his hands

thrust deep into the pockets of his robe. Could she stand to know the truth? Would she still love him if she knew what he'd become—and worse still, the things he'd done, things for which he could never forgive himself, much less ask the forgiveness of others?

"Do you really want to know?" the vampire asked, his voice sepulchral.

"Of course," Bailey said. "I want to know everything."

"As you wish," Lazaro said, turning slowly, looking at her intensely. "But you must promise not to hate me for it."

Treinta y Cuatro

✧

FATHER XAVIER WENT up the darkened street toward the modest rectory, doing his best to walk in a straight line after having more mescal than he could remember drinking. The outline of his house materialized a few hundred meters ahead, a small, squat shadow compared to the larger, more vertical shadow of the church.

The priest stopped, swaying to one side, overcorrecting when he leaned back in the opposite direction. He would have fallen if he hadn't taken several quick shuffling steps to the side.

At first he couldn't remember why he stopped, but then it came to him. He felt for the pistol in his back pocket. It was still there. Reassuring.

Except for the lights of the cantina behind him, Paradisio was completely dark. The residents rose and went to bed with the sun, living a life from a different century. Still, the provincials were not nearly so innocent as they had first appeared. The rain forest harbored an evil—an ancient evil that retained its power to pervert men's hearts and steal their souls.

Father Xavier touched the pistol again, running his fingers over the machined metal. Very reassuring indeed.

The priest stepped over a deep rut in the street. Were Paradisio's residents asleep in their beds, or off in the rain forest, dancing around a pagan bonfire with Roberto? Or had Roberto fled the province? Vincent believed that Roberto was long gone. Vincent suspected don Lazaro had helped Roberto escape, since he had done little or nothing to ensure the fugitive's apprehension.

Father Xavier regretted that he again hadn't spoken to Dr. Harrison while he was at La Esmerelda. He wanted to warn her about Roberto.

And what of that other strange fellow at La Esmerelda? "Samsa," Father Xavier said out loud, testing the name against his ear.

There was something familiar about Ludwig Samsa, don Lazaro's German guest. The protagonist of Kafka's *Metamorphosis* was named Samsa, if Father Xavier remembered correctly in his state of carefully achieved drunkenness. *Gregor* Samsa, though, not *Ludwig*. A German named Samsa interested in butterflies, the quintessential creature of metamorphosis; a tortured fictional character named Samsa from the existentialist *Metamorphosis*, a man who woke up one day to discover he'd turned into a cockroach. Strange coincidences, but then life was filled with strange coincidences.

A figure emerged from the shadows ahead, coming out the side street that ran next to Father Xavier's house. The figure stood rooted in the street, looking at Father Xavier a moment, and then was gone, disappearing into the darkness on the other side of the street.

Roberto?

Father Xavier pulled the pistol from his pocket and fumbled with it, dropping the gun in the street. The priest cringed and turned away, expecting the weapon to go off, but it didn't. He quickly retrieved the pistol, holding it in his unsteady hands as he moved cautiously toward his house. He soon abandoned his pretense of caution and dashed up the steps and through the door, slamming it behind himself, falling against it.

Father Xavier's heart was racing. Sweat trickled down the side of his face.

It had not been Roberto, or even one of his minions, Father Xavier told himself. It was probably Enrique or one of the other young men living near the church, returning from an assignation with a girl and not wanting to be subjected to the priest's questions.

Father Xavier put the gun down on the table by the door and shook his head in the darkness.

"Nerves," he muttered.

He had been a little worried about his drinking, but a stiff drink was the best tonic available in Paradisio. It was not as if he could visit a friendly physician, as he might have back in Mexico City, to ask for a prescription of Valium to compensate for his anxiety. Half the priests Father Xavier knew back in Mexico City had some sort of tranquilizer in their medicine cabinets. The ones in the wealthier dioceses had a good bottle of single-malt Scotch in the cupboard, too.

Father Xavier struck a wooden kitchen match.

"Damn!"

He suddenly dropped the match and put his fingers in

his mouth. The match went out before it hit the floor, plunging the room back into blackness.

Father Xavier felt around until he located a second match. He lit it, more careful this time, and bent to light the hurricane lantern on the desk. The wick flared as he shook the match and dropped it into the ashtray. He adjusted the lantern so that it filled the room with a warm golden light.

Behind the priest on the trestle table against the wall opposite the desk was a simple wooden cross, nearly two feet high, made of oil-rubbed teak set into a heavy onyx base. Father Xavier turned from the lamp, seeing the cross, his mouth falling open.

Someone had captured an iguana from the rain forest and nailed it to the cross, carpet tacks driven through each of the lizard's four clawed feet.

"My dear God," Father Xavier gasped.

There was a piece of paper tacked to the wooden cross beneath the iguana, the tattered and water-stained remains of what had once been a sheet of elegant stationery. It was the letter Margarita Alvarez Corona had written him, the wounding note that had blown away into the rain forest during the storm.

Xavier felt a pain in his chest, a constriction, as if his heart were tightening.

How many times had the love letter been read, discussed, snickered over, passed on? No wonder he had been unable to keep the peasants from slouching off to worship Roberto's dark gods. Xavier had no moral credibility with the Indians. His mortal sin had followed him to Paradisio, a stain that would remain on his soul until the day he could get down on his knees and truly repent for breaking his priestly vows by making love to Margarita Alvarez Corona.

The lizard's entire body jerked in a single futile spasm, shaking the cross's heavy stone base.

The iguana had been nailed to the cross alive.

Treinta y Cinco

✧

"**C**ONCEIT AND FOLLY," the vampire began, speaking in a slow, quiet, almost depressed voice. "I have come to understand many things during my life, but perhaps I know these two things best of all. Indeed, I am on the most intimate of terms with these subjects, having made a long and detailed study of them while filling the many idle hours here at La Esmerelda.

"Our greatest conceit," Lazaro said with greater assurance, warming to his topic, "is to think we can know the truth, possessing it the way a rich man might possess a rare and precious object. Our greatest folly is to believe, through fallacious inference, that other versions of the truth are counterfeit, and inferior, and need to be corrected. But the truth, my dear Bailey, the *real* truth . . ."

Lazaro opened his hands and looked at them bleakly.

". . . it is too big for any of us to understand. We look out but darkly through the fog that shrouds our lives, seeing no more than outlines. To think that we know more than we do, and to use it to justify forcing our private visions of truth on others, this is too often the sin of powerful people who make the mistake of thinking themselves wise when they are really only deluded.

"This, Bailey, has been my sin."

Lazaro glanced at the room around him.

"And this—La Esmerelda—is my Hell. A pleasant Hell, you may think, but a Hell nevertheless. It is a Hell of my own making, as Hell invariably is. I can never escape it. Unless, by some miracle, an angel is sent to free me."

Lazaro smiled at his lover for a long moment. Then the focus in his eyes changed. Don Lazaro Ruiz Cortinez looked through her, past her, past his failures, to another place, another time.

"I was born in Medellín, a town in southwestern Spain, where both my father's and mother's families had lived for as long as anybody could remember. Medellín's dubious claim to distinction is that it was where Hernán Cortés was born.

"I was the youngest of five children, all boys. My mother was the daughter of an apothecary. My father's family was peasant stock but had come up in the world. My grandfather had been a notary, and my father had a position as a minor functionary in the provincial government. My parents were both extremely kind and patient people, although I do not think my father was an especially happy man. He was ambitious but lacked the family and education to reach the heights to which he aspired. My mother, on the other hand, was not ambitious except in one respect: She wanted her children to grow up to have better fortune than their parents had enjoyed. Which is, or ought to be, the goal of all parents.

"My own childhood was happy. I was the youngest, the baby, born late in life for my parents, and they doted on me. I was seven years younger than Leon, my closest brother, while my eldest brother was already working at his first job in my father's offices when I was born. I grew up with all the love and attention a child could hope for, and with every modest advantage that it was within my family's power to give me.

"My mother, a talented amateur artist, taught me to draw. Father would collect scraps of paper from the office where he worked, and Mother and I would sit for hours sketching all manner of things or drawing hilarious caricatures of the neighbors. Father taught me to write my name when I was three, and it wasn't long before I was keeping a private diary of my simple childhood experiences. I did not realize at the time the advantage this gave me over the boys my age in Medellín. Few children there went to school; few adults could read or write.

"My family somehow scraped together enough money for me to attend the finest school in Medellín, St. Joseph's College, which was not a college in the American sense but an academy for boys ages seven through eighteen run by the church. I did extremely well at my studies, no doubt because of the early encouragement Mother and Father had given me. While others in my form were learning to scratch out the alphabet, I was already beginning with the Greek and Latin grammars.

"The better students at St. Joseph's went on to the university in Seville. The best students, however, the chosen few, the top two or three from each class, were encouraged to join the priesthood."

Lazaro shifted uncomfortably in his chair.

"It is difficult for me to put myself back into the frame of mind I had in those days, to remember why I thought the things I thought, reaching conclusions that it would be impossible for me to arrive at today. Yet if the logic of it all escapes me, I will never forget the feelings. How perfectly I recall the awe I experienced witnessing the Church's solemn rites, hypnotized by the golden incense censers that swung in time with the gold brocade robes the priests wore as they paraded toward the sanctuary. Growing up in humble circumstances, having attended a school where ornament was entirely foreign, it was only in church that I had an opportunity to experience and be awed by the beauty of exquisite altar paintings. And the music—such heavenly sounds! I loved to hear the mystical intoning of Latin canticles, the cantor's voice echoing back from the vaulted recesses of the gothic cathedral where my family attended Mass."

Lazaro reached out and touched one of the newly cut flowers on the coffee table between them and the fire.

"I remember how it felt to believe, even if I can no longer believe. I have been blessed, or perhaps cursed, with a perfect memory. One particular Sunday stands out among all the others in my youth. When I close my eyes, I can see it down to the smallest detail: the place, the angle of the light coming through the stained-glass windows. I can see myself, my hands clasped before me in prayer, my head bowed, my eyes lowered. I remember the ritual perfectly, each word of the Latin I took, consecrating myself and my life to working for the church."

Bailey sat forward, a stunned expression on her face. "You became a *priest*?"

Lazaro, startled, opened his eyes to discover himself back in La Esmerelda.

"Yes," he said in a voice that was almost a whisper. "But that was many years ago. I have long since lost my faith and renounced my vows. Or perhaps it was my faith that lost me. I do not know which, only that I couldn't go on, not after the things I had seen and done, not after I recognized my sin and the evil it had all caused."

"Lazaro . . ."

"I know I am getting ahead of myself. Forgive me. Let me paint in the middle ground and the picture will become plain enough.

"I took my vows and was sent to Rome to study. You can imagine how cosmopolitan and romantic Rome seemed to a boy from a dusty provincial town like Medellín. The grand cathedrals, the palazzi where the nobles and rich merchants lived, the glorious opera where angels descended from heaven to sing enchanted music—it seemed to be the most wondrous city on earth.

"And the ruins! I spent many hours in melancholic reverie, contemplating the ruins of the Colosseum, the Baths of Caracalla, the lonesome pillars and skeletons of palaces and temples still standing in the Forum. These relics of Imperial Rome, nearly as eternal as the marble from which they were made, were so perfect in proportion and noble in their form that they seemed to have been left behind by a departed race of gods. Yet Julius and Augustus and the rest of them had not been gods, as they claimed, but mere men, men whom time had swept away as it does all men, men capable of sin. After all, such men sent Christ to the cross.

"With time, I came to regard the Roman ruins not as an enduring symbol of the greatness of the human spirit, but as evidence that man was a puny and corrupt creature, whose greatest monuments were only monuments to folly doomed to vanish beneath the tide of time like footprints left in the sand. Only two things were eternal: God and the Church.

"Instead of opening my heart, the exposure to Italian culture and greatness turned something off inside my soul. At a time when my spirit should have grown, it became smaller and meaner. The change in me was subtle, so subtle that it was not until much later that I completely came to understand the transformation I underwent in Rome. But the die was cast for me. I grew restless and dissatisfied. I wanted to take up a sword for the Church, to bring others to see the truth I had found, by whatever means necessary. I wanted to force the world to bow down to the truth I'd found in the Church.

"And so I chose to go to the New World to spread the Gospel, where there were entire nations of godless heathens waiting to be brought to the light. As the great ecclesiastical bureaucracy went to work digesting my request, which was with due process and in due time approved and blessed, I left Rome to return to the city of my birth for one final visit.

"During the journey to Medellín, I passed through a province famous for its waving fields of golden wheat. A plague of locusts had come through the region some time earlier, denuding the earth of every bit of living vegetation. The government, inefficient and ineffectual as always, had failed miserably in its efforts to organize relief. Full-scale famine was getting under way as I passed through the bleak and dusty wasteland, beset on all sides by pathetically hungry beggars, many of them children."

Guilt crept into Lazaro's eyes.

"I am ashamed to admit it now, but I blamed the starving peasants' impiety for the plague. If they had prayed more often, God would have spared them the locusts, I thought. Fanaticism turned my heart to stone.

"I returned to Medellín, all the more impatient to leave for the New World. Happily, I treated my elderly parents and the rest of my family with suitable warmth and decency. Beneath my priestly robes I was still a smug and pitiless knave, but familiar surroundings led me to behave in a familiar manner. Through my family's connections I arranged to have myself attached to my fellow Medellín native, Hernán Cortés, who had just been appointed *alcalde* of Santiago de Cuba."

"Cortés?" Bailey interrupted.

Lazaro nodded.

"Hernán Cortés?"

"That is correct."

"What are you talking about, Lazaro?" Bailey demanded. "That's completely impossible."

"When you hear the rest of my story you will realize that it is not impossible."

Bailey shook her head, not believing but not knowing what to say.

"You said you wanted to know everything, and you

shall. I was the same age as Cortés when I set sail to join him in the New World. We were both twenty-six years old. The year was 1511."

Treinta y Seis

✧

"I DON'T KNOW if you're talking about reincarnation or channeling or what, Lazaro. I'm a physician and a scientist. This kind of irrational talk is more than I can—"

The vampire gave Bailey a fierce stare, stopping her words. The irritation and disbelief in her face began to diminish, exorcised by the power in Lazaro's dark eyes.

"A little patience and your insistence on empirical reality will be satisfied. My story is indeed extraordinary, but its logic is inexorable and perfectly consonant with the phenomenon you have observed in your lab."

Lazaro gave Bailey an enigmatic smile, his tone softening. "There is no place on earth like this rain forest. At once wonderful and terrifying, it is a place where myth and reality converge. When you look at me, you see the living substance that lies at the heart of the myth of the—"

Lazaro held up his arm, as if signaling himself to stop.

"But again I get ahead of myself. I must tell the story correctly for you to understand."

Bailey nodded for him to continue.

"Hernán Cortés: He was as ambitious a man as I, but in his own way. While I was distinguishing myself in the

libraries and salons of Rome, Cortés was helping
Velázquez conquer Cuba. Both of us were hungry for
conquest. Of course, Cortés and I were interested in
entirely different kinds of victories. His passion was to
accumulate as much gold as possible, while I was interested only in conquering souls. We used the same
methods. We marched with the same army. We employed the same ruthless means to smash all who
opposed us."

Lazaro held up his hands, palms up, moving them up
and down as if judging the relative weights of two similar
objects.

"Were you to ask who was the greater criminal, I
would have to claim the prize for myself. Cortés, Pizarro,
Velázquez, and the rest of the conquistador scum were
interested only in gold. Gold has always ended up in possession of the people with the most power, to a greater or
lesser degree. Render unto Caesar that which is Caesar's,
it says in the Bible. If you rob a man of his wealth, he is
still the same man, albeit poorer. The conquistadors were
nothing more than glorified thieves.

"I, however, set out to do something much more
nefarious. I wanted to conquer souls, not armies. The
unacknowledged part of my mission was to destroy
native civilizations, to throw down pagan cultures and
replace them with the One True Faith."

Lazaro ran one hand over his face as if trying vainly to
wipe away the stain of his sin.

"Cortés was already gone from Santiago by the time
my ship deposited me there. He had gone on into
Mexico, searching out new opportunities for pillage. He
was a genius at his work, as much a fanatic as I. When he

landed at Veracruz and realized he was hopelessly out-numbered by his enemy, he secretly ordered his captains to burn their own ships. His men's only chance of survival then was to follow him, dedicating themselves to whatever extremes of savagery were required to keep from being wiped out.

"Cortés was lucky his soldiers didn't murder him by the light of their burning ships. Indeed, they might have, had I not arrived in time to intercede; they would have killed an officer of the crown but never a priest. Reassured of the righteousness of our crusade, we set out from Veracruz, in pursuit of our unholy grail, the sacking of Mexico.

"We were attacked immediately. Our small force was outnumbered three hundred to one and should have been annihilated in minutes. I got down on my knees and prayed for a miracle, and a miracle occurred, although it must have been Satan, not God, who answered my plea. The Indians had never seen horses. They thought we were gods riding on the backs of demons, our crude firearms shooting thunderbolts. They had no idea how to do battle against such demigods. The Aztecs attacked individually, thinking of battle as a means to capture prisoners and to achieve glory through individual acts of bravery. Cortés's disciplined men stayed in formation and fought with one end in mind: to kill the enemy, which they did with ruthless efficiency.

"We did not have to attack when we reached Tenochti-tlán, as Mexico City was then known. I employed diplomacy to ingratiate us with the Aztecs. We pretended to be Montezuma's ally against his warring enemies, then murdered him and six hundred of his nobles. A river of blood—literally an ankle-deep river of blood—flowed through the street in front of Montezuma's palace. I did not participate in the violence, but I conceived and sanctioned it. The Aztecs' religious practices, which included ritual human sacrifice, sickened me. Any means was justified in ending such blasphemy.

"I left Cortés behind in Tenochtitlán to count his booty and sort out political problems with Velázquez, who was jealous of his subordinate's success and greedy for his share of gold and glory. Anxious to continue my good work, I accompanied one of Cortés's captains, Francesco, to Veracruz. There we boarded ships and sailed for a land farther to the south, a forbidden country the Aztecs called the Nation of the Gods, where there was rumored to be a city named Zonatitucan built entirely of gold.

"We disembarked in the malarial swamps on the Atlantic side of what is now Costa Rica. The privations we suffered would fill a volume, if I had the heart to set them down to paper. We wandered up and down the isthmus, crossing mountains, traversing mangrove swamps, hacking our way through rain forests, fighting. Finally, after two long years of this walking nightmare, we arrived at a high pass between two volcanoes and looked down upon Zonatitucan.

"By that time our bodies were wasted and at the brink of exhaustion, and our force was cut in half by sickness, death, and battle with hostiles. We could barely walk, much less fight. It was only through the grace of the Great Zona, the priest-king ruler of Zonatitucan, that we were allowed to enter the city. I learned later that their ruler had been cleverly manipulating our movements, letting us into his world a bit at a time, studying—and weakening—us. Only when he was certain we had no chance of escape or reinforcement did he bring our wandering in the wilderness to an end.

"Zonatitucan was a tremendous disappointment for Francesco. Though there were many golden objects and jeweled ornaments on display throughout the beautiful city, these items had been acquired through trade and battle, not the native richness of the land. The temples and pyramids, though the most elaborate and impressive we had seen during all our travels, were built of simple stone, not gold. Zonatitucan's material wealth was pale next to Mexico City's.

"My reaction to Zonatitucan was entirely different from Francesco's. The pagan Indians were adepts in a monstrous religion, the destruction of which would be a tremendous victory for the Church. The Zona nation was exactly the sort of treasure I sought. Like the Aztecs, the Zonas' holiest sacrament involved tearing the beating hearts from prisoners of war atop an unholy pagan pyramid to celebrate certain phases of the moon. The Zona were cannibals—they *ate* their victims' hearts. There was no place my work was needed more.

"We spent several weeks as the Great Zona's guests while our men recovered their strength. In the meantime, Francesco and I studied the situation, looking for weaknesses, plotting to overthrow the Great Zona. Though we were treated as honored friends, we were virtual prisoners in the city. At night, we were closed into our rooms, never permitted to go outdoors or even open the shutters of our windows after sunset. I took this prohibition as a sign of the Indians' natural shame at their religious practices. The screams we heard while closed in our rooms were more horrible than you can imagine.

"We'd been in Zonatitucan nearly a month when the Indians' paganism became too much for me to bear. Perhaps it was because the voices that particular night all seemed to belong to women. It was impossible for me to stand by and allow such blasphemy to continue. I broke open my door and rushed outside. I don't have any idea how I planned to stop them. All I knew was that I was going to go mad if I had to continue listening to the screams of people having their hearts torn out and offered up to the moon in sacrifice.

"I didn't get far before the guards threw me back into my room. However, my brief freedom lasted long enough for me to see the plaza filled with warriors in their weird feathered ceremonial robes. The Great Zona was on top of the Pyramid of the Moon, holding above his head the heart torn from the woman held down on the altar. The darkness in the sky around the moon began to move. The blackness coalesced into a nebulous form, a cloud that descended slowly toward the heart. It was Lucifer himself, I thought, summoned forth from the earth to bless the profane sacrament. But it was not Satan. It was a horde of vampire bats from the rain forest surrounding Zonatitucan.

"I demanded that Francesco order his men to attack at the first opportunity. He was in total agreement, nervous that the Zona had taken such a keen interest in our firearms. Francesco's strategy was to attack boldly when they expected it least, overwhelming them when they didn't have their weapons at their sides. The assault was to take place a week later, when the moon was full and the citizens were engaged in one of their elaborate pageants of death.

"I did not participate in the attack. It was not because I was a coward or was opposed to violence. Indeed, I would have relished the opportunity to smash the pagan ceremony. Rather, I reasoned that it would be unseemly for me to participate in the attack, and then minister to the Indians' spiritual needs once they had been conquered."

Lazaro gave Bailey a bleak look. "My arrogance was colossal," he said with great disgust.

"Francesco gave the signal and his men broke through the doors of their chambers and charged into the plaza. Not a single shot was fired. There were no shouts, no calls to alarm, no sounds of battle. Nothing. The beating of the Indian drums continued, along with the weird music made with their reed flutes.

"I stayed in my room, kneeling in prayer, listening as the screams from the Pyramid of the Moon continued until an hour before the dawn. I recognized some of the screams, including one that sounded very much like Francesco. I was unable to fathom how the attack could have failed. The Zona had overwhelmed Francesco's forces so completely that there had been virtually no struggle. The soldiers had gone out into the Zonatitucan night, and the night had swallowed them completely.

"I remained in prayer until the next evening, believing that my fate awaited me atop the Pyramid of the Moon, that my heart would be among the next offered to Lucifer. A little before sundown, I was summoned to the imperial palace. The Great Zona was sitting alone in an enclosed courtyard. He invited me to join him as he took his supper.

"Communication between us was halting but not impossible. We had pressed a series of Indians into our service during our two years of searching for the city, and in that time I had picked up the rudiments of the dialect.

"My host refused to discuss Francesco or answer my questions about what had happened to my fellow Spaniards. In a fit of anguish and despair, I finally asked him whether he intended to tear out my heart that night.

"He smiled and shook his head. I was a man of great learning, he said, an asset to the world. He knew that I had come to Zonatitucan to teach his people about my God. Since I was obviously intelligent and capable of being educated, he intended to do me a similar favor. He would teach me the ways of his gods, instructing me personally, so that I might participate in their high holy rituals.

"He honestly thought he was doing me an honor. But this, for a Jesuit zealot, was the worst violation imaginable.

"I stood up and said I would happily die a thousand martyrs' deaths before I would once bow down to a pagan altar. The Great Zona looked up at me with a serene smile and said nothing. I stormed out of the palace, expecting to be struck down at any moment by his glowering praetorian guard. My host sent no one after me. He had complete confidence in his abilities. Who can say for certain? Had fate not intervened, he might have succeeded in converting me, the conquering priest, to his dark religion.

"The next day one of the princes was sick. Sickness was an extremely rare event in the city. The following day there were nearly fifty other Indians suffering the same illness. The glands on their necks became swollen, and tiny red dots covered their bodies.

"Their ruler summoned me to his palace and asked what I knew about the sickness. Was it the work of my sorcery? I explained that it was called the measles and said that it was nothing to be overly concerned about, that the people would recover shortly. The Great Zona nodded grimly and sent me away. I didn't know it at the time, but the prince and four others had already died. The Indians had never known measles, a disease we'd brought with us from Europe."

Lazaro let out a heavy sigh.

"I had come into Zonatitucan thinking of myself as a man of God, but in truth I was the angel of death. The Indians were unable to recover from what was, at least for a European, a relatively mild disease. The suffering and the death continued for weeks, the epidemic burning through the city like an invisible fire. Soon I was the only able-bodied man in Zonatitucan. I piled the corpses high in the gaming court behind the Jaguar Temple and burned them. It was terrible work. There were so many bodies I could hardly keep up. The pyre burned night and day, the plume of black smoke rising up from it trapped by the surrounding mountains, a smoggy haze that hung oppressively low over the city like a funeral pall, diminishing the sun into a distant and weak star.

"The stench of death hung over the city, along with the smell of burning corpses. It was nothing compared with the stink of my guilt. While only a few days earlier I would have gladly seen the Great Zona and his priests killed for their pagan practices, I never would have countenanced putting every last citizen of the city to the sword. Yet this is what I had achieved, though unwittingly, by helping to infect the Indian population with a sickness their bodies could not defend them against.

"The Great Zona had tremendous strength. He was the last to die. I nursed him, knowing it was hopeless. In his final hours he told me about the kiss of the gods that was delivered to the Zona by angelic messengers—the vampire bats living in the rain forest surrounding the city.

"I thought he was delirious when he told me the bats had made him immortal—that he was three hundred years old. He did not know that the bats carried a virus, and even if he had, I wouldn't have understood. This was long before anybody understood that something too small to see with the eye could get into our bodies and make us sick—or change us.

"The last thing he did was adopt me as his son and heir, an act of forgiveness that left me completely stunned in light of the devastation I had brought to his people. He was very religious, in his own way, and considered his dynasty's fall a judgment of the gods. Perhaps I was right, he whispered. Perhaps it was wrong to kill the people they sacrificed. His final request was that I watch over Zonatitucan when he was gone, that I keep the light of their culture from being extinguished completely.

"I cried when he died.

"That night, after I'd committed his body to the funeral pyre, I fell into an exhausted sleep. I'd left the windows in my apartments open. It was not that I was seeking the so-called kiss of the gods. I didn't believe any of what the Great Zona had told me was possible. The simple truth is that I no longer cared whether I lived or died. I had helped perpetrate a very great evil. My pride had lured me into a state of mortal sin from which I could never regain God's grace. I half hoped some viper would crawl into the room and end my mortal suffering. Instead, it was the bats that got to me.

"I awoke in the morning burning up with fever, several bite marks on my left hand. I seemed to recover, only to be bitten again and succumb to the fever a second time. After the cycle was repeated a third time, the transformation was complete. What the Great Zona had said was true: Three kisses from the gods and you are immortal."

Lazaro started to reach out toward Bailey but stopped himself.

"Do not look at me with fear. I would never hurt you. I would never hurt anybody. My needs are modest and accomplished without inflicting permanent harm. You have heard stories, many of them exceedingly foolish, about the *vampiro*."

Lazaro looked directly into Bailey's eyes.

"I owe you a very great debt of thanks. Your modern understanding has made it possible for me to think of myself as a scientific curiosity, rather than as a monster."

Lazaro raised his hands a little then folded them in his lap.

"Now you know the story of how Lazaro Ruiz Cortinez became a vampire. The remainder of my life has been one of duty, a little sad in the smallness of its effect. I built La Esmerelda and gathered the remaining

Zona around me, dedicating myself to caring for them, to keeping the flickering candle of their culture alive.

"I have prevented others from becoming *vampiros* for all the obvious reasons. I have learned to keep the Hunger from controlling me. I harm no one, taking only a little blood, just what I need to survive. There are many willing to accommodate me. I force myself on no one.

"I have taken care of Zonatitucan, as I promised the Great Zona, keeping the rain forest from swallowing the city. The Indians visit it regularly. My only prohibition is that they do not sleep in the valley, for the bats only feed at night. The saddest thing is something I have only recently come to recognize. I haven't preserved a culture so much as engendered a backward atmosphere of secrecy and superstition."

Lazaro stared at his hands, as if unable to believe the work that they had done.

"For five hundred years I have dedicated myself to keeping something from being lost. But I have saved nothing. The Zona were doomed the day Spanish ships appeared on the horizon. My life has been a waste, a feast for locusts."

"Did you kill Janis Levy?"

The unexpected question caught Lazaro by surprise. "Janis refused to stay away from Zonatitucan," he said slowly. "It was too much of a temptation for her as an archaeologist. She became infected. I had a long talk with her and tried to convince her to leave, warning her of the dangers. It takes three successive infections for the change to take hold, so she would have been perfectly fine if she'd agreed to leave. But she refused to go. She was very much like you in that respect. Extremely tenacious. She intended to stay, even if it meant undergoing the same transformation that I endured. I did everything I could to talk her out of it, but in the end I weakened and acquiesced."

"You turned her into a vampire?"

"I allowed it to happen. I was lonely, Bailey. But something went wrong. Not with the change, but with Janis. She became—different. She was ultimately unable to control her desires, although I didn't see this until it was too late. She attacked one of my men and nearly killed him. I was afraid I was going to have to take extreme measures to keep her from hurting anyone else. Before I could act, she ran off, driven mad by the Hunger. She became lost in the rain forest, and . . ."

Lazaro's voice trailed off.

"What happened?"

It was obvious to Lazaro that Bailey would be satisfied with nothing less than the complete truth.

"We are extremely hardy beings, but deprived of the one thing we must have to live—blood to feed the Hunger every fortnight—the *vampiro* dies."

"Did she suffer?"

"It would not have been pleasant."

Bailey turned away from Lazaro.

"Bailey?"

She did not answer.

"Please tell me that you understand. Please tell me that you don't hate me for what I've done, for what I've become."

Bailey's shoulders began to shake. She was crying.

"I love you more than life itself, Bailey. Surely you

can see that there is some small measure of good in me. Stay with me. Save me from this eternal curse. Make me mortal again. Help me reclaim a little of the life I have lost to the locusts."

Bailey did not answer.

PART III

The Rain Forest

Treinta y Siete

✧

"BAILEY?"

She was sitting alone in the library in her nightgown, her bare feet pulled beneath her in the chair, a glass of sherry carefully cradled in both hands. The room was draped in shadows, a single light burning on the table beside her chair.

"I hope I am not disturbing you."

"Not at all. I was just sitting here, thinking."

Beethoven sat down across from her and crossed his legs. He looked at her frown with his head tilted to one side.

"Is something the matter? I trust that you have not run into difficulties with your research."

"You might say that I have."

The furrows deepened in the vampire's brow. "I hope you're not considering abandoning your work."

"I don't mean to be rude, but what difference does it make to you?"

"It is only that, as a fellow scientist, I understand the importance of what you're trying to learn."

"I wonder if you understand far better than you let on."

"I do not understand your meaning. Perhaps my English is not all it might be."

"We both know your English is excellent."

The German bowed his head in response to Bailey's compliment.

"Who are you, Ludwig?"

"Is that an existential question?"

"This is not the time for displays of wit."

The vampire bowed his head a second time. "My humble apologies, *Doktor*."

Bailey looked at her opposite with a frankly appraising stare. "I don't think you're who you pretend to be any more than Lazaro is. I've just been sitting here, thinking about you both. I've come to the conclusion that you know exactly what is going on behind the scenes here at La Esmerelda. I think that is why you are so interested in my research."

Bailey bent forward at the waist, her tone prosecutorial. "You know that my research could unlock the secrets of something very important and strange, something bordering on the fantastic."

"I would not deny it for a minute."

"I think you came to La Esmerelda in the hopes of finding out whatever I happened to learn about the virus that has infected Lazaro. I don't know about Lazaro, but don't think you've tricked me into falling for your phony interest in morpho butterflies."

A hurt look came into the vampire's eyes. "I assure you that my interest in butterflies is entirely genuine."

"Who do you work for, the CIA? Or is it one of the big multinational pharmaceutical companies? They're always scouring the world's rain forests for new cancer-fighting drugs and genetic engineering compounds. You must think Lazaro's adaptations can be put in a pill and sold to the highest bidders."

Bailey's voice broke. For a moment she thought it was going to overwhelm her, that she would not be able to continue. She took a sip of sherry to help disguise her emotional turmoil. The drink seemed to help, allowing her to force back the almost unbearable anxiety.

"You don't have any idea what you're dealing with," she said. "This isn't the fountain of youth you may think it is. It's a curse."

"You are an extremely perceptive young woman."

"Perceptive enough to know you're not who you say you are," Bailey said, her voice rising with her anger.

Ludwig went to the piano. Still standing, he bent over the keys and began to play the *Moonlight* Sonata. Beyond him, past the open French doors, the full moon was rising past the treetops' ragged up-stretched fingertips, an enormous pumpkin in the night sky. Lazaro and the rest of them were out there in the rain forest, Bailey thought, going through the empty motions of a tradition that had died in substance centuries earlier.

"It is a little surprising you don't know me, especially now that you know the truth about Lazaro. Isn't there something familiar about my face?"

Bailey returned her attention to the German. She had long had the nagging feeling she knew him, but even now she couldn't come up with a name.

"I also would have thought my taste in music would have clued you in."

What did the *Moonlight* Sonata have to do with— The crystal sherry glass fell from her hand, shattering on the floor.

Beethoven stood to his full height, turning so she could study his face in profile. "The fact that my face has been reproduced in countless thousands of cheap busts to sit in music rooms throughout the world has caused me no end of difficulties. Fame is not without its price."

Bailey, stunned to silence, started to get up.

"Stop!" Beethoven warned, but too late. Bailey had already cut herself on a piece of broken crystal. She cried out and fell back into the chair, lifting her wounded foot into her lap. Beethoven was instantly at her side, holding her bleeding foot in his hands, a strange, hungry expression in his eyes.

"Get away from me!" she cried, drawing herself into a ball, smearing blood from her wounded foot across the chair cushion.

"I will not hurt you."

Bailey was filled with irrational terror. She knew only too well what he was—what he wanted, and needed, and craved. She held out one hand, trying to push him away. "Don't touch me," she said in a pleading voice.

"You wound me deeply," the vampire said. He reached for her injured foot, taking it firmly before she could react, pulling it toward him. Bailey trembled and watched as he wrapped it with the handkerchief from the breast pocket of his coat. She did not resist him further, partly because she knew she could not get away from him, partly because her survival instincts warned her against angering the vampire Ludwig van Beethoven.

"If you have learned nothing else from Lazaro, you

most surely know by now that self-control is at the very heart of the vampire ethic," Beethoven said, knotting the handkerchief so that it would stay wrapped around her injured foot. "Your continued well-being is proof of that. I cannot begin to express what an exquisite temptation someone so lovely is to a sensitive creature such as me."

She started to think of the hungry kisses Lazaro had showered up and down her neck while they had been making love—she had to force the memory from her mind to keep from breaking down completely.

"Please calm yourself," Beethoven said. "Remember you are a scientist. You are able to look at even the most frightening things with objective, analytical detachment."

Something in the vampire's words helped Bailey get her breathing back under control. The panic began to subside. He was right—*Beethoven* was right.

"It's a lot to assimilate," Bailey stammered.

"I'm certain that it is," Beethoven said, and began to carefully pick up the pieces of broken glass from the floor.

"You're one of them, aren't you?"

"*Ja*," he said, looking up from his chore and smiling. "What else could explain my being here today? Otherwise, I would be nothing more than dust in a tomb, which is in fact exactly what people think."

"This is almost too fantastic to believe."

Beethoven's only reply was a smile.

"Were you infected here?"

"In Costa Rica? *Nein*. My progenitor was an Old World vampire who traced her roots back to the Carpathian Mountains in eastern Europe. You must forgive the cliché, Dr. Harrison. As far as we can tell, our branch of the race rose up out of the part of the world known as Transylvania. I regret the melodrama. The reality is quite different from the picture painted by Hollywood."

"*We*, Beethoven?"

"Please do not ask about 'we,' Dr. Harrison. There are some things I am not at liberty to discuss with you at the present. Perhaps in the future. And please call me Ludwig, or Herr Samsa, if I may ask the favor. If you use my other name, my real name, it will only lead to . . ." The vampire paused a beat. ". . . confusion."

"There are no vampire bats in Transylvania," Bailey said. "They're a tropical species."

"That is true. Nor is there any evidence there ever were such creatures in Europe."

"Then how was the virus transmitted? Was another animal involved?"

Beethoven deposited the broken glass on a table and turned with a shrug. "Some believe it may have been an extinct species of wolf, but the real answer is that nobody knows. There are many things about our race that remain a mystery. That is why we are interested in your work."

"But the virus made you immortal?"

"That is our understanding. We are immortal, at least in a relative sense. We can, and do, die but usually only of the accumulated ennui of lonely existence. Our immune systems are remarkably powerful. We are able to resist most diseases."

"But apparently not measles."

Beethoven shook his head. "There is more than a little irony in the sad fate that befell the *Vampiri* Indians who built Zonatitucan. I wish that I could explain it. Indeed, I was rather hoping that you could."

"Measles are not a problem for you?"

"Not for a European vampire. Neither are smallpox, anthrax, typhus—any of the usual horrors."

"There was apparently something missing in their basic immunological makeup that left them vulnerable," Bailey said. "Survivability is usually a matter of small exposures to a population that results, over time, in acquired resistance."

Beethoven nodded.

"I would think accidental trauma would have an impact on your kind's mortality rate."

"Not to the degree you might expect. If you cut my head off, I would die. If you blew me into a million pieces or burned my body in an incinerator, I would die. But if I were merely shot, stabbed, or poisoned, it wouldn't slow me down for long. It seems to mainly be a function of metabolism. The *Vampiri* body is able to speed itself up, healing itself much more quickly than a mortal suffering the same injury."

"I'd like to see that."

She was only thinking out loud, but the vampire complied so quickly that she didn't have time to protest when she realized what he was doing.

Picking up a triangle of the broken glass from the table, Beethoven slashed an ugly gash in the palm of his hand. The vampire licked the blood away and held out his hand for her to examine. The cut was already closed, the damaged tissue drawing itself together. In the next instant it was nothing more than a red line angling across

Beethoven's hand. A moment later, all signs of injury had disappeared.

"That's incredible!"

"*Efficient* is the word I would use. The vampire has an extremely efficient physiology."

"Yet you need to drink blood."

"Yes, it is our one special need, an aspect of some congenital weakness in the structure of our blood cells. Of course, we require food and water, too, just like an ordinary mortal."

"Will any blood do?"

"I'm afraid it must be human blood. Fresh human blood. We cannot hold off the Hunger by drinking the blood of rats and dogs, as one particularly disgusting fictional account of our race claimed."

"I hope you don't mind answering such personal questions."

"Of course not," Beethoven said with a small laugh. "You are dying to know everything you can about us."

"How do you . . . eat?"

Beethoven opened his mouth wide so she could see the two glistening fangs come down from his upper jaw and lock into place. He closed his mouth gingerly. When he smiled again, the supernumerary teeth had vanished.

"What happens now depends entirely upon you, Bailey. I hope you will decide to remain at La Esmerelda and continue your research. I have more than enough resources to ensure that you will have the very finest equipment and facilities at your disposal."

"Lazaro made a similar offer," she said flatly.

"I understand there are matters of a personal nature

clouding the issue. I would simply ask that you put your duty as a scientist first in making your considerations."

Bailey sighed and looked past Beethoven at the moon. She would never again be able to look at the moon without thinking of Lazaro.

"The research possibilities are exciting," Bailey said without excitement.

"*Ja,*" the vampire said encouragingly.

"But as you said, things have become complicated."

"If I can be of assistance sorting out these complications, I am entirely at your service."

"You are part of the complications," Bailey said pointedly.

"Your work is more important than anything you or I or Lazaro might feel."

"The part of me that is a scientist knows that." Bailey looked out the window at the moon again, blinking rapidly. "But the part of me that is a woman, a part of me that has never demanded my attention, is not sure it agrees." There were tears in Bailey's eyes when she looked back at Beethoven. "I honestly don't know if I can stay here."

Treinta y Ocho

✧

A CROWD OF people moved through the trees along the ruin's western edge, the vanguard of a snake whose tail was still coming down the mountainside from the pass to La Esmerelda. The leader of the group was far out in front, alone. Don Lazaro Ruiz Cortinez was dressed shirt to boot in black. Some distance back, unable to keep up with his master's pace, was his servant Alvaro.

At the opposite end of the plaza, Roberto and his captive were already three-quarters of the way up the precipitous staircase leading to the altar atop the Pyramid of the Moon. Roberto held a machete in his right hand, in his other hand the two chains linking him to his prisoner.

Yanira Rojas, the young prostitute from Vincent's cantina, kept as close as she could to Roberto to prevent the chains from tugging painfully against the silver rings dangling from her pierced flesh. Noticing the movement below, Yanira looked down at the plaza. The dead resignation in her eyes gave way to a flicker of desperate hope when she saw don Lazaro—and don Lazaro saw her.

"Come on!" Roberto ordered, giving the chains a small tug.

Yanira whimpered, falling forward as she scrambled to do as ordered, skinning one knee against the stone steps. She bumped into Roberto and clung to him, throwing a pleading look backward at Lazaro, silently begging him for help.

Roberto paused long enough to watch Lazaro leap onto the bottom stair. He grinned at his rival, then jerked on the chains again for no reason other than to be cruel. Yanira whimpered again, lacking the strength to cry out after her long ordeal.

"*¡Rápido!*" Roberto demanded.

They continued their climb, hurrying now to reach the top before Lazaro caught them.

Lazaro watched Roberto pull the girl up onto the altar area of the pyramid's squared-off summit, the pair of them disappearing so that the only face looking down on him was the leering moon. He stopped and brought his hands to his head, as if his hands could shield him from the anguish welling up in his heart and threatening to drown his soul.

What had he ever done to give Roberto cause to hate him?

"Roberto!" Lazaro cried out, his voice filled with anguish and anger—anger at Roberto, anger at himself and the thing he had become, anger at God.

A low, growling rumble rolled through the city, a thunder that went into the earth and grew there, feeding on its primordial powers. Lazaro's torment made the city quake as if it were built of a child's wooden blocks instead of stone slabs weighing tons. He could bring the whole damn city crashing down, if he wanted. Beethoven had been right: his powers were far greater than he had imagined.

The terrified wailing brought Lazaro's mind back into focus. Below him in the plaza, stretched out all the way back to the edge of the rain forest, the people lay prostrate, expressing a lamentation that sounded as if Armageddon Day had arrived.

"How can you fear me?" Lazaro cried out.

No one answered. No one dared answer. Centuries of good works counted for nothing against the most singular aspect of his being—that he was, first and last, the *vampiro*.

Lazaro spun furiously on his heel. In the next instant, he was standing opposite Roberto, the altar—and the girl—between them. Mercifully, she had fainted.

"How could you fall so far from the light of your younger days, my son?" the vampire said, rage and sorrow within his ancient heart making his voice shake. "You were my last best hope to bring the Zona into the present. I had hoped you would grow up to free me from the burden of being their leader, that the people would learn to love and follow you. I can't turn La Esmerelda over to you now. My plans have all failed more completely than I could have imagined possible. The locusts have devoured the dubious fruits of my unworthy labor—and you along with them, my son."

"What have warriors to do with insects?" Roberto demanded, drawing himself up proudly.

"Roberto—"

"You have always been out of step with the rhythms of magic in the rain forest," Roberto said, interrupting his patron. "You never learned to read the writing carved into the walls of Zonatitucan. You substituted your view of the world for ours, flattering yourself that you'd preserved our culture because you continued to observe a few hollow rituals."

"Nothing remains the same forever, Roberto. Everything changes and, when its time is due, passes away."

"The Zona are eternal."

"No, my son," the vampire said with a bittersweet smile, "nothing of this earth is eternal, not even the *vampiro*. To pretend otherwise is to deny life itself, for life is change. Instead of honoring the old ways by maintaining them, we made them stagnate and become dead and poisonous. I have made many mistakes in my long life, but this has been the greatest mistake of all."

Roberto spat to demonstrate his contempt. "Watch carefully and I will teach you the power of the old ways, *Father* Lazaro."

"Give me the machete."

Roberto's laugh was a short, mocking bark. "I do not need a machete to tear out her heart. The machete is only for chopping off her head for the skull rack afterward. I will honor this temple with many new trophies."

"I doubt you really know what you're saying, Roberto. Something happened when you went away to Harvard, something inside your head. Let me help you."

"You have already 'helped' my people enough."

"Our people."

"*My* people!" Roberto screamed. He banged the machete against the side of the stone altar. "They are *my* people, not yours. The Zona will *never* be yours, not in their hearts and souls. We have never forgotten you are a *conquistador*."

The word stung Lazaro with an almost physical force.

"The people only follow you because they fear you, Lazaro. They know that you are not one of us. You are a pretender who has stolen fire from the gods and now masquerades as one of their immortal company."

"That is completely unfair," Lazaro said in a voice devoid of conviction.

"Let the people choose who they want to follow."

Roberto went to the edge of the stairs and held up his hands, swinging the machete above his head in a slow arc. A howl of approval went up from the crowd. Roberto touched something within the people, a violent chord that resonated even five centuries after disease had silenced the bloody music in Zonatitucan.

Lazaro went to stand beside Roberto. He was greeted with cold silence. He could see fear scattered throughout the upturned faces in the plaza below and halfway up the pyramid. Their hearts were with Roberto, but they respected and feared the *vampiro*.

"When I have become the Great Zona, I will bring back the old ways," Roberto said, turning to Lazaro. "My people will grow strong again with the power of my sacrifices. I will not offer up beef hearts, your pale approximation of our sacrament, but human hearts—steaming in the night air, still beating in my hands—as the true ritual demands."

"Roberto . . ."

"If you try to stop me, the people will tear you apart. And even if they don't, they will do something you'll find even more unbearable: they'll desert you."

"You have not grown up to walk in the footsteps of the last Great Zona, no matter what you imagine."

"Empty words, priest."

"The person you remind me of most, Roberto, is myself as a young man. I, too, was a fanatic wearing blinders that prevented me from seeing anything but the object of my own private crusade. Growing up in my household has turned you not into the Great Zona, as you imagine, but into the son I wished you were. Sadly, you have also grown up to share my weakness."

Lazaro stepped closer to Roberto, wanting to put a hand on his shoulder but knowing it would only enrage the young man.

"I let my fanaticism turn me into a monster, Roberto. Don't make the same mistake. You do not want to end up like me."

"I am not at all like you," Roberto said with brutal coldness.

"What is the matter with you?" Lazaro said, looking more closely into Roberto's eyes.

"There is nothing the matter with me."

"You are burning up with fever."

Roberto brought his hand to his forehead, and then dropped it self-consciously, refusing to acknowledge the truth.

"It is the sickness of the gods." Roberto shut his eyes. "I feel the power building in me. I am at the brink of the great change."

"No, Roberto, you are sadly mistaken." Lazaro looked again at the girl, still lying insensate on the stone altar. "She has it, too—the Nicaraguan woman you have brought here."

"Do not think you can trick me."

"What have you done to yourself, Roberto?"

"Your talk is meaningless nonsense."

"I see it plainly in you, and in the girl," the vampire said. "The transformation is not going to work, Roberto. You are too ill."

"You *are* a liar."

"I would never lie to you," Lazaro said, hearing the grief in his own voice. "You are going to die, Roberto. The girl will die, too."

"You cannot stop me," Roberto said, chin down, murderous hatred in his eyes.

"Yes, I can. But there's no need for that. You have stopped yourself. You can't achieve the thing you want now. The transformation is beyond your reach."

Roberto turned away.

"It's happening again," Lazaro said, giving in to his despair. "History is repeating itself. Thank God for Bailey Harrison and others like her. They are the true saviors in the sickness-plagued realm of mortals."

The sorcerer drew back his arms, ready to pluck out Yanira's heart.

"I won't let you hurt her," Lazaro warned, his voice sharp with menace.

"It doesn't matter," Roberto said bitterly, dropping his arms. "The guardian told me I don't really need the girl."

"The guardian?"

Roberto didn't answer. The switchblade knife he'd used to cut Anonimo's throat materialized in his hand. He drew two quick slashes along his wrists, opening a flow of fresh blood. The knife clattered to the stone floor beside the altar as Roberto scrambled onto the stone block, straddling Yanira, his hands outstretched to the moon, wrists held wide apart. Roberto began to chant a prayer in the Zona dialect, calling the gods' sacred messengers to fly from their roosts in the rain forest and drink of the sacrificial blood.

The bats' keen sense of smell picked up the scent of blood immediately in the still night air. A single bat appeared almost instantly, landing on Roberto's left arm and beginning to lap his blood. A moment later a second bat was on his right arm, eager to be fed.

"This is pointless," Lazaro said. "You'll only weaken yourself."

Roberto seemed not to hear. A third bat landed on Roberto's arm, then a fourth. The sky above Roberto's head was suddenly alive with a swarm of black scalloped wings beating the air. The cloud descended, swallowing Roberto's arms. Beneath the sharp sound of tiny leather wings, Roberto softly moaned, delirious in his imagined apotheosis.

One of the bats landed on Yanira's naked belly and began to lick her skin, curling back its tiny pink lips to reveal its delicate porcelain-white teeth.

"Enough!" Lazaro cried.

A wave moved through the night, like heat rippling the air above hot concrete, a vibration extending upward and outward from Lazaro. The bats separated from Roberto and the supine woman, fluttering drunkenly, stunned and disoriented by the shock wave. They retreated quickly as they recovered, disappearing back into the night, into the darkened rain forest.

Roberto stood over Yanira, his arms a bloody mass of bites, swaying as if drunk. Lazaro caught him as he fell backward off the altar. He lowered Roberto gently to the stone floor, cradling Roberto's head against his shoulder the way he had when Roberto had been a baby, come to stay at La Esmerelda after his parents had died.

Perhaps it would have been better for Roberto if Lazaro hadn't pulled the infant from his parents' blazing house and breathed life back into him. It might have been better for Lazaro, too. Lazaro felt no less mortally wounded than Roberto, though Lazaro's sickness was confined to his heart.

"My poor boy," the vampire said, brushing the hair away from Roberto's feverish brow. "My poor, doomed boy."

Treinta y Nueve

✧

BAILEY DROVE FAST through Paradisio, gritting her teeth and hanging tight onto the steering wheel when she bounced over deep ruts in the dirt street, scattering splashes from the puddles that never completely dried. She got to the church and cranked the steering wheel right, stomping on the brake pedal. The Land Cruiser's oversize tires skidded, the truck careening to a stop with its bumper against the peeling picket fence surrounding Father Xavier's house.

Bailey rapped her knuckles on the screen door. The door rattled noisily, its joints loosened by the humidity. Through the rusted screen, she saw a single lamp burning on the desk.

"Father Xavier?" Bailey knocked again. "Hello? It's me, Bailey Harrison." She hesitated a moment, then pulled open the door and stepped inside. "Father Xavier? Are you home?"

The priest's house was tiny and felt claustrophobic after the expansiveness of La Esmerelda. The hurricane lamp on the desk was starting to sputter. Bailey tried to adjust the wick, but she turned the knob on the lamp the wrong way, extinguishing the light.

"Damn it!"

It took a few minutes before her eyes adjusted to the darkness. The full moon pouring through the front windows was nearly as bright as a streetlight would have been, had there been streetlights in Paradisio. Bailey found a box of Black Diamond matches and lit the lamp. Turning from the priest's desk, she saw the irregular pool of wetness on the trestle table. She lightly touched the tip of her finger to it, angling her hand toward the light to confirm what she already knew: she'd dipped her finger in a puddle of congealing blood.

"Father Xavier!"

She began to see signs of the priest's hasty departure. The desk drawers were ajar, and when she looked inside, she saw they were empty except for a few paper clips. The bookshelf beside the easy chair was stripped of everything but a pile of old magazines.

"Father?"

Bailey slowly opened the door to the priest's bedroom. The room was empty. The old-fashioned wardrobe beside Father Xavier's bed was ajar. It was empty except for a dozen wire hangers.

Back in the living room, Bailey found drops of blood on the floor leading into the kitchen. Carrying the hurricane lamp, she followed the blood trail through the dark and empty kitchen and out the back door. The parish Jeep was gone, the place it was usually parked marked by a rutted rectangle of dirt where the grass had died.

Father Xavier, the one person Bailey thought she could go to for advice, was gone.

*   *   *

Vincent glanced up from the well-thumbed *Playboy* as the Land Cruiser careened to a stop in front of the cantina. Dr. Harrison turned off the motor, jumped out, and ran up the cantina stairs without bothering to kill the headlights or close the truck door behind her.

"What's happened to Father Xavier?" Bailey demanded even before she was all the way into the cantina.

Vincent carefully turned the page in the two-year-old *Playboy* and examined the brunette leaning backward over the arm of the leather couch as if this were the first, not the hundredth, time he'd studied the picture. Without changing the angle of his head, he raised his eyes so that he could squint at Dr. Harrison through the ganja smoke.

"Get you something to drink?" he asked, the cigar-sized joint dangling from his mouth wagging up and down as he spoke.

"Father Xavier is gone," Bailey said, ignoring Vincent's question. "I think he might be hurt."

Vincent straightened up. "I heard his Jeep earlier. I did think it was kind of unusual for him to be out and about. He usually sticks close to home after dark."

"His clothes, his belongings, everything, are gone."

Vincent considered this bit of information thoughtfully.

"There's blood on the floor in his house."

Vincent furrowed his brow and took a drag on his spliff. "A lot of blood?"

"Enough."

"Where do you think he went, Doc?"

"I was hoping you would know. Not to La Esmerelda. I would have passed him on the road into town."

"No," Vincent said, shaking his dreadlocks. "He drove

out of town going in the other direction. Besides, he's none too happy with don Lazaro."

"Why would he have a problem with Lazaro?"

"Xavier thought he should do something about Roberto, a kid don Lazaro was close to who has killed a couple of people lately."

"Killed?" Bailey's voice was hardly more than a whisper.

"Yeah. He cut a man's throat right over there," Vincent said, nodding toward the spot. "Earlier he'd killed the man's wife in one of the houses out by La Esmerelda. Cut out her heart."

"My God!"

"Witchery," Vincent whispered. "I don't like to talk about it, Doc, but the folks here in this part of the rain forest believe some strange things. It sounds to me like Father Xavier decided it was time to get the hell out of Paradisio while the getting was good. He wouldn't be the first priest to hightail it out of here and never return."

"Injured and bleeding."

"Might have been exactly the right motivation to make him go."

"Look, Vincent, we both know you're no Boy Scout."

Vincent smiled.

"But tell me the truth. Why would Lazaro protect a killer?"

Vincent shrugged. "Don Lazaro raised Roberto since he was a baby. He considers the boy family."

"And the rest of it, the dark things—what you called 'witchery'—that doesn't have anything to do with it?"

"I don't know and I don't care, Doc. Knowing too much about that shit gets you killed. And don't give me that look."

"What look?"

"You know what look. You'll take this seriously, if you know what's good for you. I'm no Dear Abby, but if you asked me my advice . . ."

"Yes?"

"I'd tell you to get away from here as fast as you can. There is evil in the rain forest. It's real and it's out there right now, waiting."

Vincent pointed toward the darkness beyond the door, beyond the skewed beams of the Land Cruiser's headlights.

"Maybe the evil got Father Xavier. I hope not. But I know it touched him. It touched you, too, Doc. It got your name and number. If I was you, I'd put this place in my rearview mirror and never look back."

Cuarenta

✦

"THE TRANSFORMATION CANNOT occur. Roberto has contracted a disease that robs his body of its power to heal itself. I have never seen anything like it in the province before. I believe he contracted the sickness from the *puta*. Roberto had sex with her. He drank her blood. He is very weak. I do not think he has many days to live," don Lazaro said.

"And the young woman?" Beethoven said.

"She has the same unmistakable aura of death about her, although I think it will be some time before it defeats her. But Roberto weakened himself with the first two introductions to the change. It left his body vulnerable."

Beethoven leaned back in his chair and crossed his arms. He drew in a deep breath and exhaled a long and heavy sigh.

"Where is Roberto now? You realize he is too dangerous to have his freedom, no matter how sick he is."

"He's in his old room here in the hacienda. He doesn't even have the strength to get up from bed. The girl, Yanira, is staying with one of my servants."

"You realize that she, too, presents a danger."

"Yes, I know. She brought this terrible disease to Paradisio."

"I know of this illness. It came out of the African rain forest, where it has devastated entire populations. You are correct. It destroys the body's ability to fight off sickness. There is presently no cure."

"I feared as much."

"The girl must be kept from returning to her former profession," Beethoven said. "The disease is passed through sexual contact and through bodily fluids. As *Vampiri*, you and I are immune to its ravages, but the people caring for Yanira and Roberto must exercise caution."

"Maybe Bailey can help them."

"Assuming she returns to La Esmerelda."

Lazaro's entire being seemed to collapse, a dark star falling in on itself. "She is gone?"

"*Ja, mein Freund.* She is greatly disturbed by what she has found at La Esmerelda, as one might naturally expect."

"I will convince her to come back."

"*Nein.*" Beethoven held up a hand.

"You mistake my meaning. I would never force her to do anything. I love her."

"Love is the most dangerous thing of all for a vampire."

"How can love be dangerous?"

"Because of who you are, because of who she is."

"A man, a woman . . ."

"A vampire, a mortal."

"She could join me, if she loves me. She could make the change, metamorphosing like one of your butterflies."

"We are not talking about a simple marriage, Lazaro, but transformation of a human being into something quite inhuman. The implications are grave. You of all people should understand."

"But when we love one another . . ."

"Consider Roberto. Only a taste of *Vampiri* power drove him mad. Or Dr. Janis Levy, another sad example."

"Surely you're not suggesting Bailey would be capable of violence. The woman is a saint, an angel of mercy ready to sacrifice her life to defeat deadly disease."

"I do not *think* Bailey would end up badly, but I cannot say that I *know* she wouldn't, and neither can you, without giving the matter considerable analysis. We all have a killer living within us, Lazaro. There's nothing we can do about it. It's a genetic predisposition, a trait bred into us during millions of years of evolution in the rain forests and savannas, stalking animals, hunting meat, killing or being killed. Yet if we are better than mere animals, we are also worse. Do you have any idea how rare it is in nature to find creatures that routinely kill other members of their own species? What a piece of work is a man, as Shakespeare said, so like a god in some respects, yet in others resembling the most twisted fiend God ever cast into the Pit."

Beethoven pushed his long tangle of hair back behind his ears.

"It is the capacity to control our killing instinct that makes us human, Lazaro, even when we become something other than human. We must never lose touch with this aspect of our humanity when we join with the *Vam-*

piri. Still, it is important to remember that the force of will that holds the beast at bay in most of us, mortal and immortal alike, is weak. Civilization is a gossamer curtain dividing civility from savagery. Witness Janis Levy. Witness Roberto. Bailey Harrison is a brilliant, moral, and admirable human being, but the transformation you would so quickly offer her could kill the goodness within, leaving only the monster."

"That could never happen."

"Do not be so sure. The change is more than most individuals can endure. The *Illuminati* have dealt with more of these cases than you'd care to imagine."

"Ah yes, the all-powerful and secretive *Illuminati*."

"Do not mock us, Lazaro. We take our honor as seriously as you do yours."

"You came here to kill me, didn't you," Lazaro challenged.

"I came here prepared to kill you, if your actions merited such a step. I have your death warrant from the *Illuminati* High Council in my suitcase. I can show it to you, if you like. It's hand-lettered parchment and rather impressive looking."

"That won't be necessary," Lazaro said coldly.

"I must confess that I have been rather impressed with everything you have done here. Left to your own devices in a remote corner of the world, you might have indulged in a reign of terror that could have lasted many years before the *Illuminati* learned of it. Instead, your actions have been sober, even wise. It is my pleasure to extend the *Illuminati*'s friendship to you. You're no longer alone in the world. There is much we can teach you. I sense your mind is hungry for knowledge."

"But what of Bailey?"

"Her work is very important to us," Beethoven said ambiguously.

"Then I should do everything I can to convince her to return to La Esmerelda. As much as I welcome the *Illuminati*'s friendship, it does not change the fact that I love her."

The other vampire sighed. "If things are to turn out as you hope, then, Lazaro, you must allow events to take their own course. What is meant to be, will be. Bailey must decide on her own to return. She knows what she needs to know to make up her mind. If you go to her now, you will only use your powers to bend her will to yours."

"I already told you that I would never—"

"Do not try to convince me. Do not even try to convince yourself. It is inevitable that you would sway her thoughts, consciously or unconsciously. Do you want her to return to La Esmerelda because she loves you, or because you have used your *Vampiri* powers to subtly shape her thinking?"

Lazaro put his head between his hands.

"I don't know what I'd do if I lost both Bailey and Roberto," he said in a stricken voice. "I don't think I could go on living."

"That is what happens to many of us eventually, Lazaro. Even among the *Illuminati* we eventually tire of living and simply cease to be. I do not think immortality was really meant for us. God alone is strong enough to endure eternity."

"My dear God," Lazaro said, as if remembering the

name of someone he'd known long ago but had long since forgotten.

"Do not despair," the German said, leaning forward to put his hand gently on Lazaro's shoulder. "There is time for you to make amends with Bailey and Roberto. There is even time for you to make amends with God."

Lazaro's head fell forward until his chin rested against his chest.

"The secret to being a *Vampiri* is that one must learn to wait. We are such powerful beings that it is only natural that we are impatient, but therein lies danger. Not even a vampire has the power to make something happen unless it is meant to be. I apologize for sounding somewhat mystical, but the subject defies the power of language. If you wait, Lazaro—if you wait quietly and patiently—the natural shape of things will be revealed."

Beethoven stood up and walked to the French doors. He looked up at the moon, tracing its progress through the sky.

"Kafka, the creator of my useful pseudonym Samsa, said it well: 'You do not need to leave your room. Remain sitting at your table and listen. Do not even listen, simply wait. Do not even wait, become quite still and solitary. The world will freely offer itself to you to be unmasked, it has no choice, it will roll in ecstasy at your feet.' "

But Lazaro did not want to hear Beethoven's words of comfort. His pain was too great. It was an attractive proposition—to simply cease to be, five centuries of heartache exhaled with one final breath.

Lazaro thought of Dr. Bailey Harrison.

He took another breath.

As long as hope itself remained, the vampire could endure living.

Cuarenta y Uno

✧

THE BIG CAT materialized out of the darkness, motionless in the Land Cruiser's headlights.

Bailey jerked the steering wheel left. The front tires hit the ditch, hurling the Land Cruiser into the air. Bailey had the brief sensation of flying before the truck crashed into the brush to the roar of splintering timber. The Land Cruiser hit a tree with its right front fender, heaving the truck up on two wheels. It was going to roll, Bailey thought, bracing herself.

Everything went black.

The truck was angled upward when Bailey opened her eyes, as if it were a rocket about to be launched into the night sky.

The jaguar was stretched out across the hood of the Land Cruiser, its head resting on its front paws on the windshield, waiting for Bailey to awaken. When she shifted in her seat, the cat raised its head and looked in through the cracked windshield, curious about the vehicle's occupant. The jaguar slowly blinked its enormous eyes—golden and iridescent. Its fur was pure white except for the mottling of black rosettes. Its mouth hung open far enough to reveal a bubble gum–pink tongue and two curving white incisors.

Bailey was glad to have avoided killing the magnificent animal, though as her thoughts returned to focus, she realized that she had more to fear from the cat now than it had from her. It was an enormous creature, nearly seven feet long, with powerful muscles that rippled beneath its fur when it moved its head. The jaguar must have been attracted to the heat of the engine and, like an oversize house cat, stretched out there for a nap.

Bailey moved her fingers and toes. Everything seemed to work, although her forehead was beginning to throb from where it had hit the steering wheel, knocking her unconscious.

The truck had run into a clump of a half-dozen small trees, knocking them partly over, climbing them. The right front fender was crumpled. She wasn't sure how the windshield had been cracked; the truck must have clipped a low-hanging branch. She was glad she'd paid for the extra insurance when she rented the Toyota at the airport.

The engine was off, but the lights were still on, shining uselessly up into the rain-forest canopy. Maybe she could back the truck down off its perch.

Bailey wasn't sure how to get the jaguar off the hood. Watching the animal watch her through the spiderweb of cracks in the windshield, she slid her hand over to the controls on the door that operated the electric windows. She depressed the buttons and the two front windows began to rise. The cat pushed itself up until it was sitting on its haunches in the valley between the windshield and the hood.

Bailey turned the key.

The jaguar put its paw on the cracked windshield over Bailey's face as the engine started, moving so fast that Bailey wouldn't have had time to react had the windshield not been there to block the cat.

"Time for me to go," Bailey said to the jaguar, her heart pounding as she slipped the truck into reverse.

The cat jumped off the truck as the rear tires began to spin. Bailey was beginning to think she wouldn't be able to extricate herself when the tires finally caught and the truck jerked itself backward, the front end bouncing stiffly against the ground.

The jaguar growled somewhere in the darkness, a wild sound that made the hair stand up on the back of Bailey's neck. It was a strange paradox, she thought, that the most beautiful things in nature were sometimes also the most dangerous: the jaguar, crystalline viruses, Lazaro.

Love, too.

Bailey carefully backed the Land Cruiser up the short path she'd plowed into the rain forest. The truck bounced back onto the road and sat stopped with its front wheels still in the ditch, the vehicle still pointing into the trees. A glitter of gold flashed at the edge of the darkness. It was the jaguar, watching Bailey from the safety of shadows that only hinted of its presence.

Now Bailey had to decide all over again. She had been leaving the rain forest when the jaguar's ghostly materialization on the road caused her to crash. Would she continue back to safety and civilization, as she'd originally decided, or turn around and return to La Esmerelda?

The golden eyes disappeared and reappeared as the jaguar blinked.

Bailey was a physician and a scientist, but the tools and measurements used to quantify and define the things in the laboratory were useless in the rain forest. She was in a place where the usual laws did not apply. The real and the unreal—the line dividing the two dissolved in the bright tropical sunlight, and in the moonlight shining fiercely in the pure night air.

In the end, it all came down to Lazaro, though she was also attracted to his German counterpart. Were Ludwig and Lazaro fallen angels, or demons who lived on the blood of living human beings? What was her role now in this centuries-old story? Lazaro would have her believe she was his angel of mercy, come to free him from a rare medical condition that chained him to an unspeakable tradition.

The jaguar blinked again. It was still watching Bailey.

The problem for Bailey was that Lazaro was ultimately as inscrutable as the jaguar. Bailey could assign the cat motives and intentions, but she could never really know what the wild creature would do to her, given the opportunity. She could love Lazaro, but could she ever really trust him?

Bailey looked up the road in the direction of San José. She could catch the next plane and go back to Atlanta, where her reputation at the CDC might be temporarily tarnished but at least her life wouldn't be in danger.

Maybe she would send someone else to the rain forest to unlock the mystery of the *vampiro*, as Lazaro called himself.

And maybe she wouldn't. She was not sure the world

was ready to come to terms with the *vampiro*, no matter how great the potential gain—and risk.

Bailey looked in the other direction, toward La Esmerelda. Lazaro, love, and discovery awaited her in that direction—or perhaps death at the hands of the vampire she had the tragic misfortune to love.

Bailey stepped on the gas and turned the wheel.

She had driven barely a hundred yards when the jaguar leapt back into the road again in front of the Land Cruiser. The cat bared its teeth and arched its shoulders, lashing the empty air with a forepaw, the claws as long as an eagle's talons.

These encounters were beginning to unnerve Bailey, but at least she was able to keep the truck on the road.

"Come on, kitty. There's more than enough room in the rain forest for the both of us."

The jaguar growled, its golden eyes changing from gold to red in the headlights.

Maybe it was a sign that she had made the wrong choice in deciding to return to Lazaro. She shook off the idea. Unlike the superstitious Vincent, she didn't believe in "signs."

Bailey eased up on the clutch and rolled the truck forward a few inches. The jaguar reacted aggressively to the threatening gesture, rearing up on its back feet, tearing at the air with its claws. Bailey took a deep breath and reminded herself she was safe as long as she remained in the Land Cruiser.

The jaguar began to blur, as if Bailey were looking at the beast through a lens that was being backed gradually out of focus.

Bailey blinked, trying vainly to clear her vision. She must have been wrong in assessing how badly she'd injured herself in the wreck. She was going to pass out again from her earlier concussion. She shouldn't be trying to drive.

Bailey found the gearshift lever without taking her eyes off the animal, shifting the truck into neutral so that it wouldn't drive into the jaguar or a tree if she lost consciousness—if the jaguar was even really there.

The creature was now ill-defined, a swirling cloud that moved like a tornado filmed in slow motion.

Bailey leaned her head back against the seat, her hands clutched on the steering wheel. It could be a symptom of intracranial bleeding. She was trembling, the possible onset of seizure. Who knew how long it would be until the next person traveled this road? Bailey was suddenly acutely aware of how alone she was in the midst of the rain forest at night.

She might never make it back to La Esmerelda, at least not alive.

The swirling fog began to coalesce into a human form. The fog became a young man.

Bailey squinted.

The vision of Roberto *seemed* real, down to his ponytail and the paperback book he'd carried in the right rear pocket of his Levi's the night he confronted them at Zonatitucan. The jaguar, Roberto—Bailey told herself this was not witchery but hallucination. If she could make it back to Paradisio, she could send Vincent for Lazaro. Lazaro and Ludwig would take care of her.

The Land Cruiser's engine died.

Bailey reached for the keys, not daring to take her eyes

off the phantom in the road. Nothing happened when she tried to restart the truck.

Roberto's eyes began to shine the way the jaguar's eyes had shined—the rich gold changing slowly to red.

Bailey realized she was starting to hyperventilate and forced herself to slow her breathing. A hallucination could not hurt her.

The Land Cruiser's headlights went dark.

"You are a trespasser here," a familiar voice in the darkness said, the words slow, measured, and filled with menace.

Bailey sat in the Land Cruiser, her hands gripping the wheel, not moving, hardly even breathing. She sat there, waiting to see what Roberto would do next.

Lazaro stared down at Roberto's feverish face.

The body was there, but Roberto's soul was somewhere else, gone away to do God knew what while his earthly form remained behind at the hacienda, too sick to get out of bed.

"Roberto," Lazaro said.

The empty shell did not reply.

"His astral body has gone after her," Beethoven said.

"We must stop him."

"You can—if you follow after him in like manner."

"I am no sorcerer," Lazaro said with great contempt.

"Sorcery has nothing to do with it. Reach out with your spirit, Lazaro. Follow him."

"We don't have time for parlor games!"

"Do not direct your anger at me, Lazaro. Do not direct your anger at anyone. It is a waste of both energy and time. And time is the one thing we cannot afford to squander if you intend to prevent Roberto from killing Bailey."

"What should I do?" Lazaro asked, desperate.

"There," Beethoven said, pointing to a chair. "Sit down and close your eyes."

Lazaro threw himself into the chair and squeezed shut his eyes. If there had been any alternative to following the other vampire's instructions, he would have ignored them, but it seemed his only chance.

"Let go of your body and allow your spirit to float free. Follow Roberto. Your spirit will know where to go, if you let it."

A sickening vertigo overwhelmed Lazaro, making it impossible for him to continue sitting with his eyes closed. He opened his eyes, ready to declare the experiment a failure, but he was no longer in Roberto's room at La Esmerelda. He looked down and saw the moonlit treetops fly past with impossible speed. He was streaking toward Paradisio like a comet traversing the tropical night sky.

He found them a heartbeat later.

Bailey was on her back on the ground nearly three hundred meters from the stalled Land Cruiser, Roberto standing over her. He had taken the form of a jaguar, but Lazaro could easily enough see that it was Roberto, although he did not understand *how* he knew.

Roberto had encouraged Bailey to run, cruelly playing with her, chasing her through the forest until he tired of the game and brought her roughly down. Her shirt was torn half away, three lines of red drawn over her heart, oozing blood where the claws had raked her breast.

Bailey was still alive, and conscious.

"Please . . ." she moaned.

The jaguar lowered its head and licked the blood.

"Nooooo."

Roberto!

The big cat looked up at Lazaro. A jaguar cannot smile, and yet that is somehow what Roberto's spirit animal did, drawing back its lips to mock Lazaro with gleaming teeth that Nature designed for tearing living flesh. The jaguar placed one paw over Bailey's heart and lifted the other in the air, claws bared, and roared. The creature's breath stank of death and of something fetid beyond earthly decay—the obsessive hatred of life that burned forever in the Pit from whence Roberto and those like him drew their energy.

There's nothing you can do to save her, Roberto said, the jaguar form communicating with Lazaro without words. *Your powers are no match for mine on this plane. She will be my slave in death, her soul forever mine to abuse.*

The jaguar roared, and Lazaro found himself back in the chair in the hacienda.

Everything was as it had been—Beethoven standing in the corner with his hands behind him, Roberto's empty shell of a body on the bed. And Bailey—she was still in the rain forest, helpless against Roberto's sorcery.

Lazaro jumped to his feet and moved swiftly to Roberto's side, drawing back his hand as he leaned over the motionless form.

There was no time to reconsider, no time to feel the regret he knew would haunt and torture him for as long as he lived.

In the manner of the Zona priests he had seen five centuries earlier, Lazaro tore the beating heart from Roberto's chest.

Roberto's eyes snapped open. There was a flash of recognition and, Lazaro wanted very much to believe, relief at being freed from the ancient evil that had been waiting in the rain forest when the first Indians arrived to make it their home.

The young man's eyes changed focus and drifted away from Lazaro's face.

Roberto Goya de Montezuma was dead.

Cuarenta y Dos

✦

DON VINCENT WAS talking on his cellular phone, chewing out the new cantina manager, when the trucks bringing the liquor for the New Year's Eve party finally arrived. He was beginning to doubt his new employee had the brainpower to do the job.

"The guests will be here in another hour, and the truck is only now arriving," don Vincent complained. "My friends practically beat the liquor to the party."

He put down the phone with exaggerated disgust. The truth was that he enjoyed being the big boss. He liked knowing he was the only one with complete mastery of the fine points, though the days were long and his responsibilities without end.

Don Vincent took off his tuxedo jacket—he'd been dressed for more than an hour—and went out onto the veranda to supervise the unloading. Only when that was finished did he allow himself to go into the garden to drink a cup of coffee. He made it a habit to spend a few moments in quiet reflection before big meetings and important parties. He thought it important to approach these occasions with a calm, composed mind. Afterward, if everything went well, he would reward himself with a rare pipe of ganja, a habit he'd been forced to set aside in order to keep command of his myriad business concerns.

Yanira brought don Vincent a gold-rimmed china cup. He thanked her and watched her walk back toward the house.

Don Vincent had insisted that Yanira continue living at La Esmerelda. The poor woman had grown thin with the sickness. Don Vincent considered himself fortunate to have avoided contracting the disease himself. He always used protection when he had sex with the prostitutes. That, apparently, had saved him.

It had taken a long time, but Vincent's luck had finally changed. Even at the low point in his career, when he was running the cantina and Hotel Paradisio, he'd known that one day it would be different.

Jah worked in strange ways.

Dr. Bailey Harrison's colleagues in the United States had reacted to the news of her disappearance with predictable outrage. The Yankee ambassador himself had come to Paradisio with a contingent of special magistrates from San José. Finding the wrecked truck and bloodstained clothing in the rain forest indicated Dr. Harrison had met a bad end. That so heinous a crime had been committed, especially to a *gringa*—not to mention a *gringa* doctor—had led the authorities to vow a perpetrator would be quickly brought to justice.

Of course, justice never really mattered, don Vincent thought, nodding philosophically as he took a sip of Obdulia's excellent coffee. It had all been a matter of saving face.

No killer was ever found, which was fortunate. If there was any justice in the affair, it was that nobody ever went to jail for killing Dr. Harrison, since Dr. Harrison wasn't really dead. She had been well enough the last time don Vincent had seen her, except for a touch of fever she seemed to have trouble shaking. She had gone away with the German and don Lazaro, who put Vincent in charge of his ranch before leaving.

Don Lazaro had not explained why Dr. Harrison had chosen to disappear. That was her own business. Vincent knew well enough that it was sometimes expedient to disappear. He had once done so himself, although he was rich enough now to have made all traces of his earlier trouble vanish. The reason for his employer's disappearance, however, was obvious: don Lazaro was in love with Dr. Harrison.

The *policía* had not concerned themselves with Roberto's death. If they knew don Lazaro had killed Roberto, they gave no clue of it. Yanira had told don Vincent all about don Lazaro digging Roberto's grave with his own hands and crying over it. Don Lazaro was, Vincent thought, a complicated man. Vincent did not fault Lázaro for killing Roberto. Somebody needed to kill Roberto, and the fact that it had been don Lazaro did nothing but enhance don Lazaro's reputation in Vincent's mind.

Don Vincent had done a good job managing the ranch, so he was not completely surprised when a letter postmarked in Paris arrived one day from don Lazaro—his only contact with his employer in more than a year—putting Vincent in charge of the balance of don Lazaro's financial concerns. Don Vincent's employer encouraged him to manage things as he saw fit, telling him to bring the province into the twenty-first century.

Don Vincent immediately increased logging operations, cutting enough timber to please the government officials in San José, but not enough to upset the Indians. The government was anxious for the money the exports would bring into the country, and they had been long frustrated by don Lazaro's overly conservative land-management practices. Using his natural ability to make friends—and his generosity with bribes—don Vincent quickly became a popular, and powerful, man.

Don Vincent had been careful to stay on good terms with the Indians. Alvaro, don Lazaro's old butler at La Esmerelda, had become the Zona headman after don Lazaro went away. Alvaro went to live in the ruins out in the rain forest beyond the volcanoes. The Indians trooped out to Zonatitucan several times a month in the dead of night to see Alvaro. Don Vincent didn't know what the Indians did at the ruins, and he didn't want to know, his aversion to witchery one thing about him that would never change.

Don Vincent wasted little time before improving things in Paradisio, now a booming town with a paved main street and a dozen new businesses. The rebuilt Hotel Paradisio was always full of foreign investors anxious to share in the money to be made developing the province's vast resources. Each new deal enhanced don Lazaro's fortune and, by extension, don Vincent's.

Though her visit had been brief, Dr. Harrison was well remembered in Paradisio. The Indians regarded the *gringa* as a martyr. The violence of her supposed death, combined with her youth and presumed virtue, came together in the peasants' imaginations to shape the image of a saint. A shrine had been built beside the road where her truck had been found. Daily visits were made to the spot. Prayers were offered, the supplicants leaving behind flowers, notes asking for assistance, even an occasional bottle of rum or mescal. Several miracles had been attributed to Dr. Harrison's intervention. The Yankee pastor of the fast-growing new evangelical Baptist church in Paradisio referred to her as the "Angel of La Esmerelda" in his sermons.

Vincent did not expect don Lazaro to return to La Esmerelda. And if he did come back someday, Vincent knew his employer would treat him fairly in recompense for Vincent's careful stewardship of his estate. Don Lazaro was, beneath all else, a gentleman.

Don Vincent stood up and pulled on his tuxedo jacket, pushing back his nonexistent dreadlocks, a habit that lived on long after he'd cut his hair to present a more businesslike image to the world.

He checked his Rolex.

It was almost time for don Vincent's Japanese guests to arrive.

*Read on for an excerpt
from the forthcoming novel by*

Michael Romkey

The Vampire Hunter

HE WAS NO longer monstrous, at least not in outward form. He'd regained the appearance of a beautiful man, with facial features that spoke of the Italian aristocrats from whom he was descended. Nourishment had restored his shrunken carapace of a body, strengthening bones, rebuilding muscles wasted away during eighty-five years spent trapped in the *Titanic* at the bottom of the ocean, floating like a specimen suspended in preservative in a museum jar.

His reconstructed face was strikingly handsome. His good looks were of the brooding, Byronic variety—which was strangely fitting, considering his *Vampiri* patrimony. He had a broad, intelligent forehead above strongly drawn eyebrows. His eyes, large and set deep in their sockets, smoldered with the passionate inner fires that burned within the furnace of an artist's soul. Shaving his Methuselahian beard revealed prominent cheekbones, angling down to sensuous lips set over a strong, square jaw. He'd bathed and cut his thick chestnut hair to shoulder length and pulled it back into a ponytail.

He'd been five foot seven before undergoing the transformation in London in 1870, but the change had added seven inches to his stature. There was no fat on his lithe frame, and the well-developed muscles on his upper arms, chest, and abdomen were cut into his body with such exquisite definition that he might have served as a model for Michelangelo, had he been born a few centuries earlier.

The clothes he'd appropriated from the dead man were big for him, yet he wore them with such natural ease that their bagginess seemed stylish. He sat on the deck of the *Bentham Explorer* barefoot, trousers rolled up to midcalf. It was nearly midnight. The sky was undisturbed by anything but the waning moon. The breeze was cool but not chilly, blowing just hard enough to make the flame on the candle dance and occasionally gutter but not go out. He held a glass of wine in his hand, cabernet from the private stock Drake had brought aboard. Though his taste in wine ran to port—in this respect he was a typical Englishman—he savored the rich, complex flavor.

Delicious as it was, the wine would not compare to the draught Patricia Seahurst Solberg carried in her veins, awaiting his pleasure.

He did not remember how much time would pass before the Hunger returned, especially after having sated his thirst on so many. Sooner or later, though, it would be back, forcing him to take her. He looked forward to that time with the sweetest anticipation, a connoisseur patiently waiting to uncork a particularly succulent vintage casked in the dark coolness of his cellar.

He turned his wrist slightly, watching his pulse beat slow and deep in a bluish vein inside his arm. The blood was the life; to drink it was to live, a miracle and nightmare. That was the profound and eternal mystery of blood. His eyes moved to the copper Sabona bracelet around his wrist. He'd taken it from Drake's body before flinging the corpse over the railing into the sea.

The vampire rolled the wine in his glass. It reminded him of something, but he could not think of what. His hands were strong, yet seemed capable of delicate work—the hands of a surgeon, perhaps, or a pianist. Powerful as he was, he could not force down the anxiety he felt at being unable to remember who he was, what he was.

Who was he?

He reached for the thread, but it eluded him.

The candle flame was the color of rubies when he looked at it through the glass, almost the color of roses. That simple image—roses—made his heart throb with an unhappy pain that was almost physical. He felt the slow, stupid rage rise up in him and with it the Hunger.

The vampire looked at the woman seated opposite him on the ship's deck and started to smile—a smile filled with wicked malice.

Patricia had been staring off into the middle distance. She'd been in a state of shock since watching him kill her protector. She held both hands in front of her in prayerful attitude, her lucky crystal pendant clasped in her palms. Now she felt the monster's eyes upon her.

"Are you the Devil?" she asked, her voice shaking.

His brow furrowed with the intensity of his thought. "I honestly don't know," he answered after a bit. His voice was hoarse and strained, unaccustomed to speech after so many years of solitude. He had hardly spoken to the woman in the past three days beyond a few mono-syllabic commands. The thoughts that moved through his mind were still large and shadowy, impressions of things and emotions he could no longer associate with words with any precision.

"I know what you are."

"Tell me," he said, earnestly.

"You are a vampire."